SKULK

BOOK THREE OF THE FRACTURED FAERY

BY HELEN HARPER

Chapter One

It was the beeping that told me I wasn't dead. Unless hell had a special section set aside where you were driven mad by the incessant sound of human technology. It was unlikely.

I groaned and tried to turn onto my side to get away from the sound, which was starting to feel like it was reverberating around my skull. As soon as I shifted, however, there was a clink of metal upon metal and I realised I couldn't move. I opened my eyes and glanced down. Gasbudlikins. I was in a hospital bed – and, not only that, I was cuffed to it so I couldn't escape. If it weren't for the pervasive smell of antiseptic, it would have been kinky.

'Welcome back to the land of the living.'

I glanced to my left, spotting the white-coated doctor who wasn't quite able to meet my eyes. 'What…' I croaked. 'What happened?'

'You pulled out a gun in the city centre and tried to use it,' he said. 'It wasn't a wise action on your part. If anything, I'd say it was quite mad.'

Well, I thought, wishing I didn't hurt quite so much, I *was* the Madhatter.

'You're healing remarkably quickly. The police shot you. The bullet missed your heart by centimetres. All the same, the shock alone would have killed a normal person. You are some sort of medical miracle. You should be glad.'

I was beyond thrilled. I looked around. 'Where are my clothes?' And, more to the point, where was the sphere? The magical one created by a dragon that had the potential to destroy this world? It had been in my possession just before the armed police made their move. If they hadn't impounded everything I owned for forensics and further investigation then all this had been for nought. 'My belongings?'

'We had to cut you out of your clothes. But we'll rustle up something else for you to wear before you leave. As for your belongings, the police have them. I doubt you'll get them back any time soon.'

I breathed out. Praise be. It had worked.

I'd been out of options. Confronted by Rubus and his minions, suicide by cop had seemed to be the only way to keep the destructive magic out of his hands. Maybe it wasn't my finest hour but it had served its purpose and the sphere was safe – for now. All I had to do was get the police to arrest me properly and throw me in jail, and the sphere would be locked away as evidence for good along with me. Then I froze.

'Wait a minute!' I half screeched, as the doctor's words finally filtered through my fogged brain. 'You cut me out of my clothes? Even my sexy-arse leather trousers?'

He nodded. 'Yes.'

—

3

'And my gorgeous leather corset?'

'Yes.'

I hissed in annoyance. Screw the damn dragon-created, apocalypse-inducing, magical sphere. I'd looked bloody good in that outfit.

The doctor looked unconcerned at my fashion-related loss. He pursed his lips slightly before turning to the IV drip by side and fiddling with it. I sighed. It was lucky I looked fabulous in just about everything I wore. It would be hard but I'd get over it. With time.

'So I'm going to be alright?' I asked.

'It appears that way,' he said. He glanced at the door. 'Your barrister is here to see you. Are you feeling well enough to talk to him?'

There was a lingering cloud of confusion misting my mind but I nodded anyway. When the doctor exited and Morgan appeared in his place, I almost cried.

'You're a bloody idiot, Madrona,' Morgan said, striding over to my bedside and grabbing my hand.

'Yeah,' I sniffed. 'And it seems like I've got a bartender as a lawyer, too.'

He smiled slightly, although it didn't reach his eyes. 'They are only going to keep you here until you're well enough to be moved to prison. You're being investigated on suspicion of murder, as well as discharging a firearm illegally.' His face darkened. 'An anonymous source sent them the CCTV clip of you with Charrie the Bogle.'

I bit my lip. 'You mean,' I whispered, 'the CCTV clip of me cutting off Charrie's head. I *am* a murderer, Morgan. I deserve this.'

He shook his head. 'We still don't know what really happened between the two of you. Not to mention the fact that there's no body. Finn and his brothers ensured that. We'll find out what happened and get you out.'

'The sphere…'

'The police have it. It's safe for now.'

I swallowed. 'And Rubus? Your evil brother who's seeking to destroy the world? What happened to him?'

'He was questioned and let go. We all were. I've not seen him since.' Morgan's fingers tightened round mine. 'He swore blind the gun had nothing to do with him and he can be a convincing bastard when he wants to be. The only good thing is that he'll still be recovering from the effects of the rowan poisoning. I was an idiot for not realising what he'd done sooner.'

I sighed. 'It was me who gave him the idea. All this is my fault. If I'd not told him that rowan poisoning enabled me to maintain a glamour for hours rather than minutes, he wouldn't have known. He couldn't have pretended to be Mendax the damned dragon. We wouldn't have almost handed the stupid sphere over to him.'

'If it wasn't for you,' Morgan said, 'this demesne would already have been destroyed. You're a hero.'

5

Well, there was that. 'I knew that part all along.' I half smiled. 'I'm truly wondrous.'

Morgan held my gaze. 'One day you'll realise that's actually true.' He leaned over and brushed my lips with his. 'The police want to question you. We'll need to work out what you're going to say.'

I tried to shrug, although it was remarkably awkward from the position I was in. 'I know what I'm going to say,' I said. I attempted a weak grin. Morgan raised a questioning eyebrow. 'I've got amnesia,' I whispered to him. 'I can't remember a gasbudlikin thing.'

'I'm not sure that's much of a defence.' His expression was grim. 'We can't afford for you to be locked up for a quarter of a century for murder.'

'We?' I enquired. 'Or you?'

His eyes held mine. 'I think you already know the answer to that.'

I ignored the momentary ripple of delight in the pit of my stomach and lowered my voice. 'But I deserve to be locked up, Morgan. I did decapitate that bogle. The video proves it. And more to the point,' I added, 'if I'm locked up then so is the sphere.'

I'd barely finished speaking when there was a sharp knock at the door. Whoever was outside didn't bother to wait to be granted access, however, so the knock was a wasted effort.

Morgan growled at the sight of the sharp-suited couple holding up their badges. Apparently he and they were already acquainted.

'I told you,' he said, with a protective air that made my toes curl in delight, 'I require some time alone with my client first. She's only just woken up and she's in a position of extraordinary vulnerability. This is not the place for an interrogation.'

'Perhaps,' the woman said, 'she should have thought of that before threatening the city of Manchester.'

Morgan's face darkened. 'All she did was fire a gun into the air.'

'An illegal gun.'

He held his ground. 'It didn't belong to her. She took it from her assailant. It was self-defence.'

'All the more reason for us to talk to her,' the woman's partner replied calmly. 'We need to keep her safe.'

'By handcuffing her to a hospital bed?'

'It's just procedure. Besides, there's also the question of the video evidence we've received. And her confession at the crime scene in front of the library. She said that she had already killed.'

'Video evidence that could easily have been doctored,' Morgan returned. 'And she was under great duress when she said that.'

The three of them were putting on quite a show. Under any other circumstances, I'd probably have been rather entertained. I tried to scoot upwards to make myself more comfortable but the authorities obviously weren't taking any chances. The handcuffs were far too tight and all I could manage was to shift up an inch or two on the pillow.

I shook my head from side to side in a bid to look like the glamorous sex kitten I knew I was, adorably mussed-up after a long sleep, instead of pale, chained up and with bed hair. Neither of the police officers appeared impressed. I suspected they were simply jealous.

'In any case,' the policeman said, 'you have no right to be here.'

I blinked. 'I can leave?'

He rolled his eyes. 'Not you.' He jerked his chin at Morgan. 'Him. We have searched and found no one on the Barristers' Register to match you. You're not a lawyer. Therefore,' the officer smiled unpleasantly, 'you have to go.'

'She is entitled to legal representation!'

'Then go and find some.'

Morgan opened his mouth to argue some more. It was rather heartening given that, not all that long ago, he'd have quite happily allowed the police to lock me away forever. All the same, I interrupted him before he could begin his tirade. It was for his own good; he'd only feel bereft and useless when I talked my way into a life sentence without his help.

'It's fine, Morgan,' I said softly. 'I'll deal with this. I'll answer their questions. You stay focused on Rubus and what he's planning.'

Neither police officer would have made a great poker player. Their stoic expressions cracked

—

when I mentioned Rubus's name. Aha.

I smiled serenely. I was an uber villain; I deserved to be locked away. But if I could bring Rubus down with me, you could bet my curvy, gorgeous arse that I'd do it.

After Morgan reluctantly departed and the door closed firmly behind him, I fixed my attention on the police. 'He did have a point,' I said. I jiggled the handcuffs. 'I have no lawyer and I'm completely vulnerable and helpless. This is not a good place for an interrogation.'

'We're not here to interrogate you,' the policewoman told me. 'We're just here to find out what happened. You're very welcome to get legal advice before we proceed but, honestly, we're on your side. This is merely an exploratory chat.'

'Exploratory? Then you're saying you're like Christopher Columbus.'

She appeared slightly discomfited. 'Not exactly but...'

'Because he was an incompetent tyrant.' I raised an eyebrow. 'I've not had dealings with the police in the past but I'd rather hoped for better than that.'

Rather than unbalancing my pair of PC Plods, they both seemed to brighten. Uh-oh. Maybe I did have direct experience with the arm of the law. It was entirely possible. Thanks to my ongoing amnesia, I couldn't remember.

'I can assure you that we are not tyrants.' The policeman smiled as if he were my brand new best friend. That could not be a good thing. 'Let's start over, shall we? I'm Detective Inspector Mulroney and this is Detective Constable Jones.' The policewoman smiled thinly. 'Our records indicate that you are Madrona Hatter.'

I beamed. I couldn't help myself. 'Madrona Hatter? That's awesome.' Then I realised what I'd said. 'What I mean is, yes.' I coughed. 'I am Madrona Hatter.'

'Where are you from, Madrona?' Mulroney's expression was friendly enough but there was something about his tone of voice that gave me pause.

'Er … is that relevant?'

'You are not registered as a British citizen. Neither is there any information at border control about which country you arrived from. Are you here illegally?'

I stared at him. Before I could answer, DC Jones stepped in to tag-team him. 'You've been in trouble before now, Madrona. Anti-social behaviour…'

I spluttered. 'I'm a very social person! Everyone who meets me loves me!' That was a blatant lie. Oh well. She wasn't to know that.

'Drunk and disorderly…'

'Being drunk is a crime? Come on!'

'Public disorder…'

I shook my head. 'You've got the wrong person. Ordering the public around is very important to me.'

Jones was not amused. 'That is not what public disorder refers to. There is a litany of petty crimes attached to your name but we haven't been able to follow up any of them because you're an illegal immigrant who thinks she's above the law. Isn't that correct?'

I considered possible responses. Really, there was only one way to go: the truth, the whole truth and nothing but the truth.

'I thought I was above the law for a few days,' I agreed. 'That's because I thought I was a superhero. It's not true, though. I've got amnesia so I don't remember my background or where I came from. However, I have it on good authority that I'm really a faery. I come from a place called Mag Mell and I've got special magical powers. So I probably am here illegally but, you see, I can't leave. Mag Mell is closed off. No faeries can return. Like it or not, I'm stuck here.' I tried to shrug but it wasn't easy, given my supine position. 'I'd go home if I could.'

Mulroney didn't blink. Maybe he was actually a lizard rather than a man. Frankly, these days nothing would be surprise me. 'You're telling us that you have amnesia?' he said.

'Yes.'

'And that you're a faery?'

'Yes.'

'But you're trapped here?'

'Yes.'

'And you have magical powers?'

I beamed. 'Now you're getting it!'

He leaned down. 'Tell me, Madrona. Do these magical powers extend to the ability to chop off someone's head? Because we have evidence that's what you did.'

'I don't remember anything about that.'

'Because you've got amnesia.'

'Yes!'

Mulroney shook his head sadly. 'I thought you were going to help us, Madrona. Instead, you're just being obstructive. As soon as the doctors agree that you're well enough to be released, which I believe will be very soon, you will be arrested on suspicion of murder and serious public affray. You do not have to say anything. But it may harm your defence if you do not mention when questioned something you later rely on in court. Anything you do say may be given in evidence.'

I did my best to look crestfallen but it wasn't easy. This was what I wanted. Being locked up in prison meant that the sphere would also be locked up in an evidence room somewhere so that Rubus couldn't get his grubby hands on it. The world was lucky that I was such a self-sacrificing person.

I just hoped that prison food was going to be palatable. I'd keep my fingers crossed for kebabs.

Chapter Two

Part of me expected to be shoved into an orange jumpsuit after a brisk cavity search and then sent to a large grey building with lots of bars where my only exercise would be swinging a pickaxe at chunks of rock and avoiding eye contact in the showers. It was almost disappointing when I was taken straight from the hospital to nowhere more interesting than a police station. That was nothing compared to the baggy jeans and boring T-shirt that were forced on me before I left the hospital. If it had been a month or two earlier – and a few degrees warmer – I'd have simply strolled out naked. Instead, I suffered the indignity of looking like everyone else.

My rights were read to me again, presumably on the off chance I'd had another bout of amnesia in the past hour, before I was deposited on an uncomfortable aluminium chair in a small interrogation room.

The fact that the chair was bolted to the floor wasn't lost on me. It was good that the police were wary of me; it made putting up with more questioning slightly more palatable. Small mercies, I reminded myself. If this was what it took to get the coppers to lock me up and throw away the key, this was what I'd do.

The first person to enter the room wasn't another police officer, however. It was a slim, middle-aged woman with fiery green eyes. 'Don't get up,' she told me.

'I'm cuffed to the chair by my ankles,' I said. 'I couldn't get up even if I wanted to. And believe me, I don't want to.'

Viburna grimaced. We'd only met once before, when I was trapped in the body of a large bearded man and she'd used Truth Draw magic to find out who I really was. I hadn't liked the Fey woman much then; somehow I didn't think my feelings were going to change now.

She took the adjacent chair, although I noted that she angled herself away from me as if she were afraid that I'd contaminate her with my very presence. Our dislike was mutual, then. This *was* going to be fun.

'I will represent you,' she said. 'Unlike Morganus, I am actually registered as a barrister. I've been a practising lawyer for several years now and I deal with a lot of Fey and human criminal deeds. The police will take no issue with me.'

'What if *I* take issue with you?' I enquired.

She gestured as if it were no concern of hers. 'That's your right.'

I peered at her. I had the impression she was hoping that was exactly what I would do. 'You heard then,' I said. 'About what I did.'

'You mean that it's your fault we are all trapped here? That you were the one who forced the borders between this demesne and our own to be closed?' Her voice was cold. 'Yes, I heard. But it will not hinder my ability to do my job, if that's what you're worried about.'

'Morgan and Artemesia weren't bothered by the revelation. In fact, they were almost relieved to learn the truth.'

Viburna didn't miss a beat. 'They are entitled to their opinion.'

I couldn't stop myself from grinning. It was quite something to realise that I inspired absolute revulsion and hatred in another person. Most people garnered apathy and ambivalence. Not me; I was too cool for that.

'Well,' I said, 'your job in this scenario is to ensure that I'm properly locked away.'

The Fey woman blinked in surprise. 'Pardon?'

I waved a hand. 'You heard me. We have to keep the sphere away from Rubus. As long as I'm in jail, that's exactly what will happen. Given that the police are already onto him, I doubt that even Rubus will try to sneak his way in here to nab it. It's my job to keep it as far away from him as possible.'

'You're martyring yourself?' Viburna asked with a doubtful – and rather disparaging – sneer.

'I want the songs,' I said.

Her brow furrowed. 'Excuse me?'

'The songs. All good martyrs have songs

written about them. Once they've thrown away the key I expect you, as my lawyer, to contact Right Said Fred.'

'What on earth are you on about?'

Clearly, human pop culture was beyond Viburna's frame of reference. 'Right Said Fred. They're a British pop duo. Their original hit 'I'm Too Sexy' could easily be re-worked for me. I'm even prepared to help them out with the lyrics. Or if Right Said Fred are too busy, perhaps The Specials could re-write 'Free Nelson Mandela' for me.' I pursed my lips. 'It's a good tune.'

I'd managed to flummox her into momentary silence by comparing myself to Mandela. Unfortunately, she recovered quickly. 'Morganus wants me to ensure your release,' she said, ignoring my musical suggestions.

'He'll have to manage without me. *You* have to ensure that my release doesn't happen.'

For the first time, Viburna smiled. 'If you insist. But you can't tell the police you're guilty and end up in prison just like that. They're still going to want to ask questions. A lot of questions. We probably don't want to appear too eager to get you charged with the crimes either, or they'll suspect something is up. Generally speaking, people who are keen to end up in jail are hiding more than they let on. The police and the world at large are far happier if you at least pretend to put up a fight. You will also be more convincing if you actually tell the truth. Within reason, of course.'

I inclined my head. 'I bow to your wisdom.' I paused. 'Metaphorically, I mean. I'm not actually going to bow to you. And I'm not yet convinced by your wisdom.'

'The feeling's mutual,' she grunted. She got to her feet, walked to the door and knocked on it. When it opened, she told the duty officer outside that we were ready.

I rubbed my palms in anticipation. I'd played a lot of roles in recent times. This one might prove to be my best yet.

Jones and Mulroney ambled inside, taking the chairs on the opposite side of the table. Jones took out a digital recorder and placed it between us. I made as if to reach for it and she glared at me.

'Not a gift for me then?' I asked.

Her glare increased. 'For the purposes of the tape,' Mulroney said, 'present in the room are myself, DI Mulroney, and DC Jones.'

'Good morning,' Jones said.

'Representing Ms Hatter is...'

Viburna cleared her throat. 'Viburna Smith QC.'

Mulroney gestured at me. 'Please state your full name.'

I deepened my voice to a villainous half-cackle. 'Madrona Hatter.' I inhaled deeply, holding the stale air inside my lungs. 'I'm guilty of murder. I confess. I did it. I deserve whatever happens next.'

'You admit to murder?'

Viburna muttered under her breath,

obviously annoyed that I'd ignored all her instructions.

'Yes.' I nodded vigorously.

Unfortunately Mulroney and Jones's disbelief at my immediate confession was so obvious that I began to suspect Viburna had been right: my rush to admit my guilt merely raised doubts rather than dispersing them. I had to backtrack somehow. If I made matters too easy for them, they'd remain suspicious. People like to work a bit to get what they want because it makes the desired outcome much sweeter when it arrives. I should have realised that earlier – or Viburna should have explained it more clearly.

I was fortunate that Mulroney gave me the opening I needed. 'I thought you had amnesia,' he said.

'Yes.' I nodded wisely. 'I don't remember killing anyone. But I don't remember *not* killing anyone either.' I raised my shoulders helplessly. 'I'm a danger to the public. Send me to prison!'

Mulroney sighed. Rather than ending the proceedings because of my botched confession, he started with his other questions. 'Ms Hatter, please explain what brought you to the vicinity of the Manchester Library on Monday 8th October.'

I sank back in my chair. I would have to try a lot harder than I'd thought to get these two to charge me properly. Didn't they know who I was? Couldn't they spot my dangerous edge? I twisted my lips into a snarl and did my best to help them along. 'I'd heard that Rubus, a local drug dealer, was going to be there and that he was up to no good. Plus, I wanted some drugs.'

Viburna shot me a narrow-eyed look.

'What is this alleged drug dealer's full name?'

I shrugged. 'Rubus Evil Bastard. I don't know his last name. I just know that he was going to be there doing bad things.' It was a sort of truth. 'When he didn't do what I wanted, I wrestled a gun from him.'

'Wrestled?'

'Well,' I said, 'someone knocked him to the ground and the gun he was holding fell with him. I took it. It was almost a wrestle.' I smiled nicely. 'Then once I had it, I shot it.'

'At who?'

'I think the question you want to ask is 'at whom'?'

Jones drummed her fingers on the table in irritation. Good. I wanted her to despise me. It was the easiest way to get this all done and dusted.

'I guess you were off school that day,' I said. 'Anyway, I shot the gun into the air. I wasn't aiming at anyone.'

I felt Viburna relax slightly now that I was doing what she'd told me to do. Even Jones appeared placated. Given that my actions could well have been filmed, just like my murder of Charrie was, I didn't feel like I could say anything else.

'You also shouted something. What did you shout?'

"I have killed before',' I intoned, "and I shall kill again'.'

Mulroney leaned forward. 'What did you mean by that?'

I frowned. 'Which words don't you understand?'

'Who had you killed before?'

A sudden knot of unexpected – and very real – tension tightened in my chest. 'I don't remember. As I keep saying, I have amnesia. But I think I might have killed a man called Charrie. I believe you have evidence that proves I did just that.'

At a nod from Mulroney, Jones took out a photo from a brown envelope and slid it across the table. I immediately recognised it; it was indeed a still from the golf-course CCTV footage, the footage that proved once and for all that I'd killed Charrie by cutting off his head with a sword.

I bit my lip. This was what I wanted, I reminded myself. 'Yeah,' I said. 'I think that's him.'

'Good,' she said, obviously pleased. 'We have his wife and children next door.'

The last of my well-intentioned, lock-me-up-now bluster flew out of the window with all the speed of a buzzard on crack. What? My mouth felt dry. 'Wife and children?'

'She's a grieving widow now. And those cute little kiddies will grow up without a father.'

All I could do was stare at the pair of them. I

supposed it would be a bad thing if I vomited all over their digital recorder.

'Charrie's wife is very keen to talk to us. She's being interviewed right now.' DC Jones sounded positively gleeful.

My shoulders sagged. 'I'm an evil bitch,' I whispered.

Mulroney raised his eyebrows. He didn't disagree. No one did. 'Your alleged amnesia—' he began.

There was another knock at the door and a head popped round the edge of it. Jones got up. Although she kept her voice low, I had keen enough hearing to hear every word. 'The entire footage?' she asked.

'We just ran corruption software on it. Some of the images are still blurry but most of it is visible. You'll want to see it. You should probably watch it on your own first, though.'

Jones sniffed. 'We have nothing to hide. We'll watch it with the suspect.'

She took the proffered laptop and returned to her seat. 'We have obtained some evidence,' she said. 'The full footage of the night in question. This is a video from Chorlton Golf Course. It was deliberately corrupted but we've managed to recover most of it. I'm sure you didn't expect that our technological abilities would be quite so advanced, Ms Hatter,' she added, implying that it was my efforts that had corrupted the footage in the first place. Not for lack of trying, I thought. Rubus, in the glamoured guise of Mendax, had gotten there before me.

'We are all seeing this for the first time.' Jones licked her lips in anticipation. I felt even more nauseous. Viburna was looking rather pale too. Either that, or she was just lacking in Vitamin D.

'We've already seen an image from a video that shows you using a sword to cut off Charrie Mickelson's head. The video was a short clip, however. Here is the scene in its entirety.' Jones smiled. 'This will be interesting.'

I didn't want to look; I didn't want to watch myself killing another living being yet again. I deserved to be made to look, though. Whoever Charrie was, I owed it to him to at least live through the experience again. And I owed it to his family, who were just next door.

Jones pressed play. Collectively, we held our breaths.

The boffin who'd handed her the laptop was right: the first images were desperately grainy. Neither did it help that the footage was from night time. It was just possible to make out a flag then, as the murkiness dissipated somewhat, I recognised the spot where I'd woken up. The spot where I'd murdered Charrie.

A moment later, the man himself wandered into view. His body appeared to be drooping and his feet were shuffling. He didn't look like someone who was thrilled to have finally obtained Chen's little magical sphere.

For several moments nothing happened. I wanted to cry out to him to run, to get away and escape while he still could. But it was pointless; the video we were watching had been taken three weeks earlier. This was the past. There was nothing I could do to change it now.

As I continued to watch the screen, wholly aware of the sickening fate that was about to befall the bogle, another person came into view. It was unmistakably me. I held up a hand towards Charrie as if in friendly greeting then walked right up to him with that damned rowan-poisoned sword in my hand. I started gesticulating and talking. I didn't appear to be threatening him, although I was waving the stupid weapon around.

Charrie's mouth moved as he replied. I squinted, desperately trying to lip-read the conversation, but with both our faces in profile it was impossible. Even an expert couldn't have worked out what we were saying.

Charrie held out his hand. Seemingly reluctantly, I passed something over to him. It looked like a small bottle or vial; when he unscrewed it and tipped the contents into his mouth, I knew I was right. What I didn't know, or couldn't remember, was what he was drinking.

It wasn't long afterwards that he collapsed, his knees giving way before his chest fell forward to the ground.

Jones paused the video screen and turned to me. 'What was that?' she demanded. 'What did you give him?'

'I don't know.'

'Bullshit!'

'I don't remember anything! I told you already, I've got amnesia! The first thing I remember is waking up next to him after he was dead. No one else was there. It must have been me who killed him. This though,' I pointed at the screen, 'I don't know what this is.'

Mulroney's gaze was hard. 'It's very convenient that you don't remember.'

'I can't prove that I've got amnesia,' I half-yelled. 'But whatever is happening on that video, I'm telling the truth. I don't remember any of it.'

The last thing I wanted was to be caught in an obvious lie. I had to tell the truth where I could – but I could still gently nudge the two police officers in the right direction. 'It could be poison though. It *must* be poison.' I warmed to my topic. 'I poisoned him. I probably lied and told him I was giving him apple juice. He wouldn't have known what he was really taking. He wouldn't have known what was going to happen.'

Mulroney's answer was cool. 'Then let's see, shall we? Let's see what happens.'

Jones started up the video again. We all watched as my past self dropped the sword and collapsed beside Charrie's fallen body, hunching over him with shaking shoulders. I was crying. Not just crying; I was sobbing my heart out. Was he dead? Had I actually killed him with a potion? Had

I tricked him into drinking it? But if that was the case, why was I so upset that it had worked?

I shook my head, my own confusion as palpable as that of the other three people in the room. From underneath the table, I was aware of Viburna's legs jiggling with nervous tension. It appeared that she was almost as thrown by all this as I was.

After what seemed like an eternity, the video showed me standing up. I spun round and walked away several steps then I walked back. I seemed to be muttering to myself. I ran my hands through my hair and kicked angrily at nothing. Throughout it all, Charrie didn't stir.

'He was already dead,' Viburna murmured. 'Whatever you gave him, whatever that was, that's what killed him.' She shook herself, apparently remembering she was supposed to be my lawyer. 'Those are not the actions of a cold-blooded murderer,' she declared to Mulroney and Jones.

I nudged her sharply with my elbow. We *wanted* them to believe I was a cold-blooded murderer. That was the entire point. 'But it's possible,' Viburna added, 'that there is indeed some culpability on my client's part.'

On the video, I took another little bottle out of my pocket. I wiped my eyes with the back of my hand before holding it up towards Charrie's body as if in a toast. Then I drank it down. As soon as I'd swallowed the contents, I grabbed the first empty vial and disappeared from view.

'Where has she gone?' Mulroney demanded.

Jones grimaced. 'The cameras only cover the course holes and teeing-off points. She could have gone anywhere.'

I rubbed my forehead. I was getting rid of the empty bottles. They hadn't been there when I woke up, so nothing else made any sense. 'But the sword. Charrie's head…'

My voice drifted off as my image returned to the screen, a grimly determined tilt to my chin. I picked up the sword again and squeezed my eyes shut. Oh no.

I continued to watch with horrified eyes as the video version of me swung the sword downwards with one strike. The weapon was clearly razor sharp. It only took one blow.

Both the me on screen and the me in the interrogation room heaved. Until this point, it had seemed that nothing made me retch. Now I knew why: I'd already reacted biologically to the worst possible thing that could happen. Nothing could top dismembering an already-dead body.

I continued to stare at the video.

On the screen, I dropped the sword before rolling Charrie's body so he was on his back. I didn't seem to notice that I'd covered the sword with his corpse. Instead, I appeared to arrange his limbs as if I wanted him to look more like he was sleeping and less like he was dead. I gently adjusted his decapitated head then leaned over and kissed his brow.

The quality of the recording made it difficult to tell for sure but I was almost certainly still crying. I leaned back on my haunches, swaying. Now it was my turn to look ill. Within seconds I also collapsed, falling sickeningly parallel to Charrie.

That was it, I realised. That was the position I'd been in when I'd woken up with amnesia. I swallowed and looked away from the laptop.

DC Jones reached over and closed the laptop lid with a loud snap. 'Wait here.' She and Mulroney got to their feet and walked out of the room.

Silence settled and stretched out as I struggled to make sense of what I'd seen. It seemed to neither entirely prove nor disprove that I was a murderer. At no point had Charrie resisted or tried to run away. While I might well have given him poison, he'd willingly drunk it. What kind of daft arsebadger would do what I told them to do?

Tension snapped in my spine. This was ridiculous. Lock me up already.

The only sound in the room was the ticking from the large clock on the wall. It continued to tick and fill the air until I couldn't stand it any more. I opened my mouth in a silent scream of frustration and horror and jerked pointlessly against my restraints until at least the rattling muffled the blasted noise.

I turned to Viburna. 'I don't understand,' I said, fully aware of the tremble in my voice. 'I don't understand what any of that was.'

She met my eyes. 'Neither do I.' Her mouth

flattened grimly. 'But I'd bet my life that you gave yourself amnesia. Whatever you drank, that must be what caused it. You did it to yourself.'

'I had to forget,' I whispered. 'I had to forget that I killed him.'

Viburna shook her head. 'No. From the way he was acting, he knew what he was getting into. Actually, I don't think you did kill him. I don't think those two coppers do, either.'

'But...'

The door re-opened and Mulroney and Jones stalked back in. This time neither of them sat down. 'You discharged a firearm in a public place,' Mulroney said.

'And that is a criminal act,' Jones added.

Mulroney clenched and unclenched his fists. 'We are dropping the murder charge. But we will not forget the rest. However, your doctor is outside. He has documentation that proves you are mentally unbalanced and belong in a hospital.' He let out a short, humourless laugh. 'After all, you did tell us that you were a faery.'

Viburna stiffened visibly. Fortunately, both Mulroney and Jones were focused on me and didn't notice.

Jones continued. 'You are to be released into your doctor's care and will remain on bail for the time being. You are *not* to leave the city of Manchester for any reason. There may be other charges to follow. Someone will be along shortly with the paperwork. Your belongings will be returned to you before you leave. We will be in touch.' They both whirled round and made for the open door again.

It took me a moment to react. 'Wait!' I screeched. 'You saw the video! I gave Charrie something that killed him. His death is my fault. You have to charge me now!'

Mulroney halted. 'New evidence has come to light,' he said over his shoulder. 'We'll give your barrister the details.'

'I shot a gun in the city centre!'

'You shot into the air.'

'I'm an illegal immigrant!'

'Your doctor has proved otherwise. He has identification for you.'

'I mutilated a corpse!'

'Corpse desecration is not, alas, a crime under English law.'

He had to be kidding me. 'But…'

'You're being released on bail, Ms Hatter. Be thankful.' He glanced at Viburna then at me again. 'Anyone would think you wanted to be locked up.' He continued on his way.

I clutched at Viburna's arm. 'Who in gasbudlikins is this doctor? Is he one of ours? Does he work for Morgan?'

She was even paler than before. 'I don't know.'

'You need to do something. They can't just let me walk out of here with that damned sphere. Rubus will —'

The white-coated figure of Carduus appeared in the doorway. The mad faery scientist, loyal only to one man. 'Rubus will what?' he enquired with a nasty smile.

My stomach dropped. Getting shot by armed police was better than this. Being cuffed to a hospital bed while fully unconscious was far, *far* better than this. Truthfully, taking a dip in a swimming pool of sewage and getting my hair caught in the filter so I slowly drowned wouldn't be as bad as this.

I squared my shoulders. I was Madrona, the maybe-not-murdering-after-all Madhatter. I'd find a way to swim out. And hopefully drown arse-badgering Carduus in the process too.

Chapter Three

The best way to attack this situation was to make some noise. Without further ado, I started to scream at the top of my voice. The piercing noise bounced off the walls until I reckoned it sounded as if I were being dismembered limb by limb.

Mulroney was back in an instant. 'What on earth is going on?'

'This man!' I screeched. 'This man is not my doctor! In fact, he's no doctor at all. Get him away from me!'

Carduus simply folded his hands together and looked concerned. 'She's obviously brain damaged. We need to get her back to the hospital and under proper care. She's been off her medication for too long.' His calm voice and placid features gave the impression of a kindly medical practitioner dealing with a crazed psychopath. Despite knowing that, I didn't let up with my shrieks.

'Viburna! Do something!'

Fortunately she finally stepped up and did her job like she was supposed to. 'My client has nothing to do with this man. He is not a doctor and, as such, his reasons for taking away Ms Hatter can be nothing but nefarious.'

Nefarious. That was a great word. I bobbed my head with considerable energy and enthusiasm and stopped yelling just long enough to speak properly. 'Yes! He's definitely nefarious! And I'm not going anywhere near him!'

Mulroney frowned. He knew there was something going on but he couldn't quite work out what. 'I'll double-check the paperwork.'

'I can assure you,' Carduus said mildly, 'it's all in order. Unfortunately, Madrona is a danger to herself. She believes herself to be a faery. If she thinks that she can fly too, and leaps off a building to prove it, well…' He shook his head in dismay.

Jones reappeared, a sheet of paper in her hand. She handed it over to Mulroney. He scanned it then held it up. Both Viburna and I stared. It was completely blank.

'I'm sorry,' DI Mulroney said, not looking in the slightest bit sorry at all. 'As you can see, the paperwork is all in order. The courts have ordered Madrona Hatter to be committed.'

My voice reached crazy decibel heights again. 'There's nothing written there! It's just a blank piece of paper!'

Carduus tutted. 'She's hallucinating now. The faster we get her transported back to hospital the better.'

I looked at Viburna. There no doubt from the expression in her eyes that she knew the paper was as unblemished as the perfect skin on my arse. Carduus or Rubus – or whoever happened to have enough magic skill – had done something to make Mulroney and the rest of the police see something completely different. It was a bloody clever glamour. But Viburna couldn't let this happen. She was the lawyer around here; it was time she did some proper lawyering stuff.

I swung round to her and put my hands on my hips. My screaming had got attention; now I needed to get her respect. I forced myself to speak calmly and levelly. 'You must be able to challenge this … court order.'

She shook herself. 'Yes. Yes, I will.' She drew herself up. 'In fact —'

'I should add,' Carduus interrupted, 'that my employer is outside waiting. He's an important man but I can always ask him to join us to help iron out this little issue.'

Viburna went white. We both knew exactly who he was referring to. Rubus was out there. And, as the only Fey no longer affected by the truce that kept the rest of us in check and prevented us from attacking each other, he'd be able to use both magic and violence to do whatever he wanted.

I could tell Mulroney that Rubus was out there but what was the bet that the blasted faery would conjure up another glamour for himself to maintain his anonymity?

'Viburna,' I said through gritted teeth.

'I…' Her face fell and she looked away. 'The paperwork seems to be in order legally,' she

33

muttered.

What. An. Arsebadger. So this was the new world order. Now that Rubus could hurt – or even kill – any of us, he was going to be granted permission to do whatever the hell he wanted. Even the likes of Viburna, who had a rod of steel up her arse, was too scared to go up against him.

For a moment I debated requesting that my belongings, and in particular the sphere, be released into Viburna's care but it was clear that I could no longer count on her. Not that I ever had.

'The last time I met something like you,' I told her icily, 'I flushed it.' It wasn't my best effort but I was under pressure and she got the point. Carduus just smirked. I glanced at Mulroney and Jones. 'Get her out of here. Viburna Smith QC no longer represents me.'

Mulroney shrugged. He patently couldn't give a toss what I decided to do. 'As you wish.'

DC Jones, who until this point could hardly have been described as amiable or helpful, gave all three of us an assessing look. 'The good doctor will meet you out front,' she said.

Carduus frowned. 'I'm not sure that's…'

She glared at him and he subsided. I almost smiled. At least someone around here besides me had a bit of backbone. And until Rubus had his hands on the magical sphere, I wasn't going to give up hope.

***

I was uncuffed and given enough crappy bits of paper to sign to fill up even the roomiest recycling bin. A fresh-faced uniformed cop handed me my belongings in a sealed plastic bag and I relaxed slightly when I spotted the sphere nestled in the bottom. The fat lady hadn't sung yet, regardless of who was out there on the street waiting for me.

'I need to use the loo,' I declared loudly.

He pointed me down the corridor. I sniffed, grabbed the bag and headed in that direction. I could feel Carduus's eyes boring a hole in my back from the waiting room. He could bore away; I'd always thought he was a tedious sort of faery anyway.

Once inside the toilets, I darted into the nearest cubicle and dropped the lid so I could sit down then I used my teeth to tear open the plastic bag. I shoved my wallet into my back pocket before carefully drawing out the sphere.

I'd never really paid it much close attention before. It was about the size of a golf ball, with a smooth, glistening, silver exterior. It felt slightly warm to the touch but there was nothing that indicated it was an object that had the power to destroy worlds. Not, of course, that such destruction was its main aim.

Apparently the dragon Chen had created it in order to draw magic from other demesnes into this one. He'd wanted new ways to locate treasure for himself. Unfortunately for humanity, bringing such a flood of magic would unbalance this world. As a technology-driven demesne, it couldn't cope. I didn't know the specifics but I was aware that using the sphere would tip this already precarious place into an event of apocalyptic proportions. The world's population would be decimated.

Rubus wanted the sphere because using it would re-open the borders to Mag Mell, the faery homelands. He didn't care what happened afterwards in this demesne.

I hefted the sphere from hand to hand, rolling it through my fingers and thinking. In theory I could have swallowed it but goodness only knew what it would have done to my intestines. Irritable bowel syndrome or saving the world? It was a tough choice. Perhaps I should explore other avenues first.

I could conceal it in other body cavities. There were two likely possibilities. Neither particularly appealed although, given what I knew of Rubus's distaste for germs, it would be rather enjoyable to see him try to get hold of the sphere and use it after it had been, erm, intimate with me. I pursed my lips. Given that he'd happily rip me apart to retrieve it, it probably wasn't a suitable option.

I considered leaving it here. Maybe I could find a dusty corner somewhere to hide it in – but Rubus could easily send in his many minions to locate it. I tapped my mouth. No, I needed to be clever. Luckily, I was; I just had to think a wee bit harder and a solution would present itself.

The outside door to the toilets opened and I heard footsteps followed by a trundling wheel. A moment later, there was a deep sigh and the tinny sound of music. I heard the scoosh of a spray. Curious, I stood up and unlatched the cubicle to peek out.

A young woman stood with her back to me. She was wearing grubby overalls and using a yellow cloth to wipe one of the mirrors over the row of sinks. I used my intense powers of deduction and relaxed slightly. A cleaner. Admittedly, a cleaner with blue hair, a slim figure and appalling taste in music, but not anyone I should be afraid of. She knew how to dance as well, wiggling her body in time to the beat as she rubbed at a particularly stubborn streak.

Her earphones meant that she couldn't hear me but my reflection caught me out. She jumped, startled at catching a glimpse of me in the mirror, then shot me a dazzling grin.

I stood up, flushed the toilet and ambled out towards the sinks. The woman, who couldn't have been older than twenty-four or twenty-five, made room for me so I could wash my hands. Just before she turned, I spotted her identification badge: Charlotte Page. Pixie Dust Cleaning Services.

I almost crowed aloud. Well, then. It was simply meant to be.

I dried my hands and spoke. 'Cool hair.'

She didn't hear me. I tapped her on the

shoulder and she glanced up, surprised. She took out the earphones and tilted her head questioningly towards me with a small smile that made dimples form in her cheeks. She had a snub nose that was incredibly cute and added to the overall effect of sweet wholesomeness. No wonder she worked for Pixie Dust Cleaning Services; she was less like the drug I was renowned for selling and more like something I wanted to put in my pocket and carry around with me.

'Cool hair,' I repeated.

Charlotte grinned. 'Thanks. I love blue. Did you know that it's been proved that weight lifters can lift heavier weights in blue-painted gyms?' I stared at her as she laughed and flexed her arms. Then she leaned in towards me and tapped her nose. 'I'll let you into a secret about my hair.' She paused. 'It's not natural.'

I laughed more than I should have done. I also relaxed even further. Little Miss Charlotte Page had a northern accent that couldn't be faked. This was no glamoured-up faery; she was human through and through. She was also just what I needed.

I stumbled slightly, feinting left. As expected, Charlotte put out her hand to steady me. The moment she did so, I dropped the sphere into the large pocket at the front of her work tunic.

'I'm so sorry! I'm hopelessly clumsy!' I said.

She smiled at me again. She was beginning to annoy me now that she'd served her purpose; she was almost too winsome for words, despite the daft hair. Maybe, I pondered, this was why us faeries always had green eyes. Jealousy seemed to be a running theme.

'Don't worry about it,' Charlotte burbled.

Yep, far too cheery for her own good. Still, she was going to be an excellent mule. I congratulated myself on my genius-level plan and strolled out of the bathroom. I'd done all that I could for now.

Chapter Four

Fun as it would have been to skip happily towards Carduus, I couldn't let him realise that I'd temporarily disposed of the sphere. As his figure came into sight, I dropped my happy amble in favour of a stiff-legged shuffle. I needed to appear as reluctant to reach him as possible. The sphere might be safe for the time being but I certainly wasn't.

At least there was no sign of Viburna. That bloody Fey lawyer had done enough damage.

I was almost at the door when DC Jones caught up to me. She grabbed my elbow, causing me to whirl round and almost smack her in the face.

'Sorry,' she said, not sounding sorry at all. 'I just wanted to catch you before you left. I think what you did what was a good thing. That doctor of yours gives me the heebie-jeebies but we can't argue with a court order.'

It wasn't an arsebadgering court order, it was a magicked-up sheet of blank paper. 'What good thing did I do?' I enquired irritably. It wasn't her fault that she was human and had been fooled by faery machinations – but I was still going to hold it against her.

'You helped that man,' she said. 'Mr Mickelson.'

For a moment I didn't have the faintest idea who she was talking about. I scratched my head before abruptly realising. 'Oh, you mean Charrie the Bogle.'

'Bogle?'

Uh-oh. Me and my big mouth. 'Bogle?' I repeated, as if I'd never heard the word.

'That's what you said.'

I shook my head. 'No, I didn't. You must be hearing things.' Time to change the subject. 'And how in gasbudlikin hell did I help him?'

A faint line furrowed her brow. 'You really do have amnesia.'

Good grief. Why did no one ever believe me about that? I gestured irritably. 'As I have said.'

'His family told us what you did. His wife. And his children. They all backed it up.'

Tense now, I watched her carefully for signs of subterfuge. 'What exactly did I do?' I asked carefully.

'He had cancer. You gave him something to…' she swallowed. 'Look, I'm not supposed to agree with euthanasia. It's against the law here. But I don't think you did a bad thing.'

'That bottle I gave him,' I said, realising. 'It *was* poison.'

DC Jones nodded. 'His wife said he'd forced you into getting some. He wanted to die on his own terms. You cut off his head afterwards to make it look like murder so she could still collect on the life insurance.'

Uh...

'Of course,' Jones added with another frown, 'it doesn't explain what happened to his body. But it puts you in the clear. You didn't force him to drink poison, he made that decision of his own volition.'

It was a strange day when the police were letting me walk free after it had been proved I'd given a man a vial of poison that had caused his death and then I'd chopped off his head afterwards. Human law was a very odd thing indeed.

'Okay, then.' I pointed towards Carduus, who was watching us through the glass door with narrowed eyes. 'I don't suppose there's anything you can do about him?'

'I told you I can't. I'm sorry. I do believe you're a good person, Ms Hatter.'

'I'm a very bad person.'

'You're not. Misguided, perhaps. But not really bad.'

I put my hands on my hips. 'I'm an evil bitch. It's already been agreed.' Then it occurred to me that arguing with the police about how truly villainous I was probably wasn't a good idea, not now that my release was already happening and the sphere was relatively safe. 'No,' I said. 'You're right. I'm actually very heroic.'

'You are to Mr Mickelson's family.' Jones smiled faintly. 'Just don't go shooting up any more of our city.'

'I'm about to be committed,' I told her. 'I don't think I'll have the chance.'

She grimaced. 'Yeah. Well, I've heard straitjackets can be quite comfortable. And at least you'll have a nice padded cell.'

I gazed at her. She smiled back. 'You're all heart,' I told her.

She curtsied in response then reached into her pocket and pulled out a small card. 'Just in case,' she said with a smile. 'My number is there.'

I felt that the police had failed more than enough by now; I was on my own, whether I liked it or not. I offered her a bob of my head and waited while she pressed the door-release button. Muttering under my breath, and still not sure whether the policewoman had been trying to be nice or trying to be nasty, I walked out.

Carduus flapped towards me as if he were certain I was about to make a run for it. Given that the street outside was probably teeming with Fey loyal to Rubus, it seemed a rather pointless measure on his part.

'Ms Hatter,' he boomed. 'We'll get you back to the hospital and feeling as right as rain in no time.'

I rolled my eyes. The only person present to hear him was the desk sergeant and he looked about as interested in Carduus and me as a Goth teenager would be in a rainbow fun house. 'As right as acid rain,' I muttered.

Carduus chuckled and took my arm. 'Aren't

you funny?' Then he dipped his head toward mine and lowered his voice. 'Where's the fucking sphere, you bitch?'

'My, my,' I said. 'Just when I thought we were getting along so well.'

He glared at me and steered me out of the police station. 'I don't know what you think you're playing at,' he spat, as soon as we were safely out of earshot of any helpful police officers. 'But you will tell us where the sphere is and you will tell us now.'

'Poor Carduus. All that time and effort that you and Rubus put into fooling me and in the end it was for nothing. You still didn't get the sphere. You're still stuck here just like the rest of us.'

'And we all know whose fault that is, don't we?' His malevolence was quite extraordinary; until now, I'd had no idea that underneath his wrinkled façade was such a seething mass of hatred. He was an even better actor than Rubus.

I yanked my elbow away from him and threw out my arms. 'Yes! We do know. I caused the borders to close! I trapped everyone here! But that doesn't make what you're doing right. If you use that sphere, you'll effectively destroy this demesne. Magic isn't supposed to live here. If you bring it, you'll end the lives of millions – no, billions – of people.'

'Since when did you become a saviour of the human race?' Carduus sneered. 'The only person you've ever cared about is yourself, Madrona. Now give me the sphere.'

I shrugged. 'I don't have it.'

'Of course you do!'

'Nope.' Out of the corner of my eye, I spotted several car doors opening across the street. Numerous Fey, most of whom I recognised, stepped out. Included in their number was Rubus. He looked pale; no doubt he was still recovering from his self-inflicted bout of rowan poisoning. All the same, he managed a nasty smile in my direction. I beamed and waved at him. My actions didn't seem to improve his mood.

'Play the joker all you like,' Carduus said. 'Do you have any idea what Rubus will do to you if you don't hand over the sphere? I might not be your biggest fan but I'm doing you a favour. I'm trying to help you, Madrona. You'll save yourself considerable pain and anguish if you just give it to us.'

'I can't give you what I don't have,' I replied mildly.

'You think you're so clever. Getting yourself locked up, offering up the video evidence to keep you there, using Viburna as a lawyer. Your problem is that you're not as smart as you think you are. The fact that we pulled the wool over your eyes and got you to believe that Mendax the dragon even existed proves that you have the brain capacity of a slug.'

I considered this. 'Fair enough,' I agreed. 'But you have to admit that I'm a pretty sexy slug.' Then I thought over what he'd said. 'Hang on. Didn't *you* give the police the video evidence?'

'Pah.' He grabbed me again and all but dragged me across the street towards Rubus. We'd barely got halfway across the street, however, when another car appeared, screeching to a halt and blocking our path.

Morgan jumped out, his body tense and his expression grim. I beamed. My hero.

'Let her go, Carduus,' Morgan said. I was hoping for a crack of thunder to add weight to his words. The sky did look ominously grey but there wasn't so much as the sound of car backfiring. Shame.

The Fey scientist curled his lip. 'No.'

'Do it.'

'Or what? You can't hurt me. You can't do anything to stop me.' Carduus pointed a bony finger. 'Your brother can though.'

As if to give weight to Carduus's words, Rubus smiled and jerked his head. A moment later, a struggling Viburna was pulled out of his car. My stomach dropped. He must have grabbed her as soon as she left the police station. There was a red imprint on her cheek, finger marks painfully visible against her pale skin. For effect, I thought scornfully. He wanted to remind us that he was the only Fey in this entire demesne who possessed the capability to hurt another Fey.

'I think,' he called out, 'that a little demonstration is probably in order. Just in case you've forgotten what I'm actually capable of now.' His smile broadened. 'Thanks to you, little brother.'

Carduus let go of my arm. 'You can stop this, Madrona. Just give us the sphere and we'll release Viburna.'

I looked past him to Morgan. 'I can't give it to you.'

Morgan nodded. 'Don't.' His gaze hardened and he turned to address Rubus. 'We don't negotiate with terrorists. Besides,' he added, 'what are you going to do? We're in front of a police station.'

Rubus laughed. 'Like I care! Am I supposed to be scared of a few humans wearing silly uniforms? Our cause is more important than anything they could conjure up.' His green eyes, so similar to Morgan's, flashed. 'You can still join me. You can still be part of the team that returns us to Mag Mell and makes everything right again. The humans don't matter. They're inferior. But we faeries deserve better.'

'You're a megalomaniac.'

Rubus smirked. 'So's your girlfriend. I'll take that as a no, then. Remember that in the future when you think of Viburna. This was your choice.' He tilted his head at me. 'And yours.'

Even from several metres away, I could see that Viburna was trembling. She started walking backwards with her palms up in a desperate bid to escape. 'Don't hurt me! I've not done anything! I don't have the sphere! Madrona will have it now. You need to talk to her. This is nothing to do with me.'

Morgan started to move towards her but several of Rubus's Fey minions jumped forward to bar his progress. All the while, Rubus continued to advance on Viburna.

'Leave her alone!' I yelled. 'You're not interested in her.'

Rubus kept his eyes on her. 'She's a means to an end.'

I gestured desperately at the other Fey. 'Are you really going to let him do this? You're going to let him harm one of us for no reason?'

Several of them looked uneasy; there was even doubt in a few eyes. With enough time, I could get them to see that this was wrong.

'The truce is there for a reason! We're not supposed to fight each other,' I shouted.

'Then give me the sphere, Madrona,' Rubus responded calmly. 'You can stop this.'

'I don't have the sphere! The police have still got it.'

He shook his head. He was only a few steps from Viburna now. She'd backed herself up against a brick wall and there was nowhere for her to go. 'They'll have returned it to you when you were released.'

'Madrona!' Viburna shrieked. 'Help me! Just give him the sphere!'

Even if I'd had it on me, I wouldn't have handed it over. I had no desire to see Rubus hurt Viburna but her well-being was nothing compared to the well-being of planet Earth.

Rubus reached her, angling his body so that everyone could see what he was doing. He put out his hand and stroked her cheek with the tip of his index finger. 'Poor Viburna. I don't want to do this, you know. But it's for the good of all of us. Getting the sphere will save us. How much more of living here do you think we can take? The physical ache is getting worse by the day. If we can get back to Mag Mell, we can undo all the hurt inside us. Once that's happened and the borders are re-opened, we'll be able to repair any damage here. I'm not going to lie. Using the sphere will cause problems in this demesne. But they've got problems by the bucket load as it is. In the end, I reckon it'll do them more good than harm.' He smiled gently. 'You see that, don't you?'

Viburna nodded vigorously. At that moment, she'd have agreed to anything to escape. 'I do. I do, Rubus. Let me go and I'll persuade Madrona to give you the sphere. You can trust me. Then you can use it and we'll all go back home and everything will be fine.'

Rubus's expression took on a tinge of sadness. 'I don't think you can persuade her. Not with words anyway.'

'Morgan,' I said, my voice filled with warning.

He swallowed. 'I know.' He cleared his throat. 'Rubus, just let her go. Your argument is with me, not anyone else.'

Rubus ran his tongue over his teeth. 'I need

to make you see what I'm capable of. I need everyone to see.'

'We know what you're capable of!' I shouted. 'We don't need a show and tell.'

'Oh, Maddy,' Rubus sighed. 'I think you *do* need to see.' He glanced back at Viburna. 'This gives me no pleasure, sweetheart.' Without any warning, he pulled out a curved dagger and thrust it into her heart.

There was no scream; there wasn't time for anything like that. Viburna's eyes widened with pain and her lips parted in a sudden gasp. Then, with the dagger still in her, she collapsed.

Morgan let out a strangled cry. He barrelled forward – even the wall of Fey goons didn't stop him this time. He shoved his way past them. I ran after him, ignoring Carduus's cackle at my back.

'You can't hurt me, brother,' Rubus said, bending down to take the dagger from Viburna's body. He gave her a sad look, as if he genuinely hadn't wanted to kill her, then he wiped her blood off the dagger and onto his thigh.

Morgan snarled and attacked but Rubus was right. The truce, with its invisible threads of magic, pulled Morgan back. The strain was visible on his face as he tried to push past the pain, to push past the barrier of the truce. It didn't do him any good.

Rubus smiled. A moment later, he lunged for his brother. Grabbing Morgan, he spun him round and held the dagger to his throat. 'You wouldn't sacrifice the sphere to save Viburna,' he cooed at me. 'But I bet you'd do it to save Morgan.'

I skidded to a halt in from of the pair of them. I clenched my fists and glared. 'Let him go, you arsebadger.'

Rubus frowned. 'Let me think about that for a moment.' He paused and his expression hardened. 'Um. No. Give me the fucking sphere.'

'Don't,' Morgan said. 'Don't do it.'

Why did my mouth feel so dry? I swallowed. 'Morgan,' I whispered. 'You're too good for me. Your brother is right though – I do love you.' Maybe; I certainly lusted after him enough.

My declaration, whether wholly truthful or not, would piss off Rubus. Anything that I could snatch at that would unhinge him was a good thing. I licked my lips and softened my tone. 'But it's because I feel that way about you that I can't give him the sphere.'

Morgan sagged slightly, relief lighting his eyes despite Rubus's tight grip round his neck.

'He won't get the easy death that Viburna did,' Rubus warned. 'I'll make sure he suffers. And I'll make sure that you watch.'

There was a shout from behind us. Finally one of the policemen had decided to look out of the window and realised something was going on outside. What on earth had taken them so long? 'What the hell is happening here?'

'Just a little demonstration!' Rubus called back. Almost immediately three Fey jumped up and dragged Viburna's body into one of the cars so it was out of sight. 'Nothing for you to worry about!' He looked at me. 'I'll kill those humans even more easily than Viburna, Madrona. I'll do anything to get our people back home and you know it. You need to give me the sphere right now or there will be a bloodbath.'

I didn't believe for a second that he was bluffing – but that didn't mean that I couldn't bluff. I sighed. 'Jeez, Ruby baby. Kill the humans. I don't care. I'm only trying to stop you from taking the sphere because it's what Morgan wants me to do. I don't give a fig about whether anyone other than him lives or dies. But I really don't have the sphere.'

I reached into my pockets and tossed out my wallet then pulled out the linings so he could see they were empty. 'I'll strip naked if you need me to but I genuinely don't have it.'

Rubus stared at me. So did Morgan. I could only assume that the pair of them were indeed hoping that I performed a striptease right there and then.

'Everyone get down on the ground with your hands behind your heads!' roared another voice. Apparently the police were stepping things up. Go them. But they were far too late to this party, even though it was happening on their doorstep.

'I'll kill anyone who gets in my way,' Rubus said to me. 'This is your last chance.'

'You can't do it, Maddy,' Morgan said in a strained voice.

I ignored him. 'Let Morgan go and I'll come

with you, Rubus. That way the police no longer have to be involved and things don't get any messier than they already are.'

Rubus sighed. 'But I *want* things to be messy. Don't you see that?'

Gasbudlikins. I was running out of options. 'I...'

Suddenly, and without any warning, the sky darkened. There was a dull boom and the ground juddered. I lost my footing, stumbling forwards onto the pavement – and I wasn't the only one. Every single person did the same. I didn't have the faintest idea what was happening but I couldn't let this moment pass.

Rolling in a manner that a gymnastics teacher would have been proud of, I got hold of Morgan and yanked at his leg. Rubus could probably have stopped me if it weren't for the strange skittering sound over his head. A second later, an undulating brown mass appeared from the top of the wall, cascading downwards on top of him. It was only the odd whisker and dragging tail that made me realise what the strange wave was. Rats. Hundreds of them.

Rubus shrieked, cowering into a foetal ball and covering his face. He released his grip on Morgan. The mass of rats swarmed over him and reached Morgan's feet at the same time as I pulled him towards me. I yanked him upwards and we both took to our heels.

Shrieks and shouts were filling the air, not

just from this street but from the ones beyond as well. The horrific stench of sewage filled the air. I glanced to my right and spotted dirty water bubbling up from all the nearby drains.

'Car,' Morgan gasped. 'Get to the car.'

Luckily he'd left it in the middle of the road. One or two of Rubus's loyal arsebadgers made half-hearted attempts to stop us but most of them had their own problems. There was a keening in the air and, as if to help the still-advancing army of rats, a mass of ravens appeared, swooping and diving at anyone who was daft enough to be in the open.

I shoved Morgan into the passenger seat, dashed round and jumped into the driver's side. I slammed the door shut just before the tidal wave of rats reached us. There were several clunks on the car roof as the ravens continued to dive bomb us.

I didn't waste any time questioning the provenance of these unearthly creatures and unnatural happenings. I just thrust the car into gear and sped off.

Chapter Five

Ignoring the double yellow lines, I pulled up directly outside the Metropolitan Bar and turned off the engine. Morgan was gripping the armrest so hard I virtually had to prise his fingers off and help him unclip his seatbelt.

'I'm sorry about Viburna. I know Rubus killed Finn's brother, Jinn, just as callously but somehow I didn't think he'd do it to another faery. She was your friend and for that I'm sorry.' I surprised myself with my words. I sounded sincere. Gasbudlikins, I *felt* sincere.

Morgan nodded, although it didn't seem that he could bring himself to speak about her. He jerked his head up towards the sky. 'It's clearing up.' His voice was hoarse.

I peered out. He was right; there was the faintest glimmer of sunlight and it seemed that things were returning to normal. Admittedly, there were no people on the streets but there weren't any surging rats or crazy raven bombs to deal with either.

'Let's get inside,' I urged. 'It might not be any safer in the bar but at least there will be vodka. I could do with a stiff drink.'

He glanced at me. 'On the count of three.'

'Three. Two.' I opened the door. 'One.' We sprang out. There was a strange lingering smell in the air that was almost sulphurous. Other than that, there was nothing remarkable. I wasn't taking any chances, though; I hotfooted it to the door of the pub and pulled it open for Morgan before following him in.

There were more people inside than I expected. At least forty pairs of eyes swivelled in my direction and the television, which been blaring full blast, was immediately muted. With the exception of Jodie, the human bartender who worked for Morgan, and Julie, my soap-star vampire friend, every eye was moss green.

Every single one of them sagged in relief. Under any other circumstances, I'd have expected a standing ovation and at least a dozen rousing choruses of 'hip, hip, hooray' but somehow, at this point, my heart wasn't in it – even if it did make a change to have people happy to see me instead of recoiling.

'You made it!' Jodie exclaimed, rushing forward to hug Morgan. 'Where's the sphere?'

Morgan glanced at me and I shrugged. I noticed Paeonia, Timmons and Vandrake at the back of the crowd, but there were at least thirty-seven other Fey people in here that I didn't know. 'I don't have it,' I said.

Another vaguely familiar man pushed his way forward. 'Where's Viburna?' he demanded.

'Why isn't she with you?'

Cravat Man, minus the cravat he'd been wearing the last time I'd met him. His shirt was open at the neck and he looked dishevelled. Him and me both. I grimaced; he'd been with Viburna when I'd first met her. I strained my brain to remember his name. It was the least I could do.

'Opulus,' Morgan sighed. 'She...'

It wasn't fair that Morgan had to deliver the bad news. 'She's dead,' I finished for him. Let Opulus despise me for being the messenger; I reckoned Morgan needed a break.

Rather than get angry, however, Opulus seemed to diminish right in front of my eyes. His body sank into itself. I grabbed a chair and held it out for him. Barely noticing, he collapsed into it.

A murmur of shock rippled across the room. 'How?' someone asked. 'Was it because of what happened outside? With the sky and the...'

I shook my head. 'It was Rubus. Rubus killed her.'

The horror on the assembled faces was clear to see. 'The bastard!'

'How dare he!'

'We have to do something!'

From the back of the bar, there was a loud cough and Finn's hulking figure appeared. I hadn't spotted the Redcap before now; considering his size, staying out of sight was no mean feat for him. 'So now you're upset?' he enquired, his voice trembling with rage. 'It wasn't a problem when he killed my brother but now he's killed one of yours, you've decided you have to act?'

'The big man with the cauliflower ears makes a very valid point,' I said.

There was an angry hiss in my direction from one of the assembled Fey. 'Like you can talk. You worked for him! She could be a spy, Morganus! Get her out of here!'

Morgan rubbed his hand across his eyes. 'She's one of us. Leave her be.'

'One of us? Did you see what happened with the sky? With the animals? It's not natural. I bet she had something to do with that.'

I glared at my accuser then I drew myself up. 'I wasn't born with enough middle fingers to let you lot know how I feel about you right now. You've all been burying your heads in the sand and hoping Rubus would go away. At least I've been trying to do something about him. You want to blame me for all this? Go ahead. I deserve a lot of your censure. But complaining about me now isn't going to help matters. You've had ten years to do something about him. Some of you,' I glared, 'took his damned pixie dust and just smiled politely.'

'*You* sold us that damned pixie dust!' a brave voice yelled.

I put my hands on my hips. 'Yeah,' I said. 'I did. Not that I remember doing so. But you could have said no. You're like a bunch of witches, whispering and plotting and doing nothing. It's always someone else's responsibility to sort things out. It's someone else's fault and someone else should smooth things over so that your lives are made better. It's not *your* fault we're trapped here. It's not *your* fault that Rubus is a fucking arsebadger. But maybe it's your responsibility to do something about it. We're all faeries here. By not acting sooner we *all* have a hand in this. Stop worrying about who's to blame and start thinking about what we can do about it. You've had plenty of warning. As Finn said, his brother was killed by Rubus just as callously as Viburna. Where were you when that happened? He might not be Fey but he's still one of us! Quit your cackling or get out of here.'

Finn's jaw dropped open. Julie clapped. Several others turned to Morgan as if waiting for him to tell me off and send me to my room without supper.

He looked at me, a glimmer of a smile in his eyes. 'Madrona's right,' he said. 'Unless you have any bright ideas about what we can do to bring down Rubus then you can all piss off. We have more important things to worry about than your egos.'

I nodded happily. 'There's not enough room in here for another ego besides mine.'

Morgan growled under his breath, 'Don't push it, Maddy.'

I shrugged; I was only being honest.

'It's not safe outside. Have you seen what's been happening?' Paeonia pointed towards the muted television screen. 'It's chaos out there!'

'In case it escaped your attention, we've just been outside,' Morgan pointed out. 'Whatever that was, it's passed now. Go home. Think about what we can do to stop Rubus. Otherwise,' his voice hardened, 'don't get in our way.'

'Harsh,' I murmured. Then I grinned. 'But fair.'

Morgan obviously garnered considerably more respect than I did. One by one, the crowd of Fey started to disperse. They went slowly at first, as if they still didn't believe him about it being safe to leave, then more quickly when they realised that it was. Before long, there was only a handful of us left.

Julie smacked her lips. 'I need a drink.'

Vandrake also licked his lips but he was a recovering drug addict. I didn't think swapping one substance for another, regardless of the circumstances, was a good idea.

Jodie sighed. 'More gin? Haven't you had enough already?'

'Not gin.' Julie grimaced. 'To be honest, I'm feeling very strange. I need some blood.'

Finn walked around the bar towards her. 'I'll take you home to get some. We can return later.' He shot me a look. 'Thank you,' he said. 'I appreciate what you said to that lot.'

I sniffed. 'I didn't do it for you.'

His response was quiet. 'That's why I'm saying thank you.' Without looking at me again, he helped Julie to her feet and the pair of them walked out.

Somewhat nervously, Timmons edged forward. 'I'd like to stay and help, if that's alright. Admittedly I might not be a lot of help, but I'd like to try.' He bit his lip and flicked me a nervy look. 'Someone once told me I should stand up for myself.'

I beamed at him. 'Me, right? It was me? I think it was me.' I looked at the others. 'It was me.'

'What about him?' Jodie's voice was quiet. 'What about Opulus?'

He remained sunk on the chair I'd given him. Truthfully, he appeared all but comatose.

Morgan frowned. 'Leave him be. He'll come round when he wants to. Just give him some time. At least here we can keep an eye on him to make sure he's alright.'

Opulus groaned slightly and lifted his head. His eyes shone with unshed tears. 'I'm fine,' he said. He clearly wasn't. 'I'll get myself some water in a minute. I just need…' He choked, unable to finish.

We all nodded. That was the thing about grief – everyone had experienced it in one form or another. Even if I didn't remember my own moments of true grieving, some part of me recognised the sensation. Everyone dealt with it differently. Opulus didn't want to be alone but he didn't want to participate either. That was wholly understandable. To prove I could continue to be a lovely empathetic faery, I reached over and squeezed his shoulder.

'Getting rid of the others wasn't just about

preventing constant in-fighting and backstabbing,' Morgan said. 'It was also about trust. I know I can trust everyone in this room with my life.' It felt like my heart was going to burst. Finally. Finally he really trusted me. 'Not just you, Maddy, so stop with the cheesy grin.'

I didn't stop. Why would I?

'Maybe,' Morgan continued quietly, 'you should give one of us the sphere to look after. Carrying it just makes you a target.'

'I don't have it.' At his look, I rolled my eyes. 'I'm telling the truth! You just said you trusted me with your life so at least trust me in this! I gave the sphere to a cleaner.'

'You did what?' Jodie asked with palpable disbelief.

I sighed and explained what had happened. 'It seemed the best thing to do at the time. I wasn't going to get away with the sphere in my possession. And I wasn't expecting the heavens to start attacking the earth in order to help out little ol' me. I simply used my inherent genius. I know the woman's name and the company she works for her. The sphere is safe for now. We'll have to find her and retrieve it soon but I reckon we have some breathing space.'

'That was a smart move,' Morgan said.

I stuck my tongue out at Jodie. 'See?'

She tutted. 'Speaking of the heavens attacking,' she said, changing the subject, 'what the fuck was all that? Was it because of you? Or was it something Rubus did?'

I held up my palms. 'Nothing to do with me.'

'Nothing to do with Rubus either,' Morgan said grimly. 'He was more terrified than the rest of us.'

'The rats recognised him as a kindred spirit,' I said. 'Like is drawn to like.' I pointed at the television. 'It wasn't just a localised thing. Turn on the sound. What's happening?'

Jodie glanced at Morgan as if she needed his permission to up the volume. He gave her a brief nod. The man certainly liked to run a tight ship; perhaps he had more in common with his brother than he realised. My mouth flattened. Perhaps we all did in our own ways.

The newscaster's voice filled the room, booming out into every nook and cranny. 'For those of you just joining us, there have been numerous reports from all over the city of Manchester of serious disturbances. In Fallowfields, concerns have been raised by eyewitness who spoke of dozens of foxes running down the streets. In Rusholme, several passers-by managed to get footage of what appears to be a pink elephant causing considerable damage.'

The screen changed, flicking to what was indeed an elephant bursting out of the front window of a small Victorian terrace house. My jaw dropped. Talk about the elephant in the room.

'That's impossible,' Jodie breathed.

Vandrake rubbed his eyes. 'I've seen a pink

elephant before.'

We all ripped our gaze away from the screen to stare at him. Even Opulus jerked his head round. When Vandrake realised he was the centre of attention, his cheeks stained red and he looked down. 'I'm fairly certain it was a hallucination,' he muttered. 'It made itself a cup of tea and sat down in my favourite armchair.'

Uh … okay then.

'Here with us,' the newscaster continued, 'is Fred Bellows from the Meteorological Office. Fred, can you explain any of this?'

The face of a harried-looking man with a dishevelled suit jacket and a barely knotted tie filled the television screen. 'Good afternoon, Tim. I certainly can't explain pink elephants. That is a phenomenon which us weather men are unfamiliar with. I can confirm, however, that there was a localised event in the Greater Manchester area that affected the skies. At this stage, we believe it was a small storm caused by a sudden rush of rising air. That accounts for the sudden darkening of the skies. It's not been confirmed yet, but we also believe there might have been a small earthquake which would have added to the situation. It's an unusual event but not beyond the realms of possibility.'

'But the swarms of wild animals which eyewitnesses have reported? Can you account for those?'

'Well, I'm no expert but it is often documented that animals are more sensitive to extreme weather changes and earth tremors than the human population.'

'Can we expect further scenes like this?'

The supposed expert shook his head. 'Oh no. There's absolutely no reason to feel alarmed. This is a simply a case of Mother Nature reminding us that she can be volatile from time to time.'

I snorted. I could be volatile from time to time – but I couldn't conjure up freaking pink elephants.

'Turn it off, Jodie,' Morgan said. He ran a distracted hand through his hair and went to the bar. He poured himself a large whisky and downed it in one long gulp. Jodie did as he asked then did the same, swallowing down a full tumbler of Scotch with barely a grimace. Unwilling to be left out of this little party, I stalked over and grabbed the bottle. One swig, however, and I was choking and spluttering.

I wiped my mouth with the back of my hand. Perhaps I'd lay off the whisky. It was probably lethal to anyone who didn't have Scottish blood. I threw a quick glance at Morgan, envisioning him in a kilt with nothing underneath. Mmmm.

'What is it, Maddy?' he asked. 'You look like you just thought of something important.'

'Yes,' I nodded, imagining getting my hands on Morgan's sporran. Then I remembered where I was and what was going on. I cleared my throat and sobered up. 'It's obvious, isn't it? This is to do with us. It's magic related. There's no other explanation, no matter what Fred Bellows or the BBC seem to think.'

Timmons scratched his head. 'It can't be the sphere. It's not been activated or we'd all know about it.'

Morgan poured another glass of whisky. I shuddered. 'I agree,' he said. 'Definitely magic and definitely not the sphere. It might not be Fey related at all though.'

'Maybe,' Vandrake suggested, 'it's the spirit of Chen coming back to haunt us for being complete idiots.'

'You might be an idiot,' I told him. 'I most certainly am not. There's no way any of this is because of us. As I said to the others, it might be our responsibility but it can't be our fault. It's impossible.'

The front door to the bar burst open and Artemesia appeared, panting for breath and sweating profusely. 'This is our fault!' she gasped. 'You saw what happened outside? It's because of us!' Her eyes swung wildly from one person to another. 'That's not all. It's going to keep happening.' She hunched her shoulders; she genuinely seemed to be terrified. 'I can promise you all one thing.' She drew in a breath. 'This is only the beginning.'

Chapter Six

It took some time to get Carduus's errant niece to calm down and explain what she knew. Apparently she had a considerable array of test equipment set up back in her makeshift laboratory. She'd been experimenting with warning systems to indicate if and when the sphere's power was tampered with. When the Manchester skies had darkened and a minor hell had been unleashed on the city, she'd sprung into action. As much as an apothecary could spring into action: I suspected that involved running over to scraps of paper and crunching numbers with a chewed pencil.

'The tests are conclusive,' she declared.

She glared at us as if expecting an argument. I was tempted, not because I had any reason to disbelieve her but because it would have been fun.

'Residual Fey magic is lingering in the atmosphere,' Artemesia went on. 'It's been building up for months. Think of it like a pressure-valve system. The magic needs an outlet and, sadly, it found one. We're just lucky that no one appears to have been seriously hurt.'

'So we're alright now? It won't happen again because enough magic has been siphoned off?' Timmons questioned.

'No,' she sighed. 'It's difficult to explain in layman's terms. As magical beings present in a non-magical demesne, our very presence causes a build-up of magic. There's nothing we can do stop it, short of leaving this demesne for good.'

Everyone snorted at that. If we could leave for good, we'd already have done it. Apart from Timmons; he'd chosen a human name over his Fey one and admitted to me that he liked it here better than Mag Mell. I guessed that, as a Travotel manager, complimentary hotel toiletries did it for him in the same way that Morgan did it for me.

'We've also been using magic,' Artemesia said. 'Not a lot but enough to add to the increase in the atmosphere. It wasn't dangerous until a few days ago when there was a far longer use of magic than I've ever seen before. It sent all my equipment skyrocketing. Of course, with everything else that was going on at the time it took me a while to get to the lab and notice. What happened today was a minimal release. It won't be long before the city reaches tipping point once again.'

'So there will be more of these magical pressure releases?' Morgan asked grimly.

Artemesia nodded. 'Yep. And I reckon that the more they happen, the worse they're likely to get.'

That didn't bode well at all. Vandrake spoke

---

up from the corner. 'This added burst of magic which pushed us over the edge,' he said. 'Can you tell where it came from? If we can pinpoint its location, we can make sure that whoever did this is warned and doesn't do it again.' The corners of his mouth turned down. 'Assuming it wasn't a deliberate act on Rubus's part.'

Artemesia grimaced. 'As far as I can tell, there was no single location. The magic was occurring across the city. It was probably one faery – and they were probably on the move at the time.'

Morgan's face was dark with fury. 'Don't people realise how dangerous it is to wield our magic around this demesne? They've been told time and time again. We have enough to deal with, given all that's happening with the sphere. We don't need rogue faeries making matters even worse.'

Suddenly I started to get a rather uneasy feeling in the pit of my stomach.

'On which day was the burst of magic?' Timmons asked.

Artemesia wrinkled her nose. 'Guess.'

Morgan shook his head in vexation. 'The day that we almost handed the sphere over to Rubus. Or rather to his Mendax glamour. That has to be it. That has to be what caused the problem.'

'No,' she said. 'That was the day the burst occurred – but the glamour Rubus created was boosted by rowan. That's a natural ingredient that is native to this land. Yes, he extended the glamour longer than he should have done but it was still a contained spell. The magic I'm talking about occurred had no other support. Whatever it was, it was certainly a powerful spell that has no place here.'

I bit my lip. 'Something like, er, altering time?'

Artemesia beamed at me as if I were her star pupil. She snapped her fingers. 'Exactly like that!'

Jodie tutted. 'But altering time is forbidden. I know it happens occasionally, despite the warnings, but never for long periods. And didn't you tell me, Morganus, that very few faeries have ever done it?'

Morgan's eyes were on mine. 'I did.' He licked his lips. 'It's a spell that I've used once or twice but never for more than a few seconds.'

I pulled my gaze away from his and did my best to look innocent. I was busy saving the world that day, not destroying it. Honest, guv.

'Maddy,' he said softly, 'you've altered time before.'

'Mmm.'

'Maddy…'

I raised my shoulders. 'Sure. I did it. But mostly before I was told that it was dangerous.' That wasn't exactly a lie.

Jodie cursed. 'So who was it? How do we stop them trying to do the same thing again and making things even worse?'

Morgan was still looking at me. 'I don't think that will be a problem. Do you, Madrona?'

I put my hands in my pockets and started to

———

whistle. That would work, right? However, when it became obvious that everyone's attention, even Opulus's, was on me, I gave in. 'Okay,' I conceded. 'There is a possibility, a teeny-tiny possibility, that this is my fault.'

Jodie rolled her eyes. 'Typical.'

I fixed a steely-eyed glare on her. 'Oi you. Things would be a whole lot worse right now if I hadn't done what I did. There was no way I could have reached the library in time to stop Morgan from handing the sphere to Mendax unless I slowed down time. Yes, it was dangerous. Yes, it was my decision and therefore my fault. But,' I held up my index finger, 'you should be thanking me. If I hadn't done it, this bar would be dust and you'd be dead. I might have slowed down time for longer than usual but it was a necessary evil.'

'You should have told us,' Artemesia snapped. 'You should have told *someone*. If we'd had some warning, I might have been able to do something to stop the pressure release. Now all bets are off. It's too late and the residual magic has been too widely dispersed.'

'When exactly was I supposed to say something?' I enquired. 'Right after the police shot me? Or was it before, when I was trying to stop Rubus from unleashing the apocalypse? There have been things to worry about other than a little bending of the rules, you know.'

She raised her eyebrows. 'A little bending of the rules? There was a pink elephant rampaging through people's houses!'

I grinned. 'I know. Isn't that cool that I did that?'

Everyone glared at me. Not pink elephant fans, then. 'Look,' I said, 'there wasn't a choice. I did what I had to. There is a bright side to all this. All those arsebadgers who are loyal to Rubus will see how dangerous a little bit of loose magic can be. Maybe it will make them realise how bad things will become if Rubus uses the sphere and there's a tsunami of magic.'

'Yeah,' Jodie said sarcastically. 'Or maybe they'll think that this demesne has become too unstable and dangerous and they'll be even more desperate to leave.'

Morgan sat down heavily on a chair. He looked more exhausted than anything else. 'How long did you keep up the time alteration?' he asked.

I tried to think. 'Maybe twenty minutes? It could have been longer.'

Artemesia expelled a long breath. 'That would be more than enough.'

So now I was responsible for trapping everyone in this demesne as well as potentially destroying it. Honestly, I made a fabulous villain whenever I was trying to be a hero. I should remember that next time I wanted to be wholly evil again.

Apologies didn't really suit me. I bit my bottom lip. 'Um. Sorry?' I sighed. 'This is clearly a job for the Madhatter. How do I stop further magic pressure releases? Just tell me what to do and I'll do it.'

'I already said I don't think they can be stopped,' Artemesia sniffed.

'All we have to do is to find another way to siphon off the residual magic. Can't we just dig a hole in the ground and send it that way?' I suggested.

The apothecary stared at me. 'And potentially destabilise the earth's core?'

Okay. Not that, then. 'Well, send it up into space. Get it past earth's atmosphere or something. How do I do that?'

'Towards the sun? What do you imagine might happen then – even if we could work out how to do it?'

I put my hands on my hips. 'Give me a break. I'm trying to be solution focused!'

'Unfortunately, Maddy,' Morgan drawled, 'your solutions tend to cause worse problems than they solve.'

Slightly stung by his censure, I glared at him. 'Are you saying I should have just let you hand over the sphere to your brother?'

'That's not what I'm saying at all. But I think that in future I should stick close by you so we can avoid any further … troubles.'

I strolled over to where he was sitting and reached down for his hand so I could hold it. Then I smiled. 'If you insist.'

Jodie looked faintly disgusted but I wasn't

imagining the faint reassuring pressure as Morgan squeezed my fingers.

Artemesia scratched her head. 'I'll keep looking for a way to manage the magic build-up.' She glanced at me. 'For what it's worth, I think I'm close to a proper antidote for your amnesia as well, although that will have to be put on the back burner for now.'

I twisted my body so I could sit on Morgan's lap. Mmm. Muscly. I felt him twitch underneath me and wiggled slightly. His body tensed in response. Magic wasn't the only thing that needed to find its way to a release.

'Speaking of that,' I said, 'it might have been self-inflicted.' I told the group about the video and the strange liquid I'd drunk just before I lopped off Charrie's head.

Morgan placed his hands loosely on my waist. 'You *were* working against Rubus at that point,' he said quietly. 'Losing your memory was the only way to avoid being forced into revealing the location of the sphere.'

'There's one way to be sure,' I said. 'I need to track down Charrie's family. They went to the police station and stood up for me but they must have left before I could talk to them. They're the main reason I was released, even though I didn't want to be. They'll have more answers.'

'The police will be back to talk to you,' Timmons warned. 'There was a standoff right in front of their headquarters. They're not going to let that slide.'

'Given what happened with the elephants and the rats and all the other crap,' I pointed out, 'they probably have their hands full right now. But, yes.' I nodded. 'They'll be back. They'll want to talk to Rubus as well. He was obviously the one who was causing all the aggression. They can't just ignore that.'

'He'll talk his way out of it,' Morgan muttered. 'He always does.'

Very reluctantly, I pulled myself upwards and away from the heat of his body. 'He'll also be in hiding. I should be too.'

Jodie raised a sceptical eyebrow. 'I thought you wanted to be arrested.'

'Only to keep the sphere safe and in police custody. That's obviously not going to happen now.'

'Because you handed it to a cleaner, you mean.'

'Yeah,' I said. 'I did. So it's out of Rubus's clutches – at least for now. Feel free to fall at my feet in gratitude.'

Artemesia shook her head. 'I don't have time for this crap. I'm going back to my lab to try to find a solution to the magic build-up.'

Morgan smiled at her. 'Good idea. Madrona and I will track down Charrie's family. Jodie and Timmons, you should work on finding this cleaner, Charlotte Page. You're less likely to scare her off than the rest of us.'

Vandrake, who'd been pretty much silent until now, piped up. 'I'll look after Opulus,' he said. 'I know a little about pain. And I should probably find us somewhere else to hide out. The human police are only going to hamper our efforts to solve all these problems. The longer we can stay away from them, the better.'

I considered. 'Actually, I have a few thoughts about that.'

'Don't strain yourself,' Jodie murmured.

I snorted. 'Darling, you wish you had my brain capacity.'

'Two words, Madrona. *Your. Fault.*'

I couldn't really argue with that. I shrugged. 'A life less ordinary.'

There was a barely audible chuckle from Morgan. 'The one thing I'd never describe you as is ordinary.'

I curtsied. I also pretended that I didn't feel ill that all this gasbudlikin crap was down to me.

Chapter Seven

The Manchester streets were still very quiet when Morgan and I finally ventured back out. I was keeping my fingers crossed for another pink elephant; another sighting might well signal the end of the world, but at least I could spend my final moments parading around with it and feeding it peanuts. And let's face it, peanuts were more than I was getting for working my fingers to the bone to prevent the apocalypse.

'How do you know where Charrie's family will be?' I asked Morgan.

'I don't,' he said. 'But I know someone who will. The bogles are a tight-knit community. They found it almost as hard as we did when the borders to other demesnes closed and they were faced by a couple of thousand faeries getting in their way. They tend to keep to themselves. It's easier to avoid suspicion that you're not quite human if you avoid spending a lot of time around humans. When we showed up – and didn't leave again like we usually did – the bogles closed ranks.'

'Not entirely,' I pointed out. 'Charrie worked for Rubus.'

'There are always one or two folks in every

community who buck the trend.' He eyed me. 'You should know that.' When I didn't immediately answer, he added, 'The path less trodden can be incredibly alluring to those who are themselves unique.'

'Mmm.' I wasn't entirely convinced that was a compliment, even if he meant it as such. 'Except my path is filled with weeds and carnivorous plants.'

Morgan's lips curved. 'And the odd, stunning, but incredibly rare and wondrous, wildflower.'

I stopped in my tracks. This wasn't the place and it certainly wasn't the time. But certain things had to be said and, in light of recent revelations, I wasn't sure I could keep quiet any longer.

'Look,' I said, watching Morgan as he too paused, 'I know we have a history. Not a particularly pleasant history either, given that I betrayed you and loped off with Rubus. I know I'm highly desirable and highly intelligent, and any man would be lucky to have me. But there's no getting away from the fact that I'm bitchy.'

Morgan opened his mouth to answer but I held up my hands. 'Please, let me finish.'

He inclined his head. 'Okay,' he said quietly.

'It's because of my actions that more than a thousand faeries are trapped here,' I said. 'Whether I meant to do it or I didn't, and whether I can remember it or I can't, these problems started because of me. I know you've already said that it doesn't matter but it should.' I drew in a breath. 'It does. Maybe I'm not responsible for murdering Charrie after all, but there's no denying that I'm involved with his death. Then there's this new revelation that I'm responsible for magic leaking out all over this city and causing utter havoc. Artemesia seems pretty convinced that it's going to happen again. And again. And again. So even though there's considerable blame to be laid at Rubus's door, there's probably just as much to be laid at mine.'

Morgan's green-eyed gaze held mine unwaveringly, although I noticed the small muscle ticking in his cheek. 'What's your point?' he asked.

'At risk of sounding like a petulant schoolchild with self-confidence issues,' I said, toeing the pavement, 'do you like me?'

His answer was immediate. 'Yes.'

My next question was obvious. With genuine curiosity, even though I was fearful of the response, I attacked it head on. 'Why?'

He smiled and I could swear that my knees went weak immediately. I reached out to grab at a lamppost just in case. Unfortunately, someone had chosen that exact spot to place a sticky wad of used chewing gum. Grimacing, I yanked away my hand and rubbed it furiously on my ridiculously baggy jeans.

'Madrona,' Morgan said, 'you are neither as sexy nor as intelligent as you pretend to think you are.' I gasped in mock horror but he raised his index finger. 'I let you finish,' he said sternly. 'Now it's your turn to do me the same courtesy.'

Fair enough. I folded my arms across my chest and waited. He'd better not take too damned long, though.

'Now,' he continued, 'that's not to say that I don't find you gloriously sexy, both in terms of your brain and your body. But you're no supermodel.'

I made a face. 'A supermodel? They're far too skinny. I've got curves in all the right places,' I purred.

'Maddy,' he warned, 'you promised to stay quiet.'

I didn't, actually. But the fact that Morgan's eyes had briefly flashed down to the curves I'd just mentioned, as if he couldn't help himself gawking, was enough to appease me.

Morgan smiled, as if he knew exactly what I was thinking. 'I've always been attracted to you,' he said. 'Even when I told myself I hated you, I was attracted to you. Now, all those things that you've done? You had reasons for them all. Naïve reasons perhaps, stupid reasons almost certainly – at least as far as the border closures go. But,' he added, 'well-intentioned reasons. Slowing down time for a prolonged period to stop us from giving the sphere to Rubus? I probably would have done the same.'

He paused and thought for a moment. 'As for what happened with Charrie, maybe we'll never really know. You keep punishing yourself for what you did. You think you deserve to be treated badly so you act terribly to pre-empt that treatment. You put up facades to fool the world and, I think, to fool even yourself. But I can still see the good that shines out of you. You've put your life on the line several times to help others. When the situation calls for it, you put your mean streak to one side. Maybe other people can't be bothered to take the time to see the real you. But, believe me, it's more than worth it.'

He smiled again. 'Just don't use any magic or do anything crazy again without checking with me first.'

'You're not my boss,' I huffed.

Morgan chuckled. 'No, I'm definitely not. You're absolutely your own woman. Don't apologise for who you are. And don't forget that we learn from failure, not from success. You can build an amazing life on the basis of your mistakes as long as you don't deny those mistakes exist. Mistakes lead to discovery.'

I considered his words. 'There are two things I'd like to point out, if I may.'

He inclined his head. 'Go on.'

'First of all,' I said, 'I'd like to be clear that I'm not apologising for who I am. I'm the Madhatter. It doesn't get any better than that. Second of all, have you considered a career in inspirational meme design?'

Morgan took a step towards me and reached for my hands. 'Maybe one day,' he breathed. 'Now there's something you have to tell me.'

I tensed. 'Okay.'

'Do *you* like *me*?'

My answer was as unequivocal as his. 'Yes.'

'Why?'

I peered at him. Wow. He actually looked... 'Nervous,' I burst out. 'You look nervous.'

'Just answer the damned question, Maddy,' he growled.

I ran my tongue over my lips. 'I can't speak for what things were like before I got amnesia,' I said quietly, 'but you have never lied to me. You've never sugar-coated the truth but you've always listened to me, too. You don't look for excuses or spend your time buried in the past, and every single atom of your soul is heroic.'

'No, it's not,' he said. He sighed. 'Back in the bar, you told the others that they'd sat back and wrung their hands at Rubus but not done anything to stop him. He's my brother and, up until the last couple of weeks, I didn't do a damned thing to try and stop him either. I'm as guilty of abjuring responsibility as everyone else. We might not have known about the sphere until recently but I've always been fully aware of how dangerous Rubus can be.'

'Perhaps that's my fault,' I told him. 'You washed your hands of him when I left you for him. But there's been no point in the last few weeks where you've stinted at bringing him down. He's still your family, Morgan, but you're not letting that stop you.'

'He's left me with no choice.'

I nodded, conceding the point. 'Going back to the original question, you can be a bit too serious. I mean, you're sex on legs and you make my stomach squirm but you do tend to live life on the very straight and very narrow. However,' I added quickly before he could interrupt, 'you do have a sense of humour that matches mine, when you feel brave enough to show it. And you see through me in a way that I can't even see through myself. You're caring and sensitive.' I shrugged. 'And I fancy the pants off you. When I'm with you, it's not always easy to think straight. When I'm not with you, all I can think about is you. Maybe your schoolmarmish approach is what inspires all my lusty feelings.'

I cast a long look up and down his muscular body. 'Have you ever thought of leather? You'd look pretty damned gorgeous in some tight-fitting, thigh-hugging leather…'

A strange noise rumbled in Morgan's chest. He grabbed my hands and pulled, leading me off the main street and down a smaller side one. Then he spun me round until my back was pressed against a wall. He braced his palms on either side of me and leaned in, his body against mine. His eyes glittered.

'Schoolmarmish?' he enquired.

'It's not a criticism,' I said, feeling my chest constrict and my stomach flip. 'Merely an observation.'

'Go on.'

83

It was becoming difficult to breathe normally. 'You're the type of person who likes to follow the rules. In fact, you like to set the rules and then follow them. I can see you striding around a blackboard with chalk in hand, patiently explaining algebraic formula and then barking at anyone who dozes off.'

He raised an eyebrow. 'You're suggesting that my lectures are dull?' He dipped his head and lowered his voice. 'Are you suggesting that I'm dull?'

'No. Just that—'

Morgan didn't give me a chance to finish. His mouth met mine, hard and insistent. I parted my lips, my hands reaching round his back. His teeth nipped at my bottom lip, tugging almost painfully. Then one of his hands stretched underneath my T-shirt, snaking upwards until his fingers found my breast. He squeezed the nipple then brushed it with the base of his thumb.

'Tell me that again, Maddy,' he said into my ear. 'Tell me I'm being schoolmarmish now.'

I answered the only way I could, dropping my hands to his waist and fumbling for the button. I managed to undo it then I pushed my fingers down. Morgan's sharp intake of breath when I stroked his hot, hard length was all the reward I needed. I curved my hand round his cock. He growled again and reached for my wrist, yanking it out. He pinned both my hands against the wall.

'No,' he said. 'There are rules. You will

follow them.' He pushed his body against mine once more. 'I'm in charge. You will do what I say.'

'And what are your rules? We're outside, Morgan. Anyone could wander by. Are your rules that we should act prim and proper?' I smirked. 'Because that's what I expect from you.'

His green eyes darkened. 'You are goading me.'

'So dole out your punishment,' I told him. 'Give me lines. Order me to do push-ups. Tell me I'm being bad.'

He stepped back, the sudden cool breeze between us making me shiver. 'You will do what I say.' His gaze travelled the length of my body. 'Take off your T-shirt.'

'Or what?' I taunted. When he didn't respond, however, I did as he instructed, baring my flesh. I dropped the offending material onto the ground and toyed with my bra strap. 'And this?'

He licked his lips. 'Do it.'

I slid the straps down my arms before unclasping the bra. With my eyes on Morgan's, I slowly removed it. 'Is this what you want?'

'Drop it,' he said. 'Drop the bra.'

I did. I didn't twirl it or tease or do anything other than let it fall. I stared at him, challenging him to continue. If he decided to stop now, regardless of our al fresco position I'd have to tie him to the nearest lamppost with my underwear and work on him myself. Fortunately, he seemed to have a better idea.

Morgan folded his arms across his chest and watched me. Maybe I should have felt vulnerable; I should certainly have felt cold. But the heat of his gaze and the anticipation firing through me was more than enough to keep me warm,.

'Turn around.'

I pivoted slowly, presenting him with my back. I heard him step towards me, the crunch of his footsteps on the gravel adding to my anticipation. Then his fingers brushed away my hair and his lips pressed against the nape of neck. His tongue dipped out, circling the first nub of my spine before moving lower and doing the same to the next and the next and the next. It was a delicious, slow torment. Clearly, Morgan had a lot more patience than I did.

I squirmed and moaned.

'Stop it,' he said, pausing long enough to speak.

I smiled. 'See?' I said. 'Schoolmarmish.'

He hissed under his breath. Grabbing me by the waist, he spun me round so that I was facing him once more. 'You always have to push your luck, don't you, Maddy? Even when the going is good and the world is on your side, you can't settle.'

I let my eyes drift down to his groin. His trousers were still open at the waist which, given the size of his erection, was probably a good thing. 'That,' I whispered, 'is because I always want more.' I lifted my gaze. 'But are you prepared to give me it?'

Morgan dropped his hands. 'I'll give you

whatever you want.'

I didn't have to ask. He pulled his shirt over his head, not wasting time undoing the buttons, and threw it onto the small pile of my clothes. Then he pushed down his trousers and kicked them off. Even if there had been any passers-by, I wouldn't have noticed. Who could pay attention to their surroundings when they were facing someone like Morgan in full naked splendour? I stripped off my jeans and leapt at him. No more teasing.

Fortunately, he clearly felt the same way. There was a brief awkward moment as our limbs tangled together and we stumbled back against the wall but it didn't take us long to extricate ourselves. His skin was searingly hot against mine, despite the cool breeze which swirled round us. I'd have thought that he'd be too embarrassed for sex a la fresco like this, given that anyone could stumble upon us. Maybe the lack of people on the streets was giving him confidence or maybe it was the magic in the air that was making him extra horny. Then again, looking at the hot, feverish desire in his expression, maybe it was just that he wanted me enough to throw all caution to the wind.

I ran my fingers down the nubs of his spine and he groaned. He returned the favour by moving his own hands from my waist and upwards, until his fingers teasingly brushed against the under side of my breasts. I caught my breath. Was I actually trembling?

'Go on then,' he husked.

I licked my lips. 'What?'

'Tell me what you want.'

I shook my hand, registering his brief flare of panicked disappointment. 'Actually, I don't want,' I told him. 'I need.' I trailed my hands round until I could feel his hard length against my fingertips. 'I need you inside me. I need you to fill me, Morgan.' I gazed at him. 'I need you to fuck me.'

'Done,' he growled. Morgan's eyes met mine and, with one swift thrust upwards, he was inside me, filling every inch of me. I gasped aloud and he smiled back in triumph.

Pressure built up, threatening to engulf me every time our hips rose.

'Morgan,' I moaned.

'Tell me,' he ordered, still watching me. 'Tell me you need me.'

It was a struggle to get the words out. There was only the barest semblance of conscious thought. Morgan was taking over everything; every atom of my body was screaming just for him. I drew in a ragged breath and bit the words out. 'I *need* you.'

It was enough. He half-closed his eyes and thrust one last time. Finally I let go. My body shuddered into his and he groaned, his hands clutching me as he jerked and collapsed against me. Oh, man.

'I'm sorry,' he murmured into my sweat-damp hair. 'I had less control than I realised. It's been too long and I wanted you too much. Next time will be better.'

I smiled into his shoulder. 'My mind is already blown. I'm not sure my heart will take 'better'. It's still jackhammering.' I took his hand and pressed it against my chest so he could feel it too.

'Not so schoolmarmish then,' he said.

'No,' I agreed. 'It's just as well. The Madhatter doesn't do prim. We'll have to give you a suitable nickname, too.'

There was amusement in his voice. 'We did. You called me the Knave of Hearts because I stole yours. I called you the Madhatter because you drove me crazy.'

I drew back slightly. 'Not because I'm psychotic?'

Morgan grinned. 'No. Although you might be.'

I sighed, no longer smiling. 'I wish I could remember.'

He reached up and brushed a curl away from my cheek. 'I like you as you are, memory or no memory.'

There was a faint skittering sound to our left. We both turned our heads and spotted a long-tailed rat darting past us. I wondered idly whether it was one of the ones that had swarmed over Rubus. I bloody hoped its belly was full because it had taken a great big chunk out of his flesh.

'It's not the most romantic of settings, is it?' Morgan said ruefully.

'I don't need romance,' I told him. 'I only

need you.' Then I sighed. 'Although that's not actually true – I also need to stop the apocalypse. We should get moving.'

He dipped his head towards mine one last time and brushed my lips with his. 'We should probably put our clothes on first.'

I kissed him back. 'Only if you insist.'

Chapter Eight

As interludes go, what had just occurred between Morgan and I was about as pleasant as it was possible to get. No, scratch that – pleasant wasn't the right word. Toe-curling, spine-tingling, orgasm-inducing glorious deliciousness fit far better. Unfortunately, however, it didn't change what else was happening in the world around us. We were still faced with a range of seemingly insurmountable problems. More's the pity. Surely if Morgan and I could finally get it together, everyone else could fall in line. A girl could dream.

We were on the verge of entering the bogles' neighbourhood when there was the same ground-shaking tremor as there had been during the confrontation with Rubus. In theory we were now better prepared but in practice Morgan and I were flung unceremoniously to the ground.

I tried to flip back to my feet in the sort of lithe movement that someone who'd just shagged the brains out of the sexiest man on the planet should be able to achieve. Alas, my body wouldn't respond the way I wanted it to; I suspected that I looked more like a writhing worm than a dancing faery.

It was probably just as well. Before I could try to stand up for a second time, several red-tinged clouds appeared. And it wasn't rain that suddenly fell from them – it was droplets of fire.

Morgan bellowed a warning and rolled towards me, sprawling his heavy body on top of mine to protect me. Mmm.

'Ready for another round?' I purred. A fiery globule landed on my head, singeing my hair and abruptly changing my mind.

'Bus shelter,' he said through gritted teeth after he'd helped me extinguish the flames. 'Eleven o'clock.'

We made a dash for it, scrambling up and sprinting for cover. The fiery rain was picking up speed, the droplets hissing wherever they landed until the whole street sounded as if it were alive.

'Gasbudlikins!' I yelled, once we were under the shelter. 'This is nuts!'

'Tell me about it,' Morgan muttered.

A larger globule of flame hit the roof of a parked car, melting its paintwork. 'It's raining fucking fire!' Not just that, but the 'rain' was getting heavier. If this continued, the entire city would be ablaze before too long.

'We have to do something!' I glared at Morgan as if this were his fault when obviously it was mine.

'We could use magic to attack the clouds,' he said. 'But I'm worried that will disperse more loose residual magic into the atmosphere and make matters worse.'

The wind was picking up. Of course it was. Now, instead of falling to the ground, the flaming rain was slanting. I yelped as a few of the smaller drops blew into the bus shelter. One landed on Morgan's back. Screeching, I slammed my hand against him several times to extinguish it.

'Hey!' he protested, jerking away from me.

'You can thank me later.' I swung my head round. There had to be something we could do – we were supposed to be freaking faeries, after all. Think, Madrona. 'The glamour that Rubus created,' I said suddenly.

Morgan looked at me, apparently still miffed that I'd thumped him to stop him from combusting. 'What about it?' He pulled me towards him just in time to stop me getting another singeing.

'Artemesia said it didn't contribute to the magic build-up because it was rooted in rowan. What if we use magic against those clouds but root it in something else?'

Morgan's expression cleared. 'Boggart Hole.'

I blinked. 'Well, there's no reason to be rude about my lady bits.'

He rolled his eyes. 'That's not what I was referring to.' He paused and leaned in slightly. 'It's not what I'd call your *lady bits* either. It's the name of an ancient park near here. There's a brook running through it. It has mystical properties. It's one of the reasons why the bogles live here. We might just be able to harness it.'

I peered out doubtfully. 'When you say near here, I hope you mean within sprinting distance.'

'Quarter of a mile,' Morgan said with a zesty confidence that was obviously exaggerated. For once, I decided not to call him on it. It wasn't as if we had any other options.

'Great.' I glanced at him. 'Before we go, what *would* you call my lady bits?'

'Focus, Maddy,' he growled, with just the faintest tinge of adorable pink on his cheeks. 'The sky is spitting fire.'

Yeah, okay. I shook my arms and legs before stretching my hamstrings, not because I thought it would help but because I decided it would make me look less terrified. Then I put my hands over my head to shield myself from the worst of the fire. A moment later, Morgan and I were running like hell itself was hot on our heels, which in a way it actually was.

We did our best to weave in and out of the fiery rain but soon I was covered in minor burns and scorch marks. We moved far faster than any humans could have done but it still wasn't fast enough.

When we reached a line of trees and ended up in a small wood, I thought that things might be about to improve; at least the leaves and branches would afford us some cover. Unfortunately, what happened was that the foliage started to catch fire and drift downwards. Now it wasn't just the rain we had to worry about, it was flaming debris too.

I screeched and ran even faster. Just ahead of me, through the gaps in the trees, I could see the glitter of water. Praise be. As I put on one final spurt, something landed on my shoulders. Without thinking, I threw myself into the small lake, startling several ducks that were already nervous enough thanks to the flaming skies. They were far better at dodging the falling fire than I was though – they'd cope.

The water wasn't deep and there was a scummy layer on the surface. When I finally felt brave enough to emerge, I suspected I looked like the creature from the black lagoon. The fact that Morgan hadn't deigned to plunge in after me, despite the continuing drizzle of flames, suggested that the lake held more potential horrors than the skies.

I glanced around. The ducks, despite being terrified and quacking in a relentless cacophony, didn't appear unhealthy. I was probably safe. But perhaps rather slimy, too.

'How will this work?' I called. I was already wet; I might as well stay where I was. All the better to save my eyebrows, I figured.

Morgan pursed his lips. 'You remember way back when you used magic to hit the sniper?'

I nodded. That had been in front of the Travotel, right before I'd had the dubious joy of meeting Rubus for the first time. The sniper had been there for Julie, not us, another little reminder that this world could be a highly dangerous place for almost anyone.

'Well,' he continued, 'if we combine our magic and try the same thing but aim for the most reflective parts of the lake, in theory we can mirror the magic and send the water upwards towards the worst of the clouds.' He looked beyond me. 'There,' he said, pointing. 'About twenty feet to your right.'

I spun round, sending a spray of dirty water with me. The ducks quacked louder in further protest; I could swear several of them were giving me evil looks. 'Has a duck ever killed anyone?' I enquired.

Morgan didn't answer; he was too focused on the reflective patch of water. I sighed and zoomed in on it. The sky might be aflame but it was pretty damned shivery and cold in this lake. Hopefully this wouldn't take long.

'Ready?' I called.

'Ready,' he returned.

I heaved in a breath. 'One. Two. *Three.*'

Together we raised our hands and started blasting. At some point our magic combined above my head before shooting down towards the water at an angle. It was kind of like snooker, I decided, but perhaps a tad messier.

I couldn't actually see how it was going to work. The water droplets we dispersed upwards created a fine spray, which initially appeared to do little more than pissing off the ducks. I should have trusted more in the magic, however, along with Morgan's instincts.

The force of our combined spell sent the water upwards and the magic imbued in it did as he intended. Slowly the fiery globules falling from the sky transformed into nothing more than fat raindrops, spreading first from the lake and then outwards, as if each one were infecting the other. I kept up the stream of magic until I heard Morgan yell at me to stop. Even then I continued for a moment or two longer just to be sure. My hair was already singed and burnt; I wasn't going to take any more chances.

I cast my gaze over the horizon. The clouds were no longer tinged with red and, as far as I could see, there was no more falling fire. Just as bloody well. I glanced at Morgan and pumped the air in triumph. 'We did it!' I grinned.

He didn't smile back. 'We did.'

'You could be a bit happier about it.'

'I'm happy it's stopped,' he said. 'But the fact that it happened in the first place does not fill me with joy. It makes me worried about what's going to happen next.'

Spotting the large crowd of people advancing out of the trees towards Morgan and lake's edge, I also had a bad feeling about what was going to happen next. None of them looked particularly happy and they all had a slightly unnatural green tinge to their skin. Bogles. Lots of them.

Despite the freezing temperature, I was tempted to stay where I was in the lake and let Morgan deal with them. Much as I hated to admit it, he was far better with people than I was. The only reason I started to wade out to join him was that the largest duck was still giving me nasty glares and starting to paddle towards me. Give me angry bogles over furious ducks any day. At least the bogles were unlikely to peck me to death.

Morgan had obviously heard the bogles' approach. He turned to face them, his palms extended outwards in a gesture of peace. Before he could say anything, though, I flicked back my hair, extricated a sodden, stringy weed from where it had plastered itself against my cheek and cleared my throat.

'Take us to your leader,' I boomed.

A small male bogle stepped forward and raised an eyebrow at Morgan. 'Is she for real?'

'You're little green men,' I called out. 'What else am I going to say?'

I couldn't see the expression on Morgan's face but I was certain he was chuckling. With such a hearty, clever wit as mine, it was nigh on impossible to keep a straight face. The bogles, alas, were managing it well enough. They were probably worried that more fireballs might descend from the heavens.

While I heaved myself out of the lake, Morgan inclined his head respectfully. 'I am Morganus.'

The lead bogle still didn't crack a smile. 'You're Fey.'

'Yes.'

'Why have you come here?'

'We are looking for the family of Charrie.'

The bogle sniffed. 'He is dead.'

Morgan remained calm and stoic. He was good at that. 'We know. That's why we want to talk to his wife.' He gestured at me. 'My companion, Madrona, was involved in his demise.'

As one, the bogles' heads turned towards me. Their expressions didn't alter but I suddenly felt the weight of responsibility for Charrie's death, regardless of how it actually went down on the night or whether I remembered the details. Their friend, their brother, their son, was dead. And it was my fault.

The lead bogle, who still hadn't deigned to give us his name, broke away from the group and strode towards me. Before he reached me, he stretched his hands behind his back and, in one swift, fluid movement, drew out a long sharp sword.

I hissed.

Morgan moved towards me, as if to barricade the bogle's advance. 'We're not here to fight,' he said, his tone laced with a dangerous warning of what could be about to ensue.

'I've got this,' I snarled. Bogles weren't affected by the truce. If this arsebadger tried anything, I'd have him on the ground in a heartbeat. He'd rue the day he'd tried to cross me. His children would rue the day. His grandchildren would...

The bogle spun the sword deftly in his hands

and presented the hilt to me before dropping to his knees. 'Thank you,' he said. 'From the bottom of our hearts we thank you.'

I blinked. Er…

The confusion must have been apparent on both my face and Morgan's. The bogle smiled slightly, an expression that was tinged with warmth rather than mockery. 'It is not often that one of your kind respects our ways and acts accordingly,' he said. 'You aided Charrie and you aided his family. For that, we shall forever be in your debt.'

I was still flummoxed. 'You know I might have killed him, right? I can't remember because I have this amnesia thing going on, but there's evidence that suggests I poisoned him. At the very least I dismembered his corpse.' I frowned at the outstretched sword. Did the bogle want me to do the same to him? 'That's a pretty icky thing to do.'

'We know what you did,' he said. 'And we know it was at Charrie's request.'

I stepped back, forgetting that I was standing at the edge of the lake. Instead of meeting solid ground, my foot found nothing but air – and then water. My arms flailed helplessly as I pitched backwards. Morgan started towards me but the bogle got there first, lunging forward with his sword and snagging it deftly on the side seam of my baggy jeans before bringing me back up to my feet.

I stared at him. 'That was a pretty slick move.'

'Duh. I'm a bogle. Sword play is what we

do.' He flashed me a wink. 'Not bad for a little green man, eh?'

Not bad at all. I flicked a glance at Morgan. His arms were tightly folded across his chest. He didn't appear particularly impressed.

'Don't worry,' I said, patting his arm. 'I know you could have rescued me too. You can do it next time.'

He rolled his eyes. 'My ego is not that pathetic. Besides, you're already sopping wet. Another dunk could hardly harm you.'

The bogle squinted at him. 'I've heard of you, Morganus, although we've never met in person. I hadn't realised that you were so … so…' He cast around as if searching for the right word.

'Schoolmarmish?' I suggested.

The bogle snapped his fingers. 'Schoolmarmish. Exactly.'

I smirked. Morgan's green eyes flashed in my direction. This was kind of fun.

'Let's get to the point, shall we?' Morgan snapped. 'If you know what happened to Charrie, we'd like to hear it. As Maddy said, she has amnesia. She can't remember any of it. We're hoping more information will help us with Rubus. He's —'

'Your brother, yes.' The bogle nodded. 'The one who's trying to bring the darned apocalypse down on our heads.' He waved a hand up towards the now clear skies. 'He may be succeeding.'

I grimaced. Perhaps the least said about the

fire rain and the rampaging pink elephants the better.

'My name is Sitri,' the bogle continued. 'If you'll permit me, I'll take you to Charrie's family. They can explain everything better than I can. After all, they knew him best.'

It could have been a trap but we were already outnumbered and I knew that our Fey magic far outstripped anything even an army of bogles could throw at us. 'Great,' I said. 'Sounds like a plan.'

Morgan shot me a look and I shrugged. After all, this was what we had come here for.

A couple of the younger bogles shuffled their feet, casting nervous glances up at the sky. 'Don't worry,' I called out. 'I have saved you all from further fireballs.' Morgan coughed. I pointed at him. 'He helped out a little bit but I did most of the work.'

'Then,' Sitri intoned, 'we are even further in your debt.' He bowed to add weight to his words, his dark curls flopping over his forehead. Morgan narrowed his eyes even further. Sitri straightened up, all his attention on me. 'Do you know what caused such a terrible event? We've never seen anything like it before.'

'Uh...' I scratched my head. 'It's crazy, right?' I fudged. Time for a sharp change in subject. 'Tell me, what exactly is a bogle? I can tell your skin is slightly green but, with my amnesia, I'm afraid I don't know much more about you.'

Sitri and the other bogles turned and started leading the way back towards the wood and the small housing estate on the other side of it.

'Well,' he said, as we walked, 'we are indigenous to this demesne, not that the humans know it. As far as we can tell, we've been here as long as they have. But as our population is considerably smaller, and humans are known to be somewhat … inconsiderate of others who are different, we take considerable pains to keep our existence hidden.'

'But you're green.' I didn't want to be rude but I had to point out the obvious. Their skin wasn't an emerald green or a deep jade but there was definitely a mossy tinge to it, which was markedly different from both Fey and humankind.

Sitri smiled. 'As far as we can tell, we used to be more obviously viridescent.'

'Viri what?'

'Green.'

Ah. I nodded knowingly. Why the gasbudlikins didn't he just say green?

As if reading my thoughts, the bogle leaned in towards me. 'The PC brigade,' he confided. 'Ever since Roswell, we've avoided describing ourselves as green.'

'Roswell?' Morgan muttered. 'I knew that was a bogle thing.'

Sitri continued as if he hadn't spoken. I was finding it rather pleasant to be thought of as the altruistic, important one. It made a change.

'Evolution affected us as much as the humans. Over the generations there have been changes to our genetic make up. Our skin has lightened, although there are parts, such as our scalps and sexual organs, that still maintain a more viridescent hue.'

I quirked up an eyebrow. 'Green balls?'

The bogle didn't take offence. 'The greenest,' he grinned.

'I'm guessing no human interbreeding then.'

'No. Anyway, we're not biologically compatible.'

I tried to imagine how I'd feel if I pulled a bloke in a club and took him home for duvet shenanigans only to discover he possessed a bright green cock, but my mind just wouldn't go there. Oddly, I suspected that it was because I couldn't imagine being in bed with anyone other than Morgan rather than because a bogle's genitals were too strange to contemplate.

'So do you have, like, magical powers?' I enquired, skipping over a fallen branch.

'We can affect the natural world,' Sitri said. 'Although our skills in that regard have diminished along with our viridescence. We can sour milk, make animals go lame, or blight the occasional crop if we're feeling up to it. Needless to say, it doesn't happen often. There's no longer any need for that sort of mischief in this technological world. We usually keep ourselves to ourselves. Or,' he added grimly, 'we did until you lot showed up and decided to stay.'

I twitched. 'As I understand it, that wasn't really a conscious decision.'

'Whatever the cause,' Sitri said darkly, 'the continued presence of the Fey does not help us.' Then he paused. 'Apart from you, Madrona. You're different.'

I glanced at Morgan in glorious triumph although I managed to restrain myself from pumping the air. Unfortunately, he wasn't paying me any attention. He was focused on keeping himself upright, which was no mean feat given that at least three of the younger bogles appeared intent on getting in his way and tripping him up. They really didn't like him much.

We veered right, crossing a small wooden bridge until we were virtually back where we'd started. I glanced around. No one was outside. Considering the scorch marks on the road and pavement, not to mention the smoke rising from various buildings, that wasn't a huge surprise. Stay inside, little humans. It's safer for you that way.

'We tried to infiltrate your ranks,' Sitri told me. 'But most of you weren't interested. The only one of us who had any real success was Charrie. He had to do some terrible things to get Rubus to trust him but it was worth it to have the inside track on what he was up to. There have been numerous occasions when Charrie's insider knowledge helped us to work against the Fey to prevent catastrophes occurring. You,' he added with an air of desperate sadness, 'were the only one who truly helped him.

You were the only one he trusted.'

I sniffed. 'Well,' I said, 'even with my amnesia, I know that I am eminently trustworthy. I work for good. I am toiling alone against the forces of darkness.' I dipped my head slightly. 'I even have a superhero costume.'

Rather than look impressed at that particular titbit, Sitri appeared slightly confused. I nudged Morgan. 'See?' I told him. 'I'm the only one Charrie trusted.'

Morgan angled his body away from the nearest bogle who, I could swear, was trying to jab him surreptitiously in the ribs with a sharpened stick concealed under his sleeve. 'I'm not surprised,' he said. 'Maybe now you can stop castigating yourself for killing him and act like a normal person.'

'Don't forget dismembering his body,' I reminded him. 'I did that too.' Then I clamped my hand over my mouth and flicked a horrified look at the bogles.

Sitri simply smiled and the others didn't so much as flinch. That was odd. I understood that they liked me and I recognised that they all but worshipped the very ground I walked on. That was only to be expected. But surely they should feel slightly concerned about what I'd done to their compatriot.

My uneasy feeling that we were walking into a trap returned.

'There.' Sitri pointed ahead. 'That's his

house.'

I followed his gaze. Part of me had expected a gloomy castle with turrets and mossy slime dripping down the walls. Instead I was gazing at a small, red-brick terraced house with shiny windows and a neatly trimmed lawn. I nodded. That made sense. They wouldn't lead us to an obvious place to spring their snare. They were trying to lull us into a false sense of security. Not this Fey. I was the Madhatter; I had eyes in the back of my head.

Something slammed into my shoulder blades. I spun round, hands raised to attack, just as the offending football bounced away down the street. Morgan laughed loudly although several bogles bellowed.

'Oi! Bally! Stop that!'

A pint-sized bogle grinned cheekily. 'Sorry!'

Judging by the smirk on his face, he wasn't sorry at all.

'This is Madrona,' Sitri said sternly.

Immediately the bogle child blanched. He stared at me, eyes wide and face pale. 'I'm sorry,' he said again, this time without the trace of a grin. In fact, he looked utterly terrified. That was more like it.

'I'll forgive you,' I said magnanimously. Then I added, 'This time.' I had my limits, after all.

'You shouldn't be outside,' Sitri scolded. 'Goodness knows what might fall from the sky next.'

'The fire's stopped,' Bally said in a small

voice. 'It's safe now. I wanted to see if there were any pink elephants.' Him and me both.

Sitri frowned and jerked his head at the house. 'Go and get your mother. Tell her Madrona wants to speak to her.'

I felt Morgan bristle slightly. 'And Morgan,' I said sunnily.

'Yeah. Him too.' Sitri shrugged.

I nudged Morgan. 'You know what this means?' I said.

'What?' he growled.

'You're now my official sidekick. I'm the hero and you're the one who holds my cape.' I arched my eyebrow. 'Get behind me, Batgirl.' Morgan frowned so I leaned in and brushed my lips against his cheek. 'This still might be a trap,' I whispered.

He stepped back, folded his arms and nodded, a tiny movement only for me. These bogles might be great at massaging my ego but I wasn't relaxing yet. Besides, Bally's football had suspiciously vanished. It could still whack me on the head again at any moment.

Bally darted forward, pulled open the door and called inside. 'Mum! She's here! The Madhatter is here!'

I shook out my hair and spread my legs, placing my hands on my hips in a classic superhero pose. It also meant that no one could tell that my knees were shaking.

A moment later, a diminutive bogle woman appeared at the door. Her face was lined, not with age but with worry and pain. I dropped my stance and shuffled forward. Actually, if she wanted to lead me into a dastardly trap, I deserved it.

She wiped her hands on her apron and stepped onto her doorstep. Her mouth remained downturned but her eyes were smiling. Then she reached forward. While I tensed up, her arms wrapped round me and she pulled me into a tight hug. 'Madrona,' she murmured. 'It's so good to see you again.'

This was her evil plan, then: she was going to smother me with warmth so that I drowned in my own guilt. Good plan. 'We know each other?' I asked, pulling away.

'I'm Alora. We've met a couple of times. And of course, Charrie told me all about you.' She sighed. 'Having you around made such a difference to him.'

I gulped. 'I don't remember.'

Her mouth tweaked up at the corners. 'I know,' she said. 'The memory potion was my idea. It seemed the safest thing to do at the time.'

My expression gave me away. She smiled slightly and gestured indoors. 'Come in. I'll make us some tea and tell you all about it.' She glanced over my shoulder. 'You can even bring your...' She fumbled for the word.

'Sidekick,' I said. 'This my sidekick. You can call him Snail Boy.'

Morgan rolled his eyes. 'My name is Morgan.' He raised his chin an inch. 'I'm her lover.'

I blinked. I hadn't been expecting that. He walked up next to me and took my hand in his, squeezing it. I squeezed back. 'I prefer Lover Boy to Snail Boy,' I whispered. Morgan smiled briefly at me.

Rather than grimacing in the manner of the other bogles, Alora's expression softened. 'Really? Charrie told me that you were in love with a Fey called Morgan. I'm so glad you finally got back together again. He said that you talked about him all the time and that you followed him whenever you had the chance. You and Charrie had a spot overlooking the Metropolitan Bar where you'd meet and chat. You'd watch Morgan while you conspired with my husband to take down Rubus.' She sighed deeply. 'He really enjoyed those moments.'

Morgan and I glanced at each other in astonishment. 'You were stalking me,' he murmured in a low undertone. 'You couldn't keep away from me.' There was an undisguised gleam of triumph in his emerald eyes.

I licked my lips, my mouth suddenly dry. 'I was probably just making sure you weren't doing anything stupid,' I said.

'No,' Alora told us. 'You just liked watching him and knowing he was alright.' She smiled again. 'Now, how about that tea?'

Morgan's hand tightened around mine. I resisted the urge to lean against him and nodded at Charrie's wife. 'Yes,' I said. 'Let's do this.'

Chapter Nine

'Chen refused to hand over the sphere,' Alora said, settling into a flowery armchair and sipping her tea. 'As long as he was alive that wasn't a problem. A dragon's hoard is bound to that dragon and, despite popular belief, can't be stolen. Chen could have given it away had he so desired, but there was no chance he would ever do that. Both you and Charrie visited him and made sure that he wouldn't pass it to Rubus under any circumstances. Apparently Chen deeply regretted creating the sphere in the first place. He'd wanted to use it to pull in items from other demesnes so that he could add to his treasures. When he realised what damage the sphere could cause if it were used, he hid it away.'

She grimaced. 'Unfortunately, he also told several people about its existence. Word got back to Rubus and…' She sighed and lapsed into silence.

'And Rubus would stop at nothing to retrieve it,' Morgan finished for her grimly. 'He tried to reason with him. Tried to barter with him. When that didn't work, he tried to kill him. The old bugger was stronger than even Rubus realised though. In the end, all he had to do was wait Chen out.'

I ran a hand through my hair, picking at its singed edges. 'It's just our bad luck that Chen died of natural causes.' I paused. 'And Chen's, of course.' I sighed. 'You'd think he'd have destroyed the thing when he knew what it was capable of.'

'A dragon's treasure becomes almost part of the dragon itself. To destroy even a small item would have caused him considerable pain. I guess he decided that he wasn't long for this life and that it wouldn't really matter to him after he was gone. I can't say for sure. He's the only dragon we've ever known – I can't speak for the entire species because I don't know any others. I've never heard of any near here and dragons don't tend to travel much because it would mean leaving their treasure behind.'

'Such as his treasure was,' I said, thinking of the hollowed-out shell that was left behind after the fire at Chen's place. It would have been helpful to know that other dragons were so rare, given Rubus's glamourised role as Mendax.

Rubus had been smart to make use of minions such as Charrie from other species. Clearly, the bogles possessed a wealth of knowledge accumulated over generations. As we Fey had only ever spent short periods of time in this demesne there were obviously a lot of secrets, especially concerning non-humans, of which we were unaware.

'Anyway,' Alora continued, 'when Chen died, all bets were off. By time, Charrie's cancer had advanced beyond any possible treatment. The best we could do was watch him slowly rot away from the inside.'

She sent me a beseeching look. 'You've seen the swords. We're warriors at heart, even if we have no enemies to attack. It's not in our genes to let disease kill us. What you did for him was a far more honourable death.'

Despite her words, she still looked upset. Charrie's loss was raw; it still chafed at her heart and his soul still ran through her veins. I could see the hurt etched on her face and in the way she held herself; she reminded me of Opulus and Finn. I suspected that, despite her pain, Alora was coping far better with the loss of her loved one than either of those two were.

Without thinking I reached for Morgan again, my fingertips brushing against the bare skin of his forearm. At my touch, he relaxed. Apparently I wasn't the only one who needed that kind of contact.

Alora's clever eyes watched us and her despondency seemed to increase.

Feeling the need to keep our conversation on an even keel, I tilted up my chin. 'What exactly did I do for Charrie?' I asked. Tension prickled across my shoulder blades. 'Because to be honest, the evidence we've seen so far doesn't paint me in a favourable light.'

'I suspected as much,' Alora said, in a clear voice that belied her unshed tears. 'That's why I went to the police station. I couldn't have you locked up for doing nothing more than helping us. It wouldn't have been right.'

Morgan shifted his body so he could reach my hand. His thumb began rubbing gentle concentric circles on my palm. I breathed out. Breathing was good, I reminded myself. It was important to keep doing it.

'Go on,' I said, sounding more tremulous than Alora did.

She raised her teacup to her mouth again and drank slowly. I didn't think she was delaying her answer deliberately; she was merely trying to sort out the right words in the right order in her head. 'At Charrie's behest,' she said finally, 'you took something called white baneberry from Carduus's laboratory.'

Morgan stiffened. I forced myself not to look at him and kept my attention on Alora. 'Let me guess,' I said. 'White baneberry is a kind of poison.'

'For us bogles, yes,' she agreed. 'I know that Charrie had to persuade you to get it. He'd managed to get hold of the sphere – he took it after Chen passed away – but he was seen with it. It was only a matter of time before Rubus caught up with him.'

She glanced out of the window to where Sitri and Bally were standing, deep in conversation. 'And us,' she added softly. 'With Charrie's cancer, it made sense for him to take the baneberry and end his life. Then Rubus wouldn't be able to question him about the sphere, threaten us and hold our lives over Charrie's head.'

She grimaced. 'Rubus still tried, though. He sent several goons here to find out what we knew. It wasn't difficult to play stupid and in the end they left us alone. That part of the plan worked. Of course, when Charrie's body vanished, everything became more complicated.'

She looked at me. 'You were supposed to take Charrie's head, drink the memory potion then wake up in complete confusion and call the police. They'd have found the sphere on his body and looked after it as evidence. You genuinely would have not had a clue about what had happened so you'd have passed muster when both the police and Rubus interrogated you. Most importantly, the sphere would have been safe.'

Morgan's gripped my hand. I shook my head. Maybe my memory wasn't as lost to me as it seemed: the residual idea had obviously lingered somewhere in the recesses of my mind because it was a very similar strategy to the one I'd had a couple of days ago – without the corpse-dismemberment part and the magical memory potion.

'I'm sorry,' I whispered. 'I'm so sorry.'

Alora shook her head and offered me a sad smile. 'Don't be sorry. You gave him an honourable death. He died saving the world. What could be better than that?'

Not dying. Not dying would be better than

that.

'You see?' Morgan said softly. 'You're not a murderer. Charrie chose this way out. You simply helped him.' He stroked my fingers. 'You're not a villain, Madrona. Quite the opposite, in fact.'

'But it was all for nothing,' I said dully. 'The sphere is still in play, even if it's temporarily hidden.' I raised my eyes to Alora's. 'There must be a way to destroy it permanently.'

'If we knew of a way to do that, it would have been done already.'

'Charrie died for nothing.'

'He was dying anyway.' She hesitated, a hint of desperation lighting her eyes. 'I don't suppose you've found his body? Do you know what happened to him? I'd like to bury him. I'd like to know where he is.'

It was Finn who'd disposed of Charrie's corpse, Finn and his brothers. They'd interrupted our supposedly foolproof plan and tried to kill me. Instead of calling the police, I'd scarpered into the night taking the damned sphere with me. 'I don't know where your husband is,' I said. 'But I know who does. We'll find out and let you know.'

For the first time, Alora seemed to relax. 'Thank you,' she breathed. 'It would make a massive difference to me. And to our children.'

I nibbled at my bottom lip. 'So I'm not wholly evil,' I said to Morgan. I should have felt like cheering but I just felt tired. 'But we're still no further forward than we were before. We still have to find a way to get rid of the sphere. I think involving the police is non-starter. We've tried it twice, sort of, and it's failed both times. There has to be a way to destroy it.'

Morgan pursed his lips. 'We could always try and find another dragon. Giving the sphere to Mendax was obviously stupid because Mendax didn't exist in the way that we thought he did. But in theory it was a good idea. A dragon could bind the sphere to himself so it would be safe from Rubus. In an even better scenario, another dragon could destroy the thing once and for all.'

'How would we do that? How do we find a damned dragon? The bogles don't know of any others and the humans don't have a clue.'

'There's the British Library,' he suggested. 'Or the internet.'

'It'd be like a finding a needle in a haystack.'

Morgan tapped his fingers against his thigh. 'You mentioned that it was our bad luck that Chen died. You were right, Maddy. Dragons have long lives, far longer than humans and probably far longer than us. We need to look through old books that might hint at their existence. I'm sure we could find some clues about *something*.'

'Instead of older books,' I said slowly, 'how about older people?'

Morgan frowned but it didn't take him long to catch up. 'Julie,' he breathed. 'She might know.'

'Or if she doesn't,' I said, 'she might know someone who does.'

Alora looked confused. 'Who's Julie?'

I beamed. 'She's a...' Searing pain flashed through my chest. I doubled over as it ripped through my body, tearing at my veins and arteries. Morgan was beside my knees in my second. I gasped and heaved, involuntary tears of agony rolling down my cheeks. I bit back the word I'd been about to say and moaned instead. It was all I was capable of.

'The tea,' Morgan growled at Alora. 'What the fuck did you put in the tea?'

I waved a hand in the air to stop him. It wasn't the damned tea. I'd barely drunk any of it.

'I didn't do anything!' Alora protested.

'She,' I choked, 'didn't.'

'Then what?' Morgan demanded. 'What's wrong with you?'

I pulled myself back up to a sitting position. 'It's...' I gasped '...the NDA.'

Morgan frowned at me, concern still flitting across his face. Suddenly his expression cleared. 'Oh.' He glanced at Alora. 'I'm sorry. It was wrong of me to accuse you.' He sat back in his chair. 'Julie is a vampire. Maddy's not allowed to speak of her vampirism because she foolishly signed a magic contract to that effect.'

Alora's eyes widened. 'A vampire? You've met one? I knew they existed but no living bogle has ever met one.'

Morgan looked smug. 'You'll love this, then. Our particular pet vamp is none other than Julie

Chivers.'

'From *St Thomas Close*? The actress who plays Stacey?'

He nodded. 'That's the one.'

'No way! I love her!' Alora remained open-mouthed. 'I always thought she looked good for her age.'

I waved weakly at the pair of them. 'Hello? I'm almost dying here.'

'You'll be fine,' Morgan said briskly.

'You don't know that,' I groaned. 'Besides, Julie's ethnicity is supposed to be a secret. It's why she made me sign the stupid NDA in the first place.' My whole body still ached and tendrils of pain were uncurling in the deepest and most unpleasant of places.

'I won't tell,' Alora breathed. She was obviously flabbergasted.

'You're just annoyed that I could tell Alora and you couldn't,' Morgan smiled.

I stuck my tongue out at him. Even that hurt. How was that even possible? 'I hate it when you're right,' I muttered.

'I'm always right,' he told me.

'I'm the super genius around here, buster,' I said, with a slight toss of my head. I couldn't move it much; it still hurt too badly. 'It was me who thought of Julie in the first place.

Alora smiled slightly. 'I can see why you two are such a good match.'

I wrinkled my nose then I grinned. 'We're

awesome, aren't we?'

Suddenly Alora's front door burst open and Sitri and Bally galloped in. Morgan leapt to his feet. I tried to, but it was more of a stumble than a leap. Damn. That NDA magic was powerful stuff. My knees buckled and I fell back into the chair. Gasbudlikins.

'Someone's coming!' Sitri burst out. 'A Fey, heading here. We have outpost sentries all over the place. There's no doubt that she's coming in this direction.'

'She? It's not Rubus?' Morgan questioned, his fists clenching.

'No, definitely not. She's not one of yours?'

'No.' Morgan looked down at me. 'Get up, Madrona. We can't sit around and drink tea when we might have been followed here. We need to find out who's approaching.'

'Hurts.'

He scowled. 'It can't be that bad. You didn't actually break the NDA. You're not dying.'

'That's easy for you to say.' I heaved myself upwards. This time I managed to get fully upright and stay that way. Progress.

Morgan made for the door and I followed, albeit at a much slower pace. With a crowd of bogles appearing from doorways along the street, we marched down to meet the newcomer.

I couldn't for the life of me imagine who it might be. Given all that I'd gone through to get to this point, whether I could remember it or otherwise, I was determined not to let anyone get in my way. Unless it was Rubus, who'd decided to glamour himself into a woman this time around. Maybe he fancied a change. I gritted my teeth. He'd learn a thing or two when he got his first period.

Beads of sweat were breaking over my forehead but at least the pain was subsiding. I did my best to catch up to Morgan. 'Are you sure that this isn't going to be one of ours?' I said, trying to catch my breath. 'It could be Artemesia. She might have done some apothecary jiggery-pokery to find us here.'

'No.' Morgan's jaw clenched. 'She has other means of contacting us. If it was an emergency, she'd use the shells. We have connecting pairs so she could call if she needed to. She wouldn't waste time trying to find us and if it's not an emergency, she won't be looking for us. Arty has more than enough on our plate. I'd have said it could be Viburna – except she's dead.' His voice was flat.

Gasbudlikins. 'Maybe the bogles are mistaken,' I said hopefully. 'Maybe it's just a human woman out for a stroll.'

'It'd be nice to think that but they're not mistaken.' He pointed up ahead. 'Look.'

I followed his finger, drawing in a breath when I saw who was there. Lunaria. We'd spent some time together when I'd tried to spy on Rubus and, despite the circumstances, I had to admit that I rather liked the lanky Fey woman. She was head over heels in love with Rubus, however; there was no chance that she was here to catch up on old times over a lazy beer.

'Let me deal with this,' I said.

I squared my shoulders, ignoring the ripple of pain the action caused. Alright already. I wasn't going to blab that Julie was a vampire; I had Morgan for that.

I'd rather hoped I could stride forward looking menacing and brave. Instead it was more of a shuffle. Lunaria had realised that she was on the edge of what was effectively the bogles' stronghold, even if that stronghold consisted of cute little houses and flower-lined gardens. She paused and watched my approach. I continued until only twenty feet separated us. Fortunately, my body was finally settling down; by the time I came to a halt, the pain had subsided into a dull ache.

'Have you got new shoes, Mads?' Lunaria asked, her head tilted slightly in confusion. 'You're walking as if you have a mass of blisters about to pop.'

'Morgan is behind me,' I said, with an attempt at a carefree grin. 'I don't want to inflame his libido by swaying my hips.'

Lunaria frowned as if she couldn't understand how that would happen.

'I'm sex on legs,' I explained. 'It's hard enough for him to keep his hands off me as it is.'

'Uh huh.'

I had no idea why she didn't believe me until I remembered that I was covered in scorch marks and wearing a skater boy's clothes. Fair enough.

'Before we continue,' I said, 'I need to know you are who you appear to be.'

Lunaria smoothed her expression and regarded me with unsurprised eyes. 'You think I might be Rubus.' She gestured at her body. 'That all this is a glamour. You know you can't take the form of someone who already exists. Glamours don't work that way.'

I shrugged. 'Humour me. Prove to me that you are indeed Lunaria.'

She sucked on her bottom lip. 'When we were both eight years old, we made a pinky promise to always be best friends and to never ever kiss any boys because they would just get in the way of our friendship.'

I gazed at her in exasperation. 'I still have amnesia. I can't remember being eight years old, Looney. Besides,' I added with a sniff, 'I'm certain I would never have agreed not to kiss boys.'

'You also promised that, if I ever grew taller than you, you'd give me your favourite doll.' She met my eyes. 'I suppose we don't always keep our promises, do we?'

I sighed. 'I suppose not.'

'Last week,' Lunaria said, 'I told you that I might leave Rubus and try for Morgan instead. It made you cross.'

'Mmm. Go on.'

'When we went clothes shopping together, you were tempted by the crotchless trousers.'

'Only for a brief second,' I protested.

She leaned in slightly. 'You also pointed to a snotty kid and said that it'd be a good thing when Rubus used the sphere because the apocalypse would mean that kid would no longer exist.'

'Yeah,' I said quietly. 'I did say that.'

'I'm not a fool, Mads. I know you were trying to get me to see the light and to realise that getting home to Mag Mell isn't worth what will happen here as a result. You like pretending that you're evil but you're not.' She looked away. 'It took me a while to appreciate that. You're pretty bitchy on the surface.'

I raised my eyebrows. 'Pretty bitchy? Puh-lease. You can do better than that.'

She twitched awkwardly. 'Alright. You're *very* bitchy.'

It seemed it was my lot in life to give Lunaria pointers. She was lucky she knew me. 'My teeth are brighter than your future,' I told her.

Lunaria blinked but she didn't say anything. I tried again. 'The expression on your face suggests you're as baffled as Adam was on Mother's Day.'

Still nothing. I ploughed ahead. 'You're—'

'I've seen wounds that are better dressed than you,' Lunaria interrupted. She pointed to a nearby bush. 'Go apologise to that plant for all the oxygen you're stealing from it,' she said sternly.

My smile stretched from ear to ear. I felt like a proud mother watching her daughter graduate from university. Not with honours, mind – she wasn't *that* impressive – but she'd done her best.

I heard a few whispers behind me from the crowd of bogles – and Morgan. It was time to stop messing around. 'Why are you here, Lunaria? Did Rubus send you?'

She swallowed, as if suddenly nervous. 'He doesn't know I'm here. I came for me, not for him.'

She twisted a strand of hair in her fingers then nodded, apparently coming to a decision. 'And I sent the CCTV footage to the police for you, not him. I haven't watched it, but you killed Charrie the bogle to save the sphere from getting back to Rubus, didn't you? The lesser of two evils. And I know you deliberately tried to get yourself sent to prison so that the sphere would be safe. That's why you shot that gun. I thought I'd help you out and give the police what they needed to lock you up.'

So that was how they got hold of that first edited video. Lunaria was cannier than I'd realised. 'You gave the police evidence that implicated me in a murder?' I questioned with a half smile. 'You truly are a good friend.' I meant it, too.

'It's not that I wanted you in jail!' she burst out. 'But I was there. I saw what Rubus was doing. He won't stop at anything. I tried to talk to him about not using the sphere because of the damage it might cause and he just didn't care. He's a hero – but if he continues down this path, he's going to end up hurting himself as well as everyone else.'

Hurting everyone? Is that what we were calling the oncoming apocalypse? And I'd thought calling me 'pretty bitchy' was an understatement. Still, it did seem that Lunaria was starting to see the light. Either that or she was being negative about his plans because Rubus had gone all gooey-eyed over Julie. Hell hath no fury like a scorned faery.

'I didn't actually kill Charrie,' I said. 'He was working with me, not against me. It's ... complicated.'

'Is that why you're here and not in prison?'

'Kind of,' I admitted. I wrinkled my nose. 'You know we can't actually trust you, right? You can tag along but we can't divulge any secrets. For all we know, you're still in love with Rubus and on his side.'

Lunaria stared at me. 'Of course I'm still in love with Rubus. Of course I'm still on his side. That's why I can't let him use the sphere. I can't have the man I adore being responsible for ending the world! Imagine how he'd feel afterwards when he came to his senses!'

I wasn't convinced that Rubus had any senses to come to but Lunaria was being entirely earnest. She wanted to save him from himself; only that way could she truly prove her love to him. I sighed. As motives went, I'd heard worse but I didn't think it was going to work out well for her in the end.

A strange light appeared in her eyes. Up until now, I'd always taken Lunaria to be remarkably dippy and far too naïve but she'd possessed a rational core. Now, however, there was a fervent air about her that was giving me pause. When things were so bad that the likes of me was getting worried about the state of someone's mind, it was almost definitely time to run for the hills.

'Talk to him, Mads,' she said. 'Talk to Rubus. He'll listen to you.'

'If he listened to me, then none of us would even be here right now. Rubus doesn't listen to anyone.' I grabbed her hands and squeezed them, attempting to bring her back down to reality. 'We have to stop him, Looney. We have to do whatever it takes to stop what he's doing. *That's* how we help him.'

'How?' she whispered. 'How do we stop him though?' Her fingers tightened round mine. 'He's a hero, Mads. A real hero. He only wants to save us all. In return we have to save him. If people die, it'll hurt him so badly.'

I was starting to get seriously irked. 'Lunaria, people have already died. And they've died because of him. *He* killed Viburna. In the most cold-blooded fashion possible. And he's done the same to others. Finn's brother met the same fate at Rubus's hands.'

Her eyes filled with tears and her bottom lip trembled.

'Stay with us,' I urged. 'If you can't stop Rubus when you're with him, then you can join us and help us to stop him.'

'No,' she said, 'I'm not here to stay with you, I'm here to help you. I don't want to know where the sphere is or what you're doing. Rubus is going crazy. You mentioned Viburna. Ever since she died, he's been stalking around like a madman. He broke Amellus's arm because he took too long to fetch his breakfast. He chopped off Citrona's pinky when he thought she was yawning. He's sent faeries out across the city to find you all. There's a group in front of the Metropolitan Bar, another searching for Artemesia, and a few dozen who are making their way here. I only managed to get in front of them because these crazy fireball things started coming from the sky. It won't be long before they're here. Rubus is going to tear this city apart to find that sphere.' She licked her lips. 'And everyone's afraid of him enough to help him to do it. The more people he hurts, the more he's going to hurt himself.'

I breathed deeply. Lunaria's words filled me with foreboding. 'How did you know I'd be here?' I asked. 'Why did you come here and not go somewhere else?'

Lunaria glanced away. 'You might not remember who you are,' she said, 'but I do. I knew you'd feel guilty about killing Charrie and that you'd want to come to see his family. If Rubus understood guilt and how it can eat away at a person, he'd have sent more Fey this way, but he thinks this is a long shot. The faeries he's sent will still do damage to the bogles, though.'

'I didn't kill Charrie,' I said absently. I did still feel guilty though. I turned round, glancing back at the assembled group. Alora was there, and Bally and lots of other kids. I had to get them out of here. 'How long do we have, Lunaria? How long till they're here?'

'I had a half-hour head start.' She bit her lip. Sanity appeared to glimmer in her eyes again. Praise be. 'There's not much time,' she whispered.

I nodded. 'Then if you're not staying with us, you'd better get out of here.' Even in her current state, she had to realise what a risk she was taking by talking to me and spilling Rubus's plans.

'Wait!' Lunaria reached out and grabbed my arm. 'Do you know why it was raining fire? Why all those animals went crazy?'

'Us,' I told her sadly. 'It was us and our use of magic that caused it. That'll only be the beginning of it, if Rubus gets his way.'

Her eyes were as wide as saucers. 'I heard there was a pink elephant.'

I paused. 'Did you see it?'

She shook her head. Gasbudlikins. I only wanted a glimpse. I met her eyes one final time. 'Thank you, Looney Tunes,' I whispered. 'Take care of yourself.'

She smiled back at me. 'You're welcome.' A moment later, she spun on her heel.

I stayed where I was, watching as she skittered away. Despite the urgency of the situation, the worry I felt for Lunaria was growing. When she finally disappeared round the corner, I shook myself. There was more than Lunaria's well-being at stake.

I ran back to the bogles. Morgan's body was

tense and his eyes scanned my face as if he wanted to check that I wasn't suffering any mortal wounds from chatting. He had good enough hearing, though; he would have picked up every word we said.

'We have to get everyone out of here. You all need to evacuate now!' I bellowed.

Nobody moved. 'Didn't you hear me? Rubus has sent a contingent of Fey here. They're looking for me and for Morgan. They're desperate to find the sphere and desperate to please their evil overlord. Forget flaming rain – that lot will burn this entire estate to the ground without even thinking about it!'

The bogles exchanged looks. Sitri stepped forward with Alora right at his back. 'This is our home,' he said. 'We're not leaving.'

I threw up my hands. 'I get that you all have sharp swords but, by your own admission, you're not properly able to attack. Your best chance is to run.'

Sitri shook his head. 'The children will be led to safety. The rest of us will stand our ground.'

'No! You can't do this. Those Fey are going to—'

'Those Fey are going to do what they're going to do. We're not cowards, Madrona. We've faced them before. We're not just going to walk away now, no matter what happens.'

'It's not about being a coward. It's about doing what's sensible.'

Alora reached out and clasped my shoulder. 'We all do what we have to. We might still be able to talk them down. We might not. But Charrie didn't cower from his challenge and we won't cower from ours.'

I stared helplessly at Morgan. Rubus's faeries were already in a state of high tension. By executing Viburna, he'd effectively said that everyone was fair game – so they wouldn't care if they hurt any bogles. Rubus had whipped them up into a frenzy and had instigated mob rules.

'Then we have to stay,' I said. 'Morgan and I can help. At least our magic will match theirs. With us, you'll have a chance.'

Sitri was adamant. 'No. Your presence will only inflame matters. You won't help.'

'But...'

He held up his palm. 'This is our choice to make.' He turned to a small group of bogles standing to one side. 'Round up the kids and get them to safety. Everyone else needs to take their places. We've prepared for this.' He glanced back at me. 'When your lot didn't leave ten years ago, we started preparing. We are ready.'

I didn't see how that was possible. 'Morgan,' I said desperately. 'We can't—'

'It's their choice, Maddy,' he said. I could see my own emotions reflected in his face. 'We have to respect that.'

'I'm the Madhatter,' I snarled. 'I don't have to respect anything.'

Morgan exchanged a look with Sitri. 'But you will,' he said quietly.

My shoulders dropped.

Sitri smiled. 'We're stronger than you think. But first we'll attempt to keep matters calm. Only if and when that fails will we defend our homes physically.' His tone brooked no argument. I wasn't going to change his mind, no matter what I did.

'We should go, Maddy,' Morgan said. 'They've made their choice. And Sitri's right – if any Fey see us, this will be a whole lot worse.'

Gasbudlikins. I sighed and shook my head. I was very tempted to stamp my feet but I doubted it would help. 'What if they use magic?' I asked. 'They could.' I pointed at the blue sky. 'What comes after raindrops of fire if even more magic is unleashed?'

'We'll be sure to point that out to them.' Sitri was almost preternaturally calm. 'Now go.'

More than twenty young bogle kids had already been ushered down a side lane. Morgan grabbed my hand and tugged. I looked at Alora but all she did was smile in return.

'We can do this, Madrona,' she told me. 'Charrie would want us to do this.' She pulled me into a quick hug. 'Stay safe. And, more importantly, focus on that sphere. Whatever happens, it can't be triggered. For all our sakes.'

I nodded. I had to focus on that; I had to keep the sphere safe. 'Take care,' I told her.

She raised her fist to her chest, touching her heart briefly. 'Always.'

Morgan and I left, initially following the children and their guardians before peeling away from them in the opposite direction. At the end of street I turned and watched as they vanished round a corner. They all seemed to know what they were doing. Sitri was right: they'd been expecting something like this for the last ten years. They knew what they were doing – but it didn't mean I couldn't help.

I pulled my hand from Morgan's and stomped over to an old phone box, which had clearly seen better days. It looked forlorn and lonely in this new digital age.

'Maddy!' Morgan barked. 'What are you doing?'

'What I can to help,' I said, staying calm. If the bogles could keep level heads, so could I. I dug into my pocket for some coins and drew out DC Jones's card at the same time.

She answered on the third ring. 'This is Detective Constable Jones,' she said, in a brisk, no-nonsense voice.

'It's Madrona Hatter. I'm in a housing estate close to Boggart Hole. I assume you saw at least some of what happened outside your police station just after I was released. Unless you want to see more of the same, you need to send the cavalry here now.' I dropped the receiver, leaving it dangling in the air while Jones's tinny voice punch out a series of rapid-fire questions. Then I left the phone box, the heavy door slamming back into place behind me.

Morgan eyed me. 'I don't think the Manchester police have cavalry.'

I shrugged. 'They'll work something out. Given all that's happened today with the magic crap, they'll be busy and in over their heads. DC Jones takes me more seriously than she lets on. She'll do her best by the bogles.' My mouth turned down. 'Even if we can't.'

'We're doing what they asked us to,' he said.

'That doesn't make it right.'

Morgan nodded, maintaining eye contact. 'I know.' He ran a hand through his hair. 'Everything's going to shit.'

I set my chin. 'We still have the sphere. Sort of. Well, at least Rubus doesn't have it. As far as I'm concerned, that counts as a win. We should start warning the others that he's sending out troops, though.'

Morgan held up a small white shell. 'I've already spoken to Artemesia. We're re-grouping back at Julie's house. Rubus knows her, of course, but I'm told her place is safe.'

'It is. She's a vampire so no one can step across her threshold without her permission.' At his look, I laughed slightly. 'I know, right? It's as if everything we've ever been told about vampires is wrong.' A faint warning flash of pain jumped through me and I sucked in a breath.

I cast a glance back at the bogles' estate. It was still quiet. For now. I sighed. The only thing I could do was wish them the best of luck. 'Let's go.'

Morgan didn't move. 'Before we do…' He dipped his head towards my ear, 'I'm proud to be your sidekick,' he whispered.

I offered him a tiny smile in return. 'If we ever make it out of this,' I told him, 'I'll get you a great costume. A thong, perhaps. And nothing else.' I winked. 'Time to vamoose, Snail Boy.'

Chapter Ten

The only person visible on Julie's street was a cocky human kid strolling with his hands in his pockets. The fact that he angled his head up to the sky every few steps or so suggested that he wasn't quite as confident as he was pretending to be. I bit back the temptation to yell at him to stay inside. I had the distinct feeling that telling him what to do would only result in the complete opposite. Instead, I caught up to him and raised my hand up for a high five.

'Hey! You're like me!' I grinned. 'We're not going to let a few things like rampaging rats and fireballs stop us from being out and about! I'm not scared in the slightest. You don't look scared either.'

The teenager glared at me for daring to talk to him. 'Piss off,' he grunted.

I widened my eyes and spun round several times until I made myself dizzy. 'Only boring, sane people are staying in their homes,' I declared loudly. 'Is it true that the army are on their way to protect us? Because I wouldn't mind stealing one of their tanks, you know. Even if they don't come, it won't do any good. This is all because of MI5. They've engineered all this crap because they're doing nuclear testing.' I tapped the side of my nose. 'I know, see? They can't fool me.'

The teenager flicked a look over my shoulder at Morgan, who just shrugged and put his hands in his pockets.

I stretched my grin even wider. 'He thinks we should go inside but I want to see the end of the world. First fire, then there will be flood.' I pointed down at a nearby drain. 'The waters will come from there. The four horsemen of the apocalypse will ride through town. There will be pestilence and —'

'Screw you, lady!' the boy yelled. 'I'm going home!' He marched away, his feet moving at double time.

I watched him as he trotted off and mentally patted myself on the back. With any luck, he would do as he said. If he believed that the only people out on the street were weirdos with questionable sanity, there was more chance he'd make the sensible choice and stay indoors for the time being. For all I knew, floods really were going to happen next.

Then a thought occurred to me. 'Hey!' I called out. 'Have you seen any pink elephants?'

He didn't answer but scarpered off round the corner.

Morgan came up to my shoulder. 'That was good of you,' he said quietly.

'I'm the Madhatter,' I intoned. 'I am keeping the mean streets clear so that children are safe.' I paused. 'He should have been more grateful. He probably didn't recognise me without my fabulous cape.'

Morgan didn't smile. That was hardly surprising: the first time I remembered meeting him, I'd been wearing the aforementioned cape. Even I had to admit that it wasn't quite as fabulous as I wished it was.

Without warning, he planted a hard kiss on my lips. Before he could pull away, I grabbed his shoulders and hooked one leg round his thigh. It wasn't right that he should taste quite this good. I'd never tried pixie dust, the addictive Fey drug that I'd been selling prior to my amnesia, but I'd bet my best knickers that it wasn't nearly as addictive as Morgan's kiss. Heady. Dizzy making. Groin tightening...

From somewhere to our left there was a loud cough. I flicked a look over long enough to register the group standing on Julie's doorstep watching us.

Breaking off the kiss, Morgan growled, 'This isn't a peep show.'

Julie started to fan herself. 'It would certainly be one of the hotter ones if it were. My goodness, darlings!'

I smiled in a smug, self-satisfied manner – then I noticed just how pale she looked. Finn, who was also there, was hovering behind her as if her legs were about to give way.

'What's wrong?' I demanded. 'I've already consigned an entire species to disaster today. I don't want to lose the only v – uh, soap star I've ever met too.' Godammit with this magic NDA crap. I quashed the repeated flare of pain.

'They all know what I am, darling,' Julie said, with a weak wave of her hand. 'Under the circumstances it seemed pertinent to reveal the truth. And thank you for asking but I'm fine. Just a little sniffle.'

It didn't look to me as if she had a little sniffle. I frowned at her. Behind her, Finn frantically waved his hands then made a cutting motion across his throat. 'What's up with you, Finn?' I enquired. 'Do you want me to cut off your head? Because I don't have any handy bogle swords with me. I suppose I could try a kitchen knife.'

He rolled his eyes in irritation and hissed at me. Julie smiled and reached back to pat his hand. 'Finn's a bit worried about me. Honestly, though, it's absolutely nothing. In you come.'

Morgan and I stepped inside while everyone else moved back. It was fortunate that Julie's house was on the grandiose side of large. Our beat-Rubus-into-the-ground-and-save-the-world crowd seemed to be growing bigger every time I turned around. It was probably just as well.

Timmons loped into view. 'I've been monitoring the police radio. There was a disturbance at the estate where the bogles live but everyone seems to have dispersed for now. Was that you guys?'

Morgan shook his head. 'No,' he said grimly. 'I'll give you three guesses as to who was responsible. The bogles knew it was coming and turfed us out so they could deal with it on their own.' He glanced at me sideways. 'It appears they did the right thing.'

I snorted. 'Only because I got the police involved. Good to know that DC Jones came through.' I couldn't deny the sharp relief I felt that the bogles were safe; I had enough crap on my conscience as it was. Then another thought occurred to me. 'Hang on,' I said to Timmons. 'You have a police radio? You?'

He looked slightly discomfited. 'I don't have my own radio. I listen in via the internet. It's a hobby.'

'A useful one.' I smiled. 'Go you.'

The compliment made Timmons' cheeks turn pink. Hmmm. It appeared that I could knock people off balance by telling them nice things. Insults weren't the only way to go.

I rose up onto my tiptoes and spotted Jodie. 'I love the way your hair looks!' I called out to her. Unfortunately it was actually rather messy and looked as if she hadn't brushed it for a month. She apparently realised this and glared at me. 'I was trying to be nice,' I mumbled.

'Keep your fake niceties to yourself,' she snapped back.

I shrugged. I couldn't blame her for her antagonism. 'If you insist,' I told her cheerfully. 'Only nastiness from here on in.'

Morgan rolled his eyes. 'We don't have time for this. We have things to do.' He looked at Julie.

'Is there somewhere we can sit down?'

'The kitchen will do,' she said. 'There are plenty of chairs round the table in there.'

We all trooped in, settling ourselves onto a variety of chairs of all shapes and sizes. I made sure to sit close to Morgan on the off-chance he was going to pounce on me again for another snogging session. I didn't mind if people watched as long as his lips remained on mine. In fact, those people could do whatever they wanted as long as I had my Morgan with me.

'I'm guessing,' Timmons said, shuffling back into his chair until he was comfortable, 'that you saw the fire dripping from the sky. It makes me wonder what's going to come next.'

Artemesia appeared from an open doorway. 'There's no telling,' she said grimly. 'We're entering uncharted territory.' She slumped onto one of the kitchen chairs opposite me.

I drummed my fingers against the table top. 'There must be some kind of pressure-release valve.'

'Well, gee,' Artemesia said, her voice dripping with sarcasm. 'Why didn't I think of that? Why don't you go look for it? I'm sure you'll locate one in seconds. After all, this entire demesne is just like a household boiler. It's probably hiding in one of Julie's cupboards. While you two have been making out, I've been trying to find a solution.'

'We weren't just making out,' I said with pursed lips. 'I took a bath with some ducks too.'

She tutted. 'The magic build-up would be a

lot easier to solve if I could stay in my lab where all my equipment is.'

'I told you on the shell,' Morgan said. 'It's too dangerous with Rubus searching for us.'

'He's always been searching for me.'

'Yeah,' I pointed out, 'but now he's particularly motivated. You're the best geek we have, Arty. We can't afford to lose you.'

'You're all heart,' she muttered. 'Anyway, what I'm trying to say is that I can't find anything to stop this magic-induced craziness. The next wave could happen at any moment. It doesn't help that Rubus and his minions are probably throwing spells and potions around whenever they want. They're only going to make matters worse. Catastrophically worse.'

I sighed. 'Perhaps we should wave a white flag temporarily and get in touch with him. He's been more adversely affected by all this stuff than we have. He was almost eaten alive by a tsunami of rats. If Carduus hasn't worked out what's happening and warned him to avoid magic, maybe we should.'

Morgan's shoulders tightened. 'He's not going to listen to anything we have to say.'

My gaze drifted to Julie, who had an odd, dreamy expression on her face. 'He might listen to her.'

Finn stiffened. 'No way. That's not happening.'

The Redcap really was over-protective of her.

'It's a reasonable suggestion,' I said. 'I don't think he'd hurt her. He's more enamoured of her than anything.'

'Darlings,' Julie drawled, 'it would be my pleasure. I'll talk to him. Set the meeting up. Tell him to bring some decent gin, though. I might as well enjoy myself at the same time.'

Finn opened his mouth to argue but Morgan waved him off. 'It's risky but we have to do it. If all of the faeries under Rubus are using magic at his behest, goodness knows what might happen. As long as he remains stuck in this demesne, he won't want to threaten its safety.'

'Speaking of which,' Jodie said, 'aren't we going to get the sphere back from that cleaning lady? What if she accidentally triggers it or something?'

Artemesia shook her head. 'It can't happen. Humans can't set it off because they don't have any magic within them.'

'It's safe for now,' Morgan agreed. 'Whilst Rubus's Fey are out on the streets, we can't afford to go anywhere near the sphere. It's as safe now as it can be. It's only a temporary solution, of course, but Maddy did well to pass it along.'

I beamed. 'I'll retrieve it later when we're sure the coast is clear,' I said. 'It shouldn't take long. There's more we need in the meantime, as well.' I looked at Julie. 'We need to find a dragon. You're ancient. You must have heard something about other creatures like Chen.'

'Darling, I wouldn't have the faintest idea where to start. I didn't even know you faeries existed until last week. I've certainly never come across any dragons.'

I gestured at the group irritably. 'How is this possible? How do all these supernatural species not know about each other?'

'You say that like it's our fault,' Morgan said drily.

'It is!'

'You're one of us, Maddy.'

'Yeah,' I pouted, 'but I've got amnesia. I get a free pass.' I raised an eyebrow at Finn. 'I remember you saying that you and your brothers were planning to contact werewolves to help the fight against Rubus. How were you going to do that? Maybe they'll know something.'

'All I have is a phone number. I think they live up in the wilds of Scotland where they have the space to roam around unchecked and unnoticed.'

'Call them,' I instructed. 'Even if they can't help with finding a dragon, we need all hands on deck. They'll have heard what's happening here and they'll have magic in their veins. What's happening in Manchester affects them too.'

Finn shrugged. 'I'll do my best to persuade them to head this way.'

My gaze hardened. 'Do better than that. We need them.'

'I can't work you out sometimes,' Jodie interjected. 'One minute you're kissing Morgan, the next you're being a bitch. Then you're being flippant. Now you're ordering everyone around.'

'I kiss Morgan because I'm in a constant state of lust when I'm around him,' I said. I didn't fail to notice the sudden gleam lighting his green eyes. 'I'm being a bitch because I am one. I act flippant because sometimes the only way to deal with disaster is with a sense of humour. I order everyone around because you need a gorgeous general like me to tell you what to do. It's not rocket science. Personality isn't an immutable force – we all change and adapt to situations. We all have good and bad parts. Mine are just more obvious because I don't give a gasbudlikin shit what you lot think of me. I have enough problems judging myself without worrying about other people's judgments.' I paused. 'Apart from Morgan's anyway.' That was a given.

I continued. 'Now, can we get back to the point? We need to find a way to find a dragon. It's the only way we can keep the sphere away from Rubus for good. Apparently dragons lead incredibly long lives – they've probably been around even longer than vampires. There must be records somewhere of their existence, even if they're hidden away. If there are records of vampires, which the hunters used to find Julie, there will be records of dragons somewhere as well.'

Julie snapped her fingers suddenly. 'Wait,' she said.

We all turned to her. 'You've thought of

someone?' I asked, keeping my fingers tightly crossed.

'No,' Julie said. 'But I think I might know where we can look.'

Everyone straightened their posture and held their breath. We needed a break and we knew it.

'Manchester Cathedral,' she said. 'There are old parish records going back five centuries. A group of us broke in during the Blitz in the 1940s and made sure the ones referring to us were destroyed. But the dragons might not have been so circumspect. There might be something there.'

'It sounds like a needle in a haystack,' Artemesia said. 'If you give me a couple of hours, I can use essence of rose and falwort and come up with a potion that might help locate the information you need more quickly.'

'The build-up of magic in the atmosphere needs to be your priority, Arty,' Morgan said. 'We can't let the city be destroyed because of it.'

She raised her hands helplessly. 'I'm at a loss. I don't know what to do about that. I think I can mitigate it slightly but not if Rubus and the others are still casting spells. I need my lab and my books.'

'In that case,' I said, 'our priority is to get Julie to meet with Rubus and warn him off using magic. After that, we travel to the cathedral and rendezvous with you lot, hopefully with Artemesia's potion to help us find out about any nearby dragons. We'll just have to keep our fingers crossed that they really do care about their hoards so much that they've not moved house since the sixteenth century. Then I'll go and get the sphere.'

'Then what?' Jodie asked. 'If we can't find a dragon to help us get rid of the sphere, what do we do?'

'Run away very fast. Preferably to Timbuktu.' I dusted off my palms and got up. 'But we won't need to do that.'

'Why not?'

'Because we can beat Rubus,' Morgan answered. 'We can be smarter than him. Right now he's the monster skulking in the shadows, waiting for his moment. But we're the cunning foxes who are going to ensure he never gets it.' He smiled at me. 'We have no other choice.'

Chapter Eleven

Morgan might have described Rubus as the monster skulking in the shadows but, with his newfound ability to circumnavigate the truce, Rubus was no longer in hiding. It only took a few quick calls to discover that he'd returned to the same lair he'd been in when I was spying on him. It was about time something went in our favour.

Buoyed up with optimism and a semi-decent plan, Morgan, Finn, Julie and I hot-footed in Morgan's car to that address. Apart from a black helicopter circling overhead, we didn't spy anyone else. Even daft teenagers with false confidence were now staying indoors. Dusk was falling and, given the events of the day so far, it was hardly surprising that people weren't venturing out. There weren't any emergency vehicles on the streets either.

I spied a cat washing its face with a paw with blithe indifference. Gusts of wind blew fire-scorched rubbish across the road like tumbleweed in some old Western movie. The city definitely had a silent, ghostly feel about it. At least half the street lights had been knocked out, presumably by the fire rain, and the houses we passed whose occupants were brave enough to leave on their lights had their curtains tightly closed as if to ward off whatever might be outside.

We were trying to avert the apocalypse but it felt as if it were already here.

Julie applied scarlet lipstick and shook out her hair. 'I want to wait until it's completely dark,' she announced to no one in particular.

I peered out of the car window. 'Five minutes, tops,' I said. 'Then the last of the daylight will have gone. No-one's around, though, if you're worried about any fans spotting you.'

'I'm not worried, darling.' She patted my hand before reaching into her bag and drawing out a small silver hip-flask. She took a delicate glug and replaced it. 'But I rather feel that Rubus will be more comfortable under the complete cover of night. After all, those rats you told me about probably damaged his face somewhat with their teeny ratty claws.'

I smirked. 'Yeah. It's almost a shame that we heal so fast. It'd be nice if all those scratch marks he received got infected.' Let's face it, he deserved far worse.

I glanced at Morgan in the driver's seat. 'I'm not suggesting we appeal to Rubus's better nature,' I said, 'but how come you're so wonderful and he's such a prick? You're brothers. You look alike. Why are you so different?'

'That's the million-pound question.' Morgan arched a look at me over his shoulder. 'Who knows why anyone is evil?'

I considered. 'I was evil for a couple of days because I thought it would be more fun.'

'Was it?' Finn asked.

'I wasn't very good at it,' I confided. 'I did my best but I didn't have the follow-through I needed to be truly skilled at it.'

He let out a mild snort. 'I find that difficult to believe.'

'I know, right? It's hard to imagine that there's anything out there that I'm not the best in the world at. Unfortunately, Rubus has me hands-down at villainy.'

'Don't worry, darling,' Julie said. 'There's time yet.' She leaned forward and fiddled with the radio. A moment or two later, it crackled into life.

'A twenty-mile exclusion zone has been set up around the perimeter of Manchester,' announced the DJ. 'The government has stated that they have no numbers of those killed but reiterate that the problems are all localised. Army troops are being mobilised and are set to enter the city limits before tomorrow morning to restore peace and maintain order. Phone lines within Manchester remain open and most homes have power and running water. If you are in the city, we urge you to remain indoors for the time being in case of further problems.'

I swung my gaze up and down the empty street. 'The army's coming to restore peace? They won't have a hard job – I've never seen this place so peaceful. They're coming to destroy the peace, more like.'

'Not if Rubus has anything to do with it,' Morgan said. 'Are you ready to get out now, Julie?'

She craned her neck upwards. The moon was full, its soft white light shining down on us. Only the vaguest glimmer of daylight hovered over the horizon. 'Yes,' she said decisively. She smiled at us. 'Don't worry. He won't know what's hit him once I get started.'

Finn still looked uncomfortable and was clearly desperate to follow at her heels. Julie gave him a reassuring grin, revealing her sharp white teeth. Then she pushed open the door and, in the white stilettos that she wore as if they were slippers, walked across the road to Rubus's door.

She didn't even knock. We watched, holding our breath, as she simply turned the handle and strolled inside.

'She's becoming more vampire-like, isn't she?' I said to Finn.

He didn't answer but I felt his tension increase. 'I won't talk about her behind her back,' he said stiffly.

'She's my friend too and I want to keep her safe. But the build-up of magic is affecting her more than she's letting on.' I ticked off my fingers. 'She looks paler. More tired. She waited until it was properly dark before she left the car. Even her teeth seem different.'

'She's exactly the same as she's always been,' he said. 'You're imagining things.'

I wasn't. I truly wasn't. 'Finn,' I began.

'I don't want to talk about it.'

I sighed. Since his brothers' demise, Finn had clung to Julie like a drowning man clings to a life vest. I knew that I could talk until I was blue in the face but he wasn't going to listen. At least I could count on him to keep a close eye on her; it was the least she deserved. With any luck, she wasn't currently being ripped apart limb by limb.

I kept my eyes trained on the door. 'Ten minutes,' I said. 'If she's not out of there in ten minutes, we go in and get her.'

'And how exactly are we going to get her out?' Finn enquired. 'Every single Fey in there has the ability to stop me. Rubus has the ability to stop you two. If he decides to keep hold of Julie, there's nothing we can do about it.'

'He won't.'

'You don't know that.'

'I told you before,' I said. 'Rubus likes her. I think he genuinely respects her. He's going to want to her to believe that he's a good guy. Hurting her won't achieve that.'

'You hope,' Finn grunted.

'Shh,' Morgan cautioned. 'Something's happening.'

I immediately tensed. The door to the Fey lair wasn't budging and I couldn't see anything through the windows. 'Where?'

'Not with Rubus,' he said. 'With the trees.' Morgan pointed down the road. There was an ominous note to his voice.

Squinting, I saw why.

All along the street, trees were planted at various intervals, sprouting out of carefully dug spots along the pavement. Until a few moments ago, none of the trees had been more than three metres tall and the largest possessed a trunk that was probably of a circumference less than the calf of my leg. I was no tree expert but they'd been pretty enough with their summer foliage. They were still pretty; they still had verdant green leaves. But they were also growing. Visibly.

I fixed on the tree nearest us, perhaps twenty feet away. As I watched, my knuckles tightening on the arm rest, the tree creaked, groaned and spread itself upwards. One foot, two feet, then three. Within moments, it had stretched above the tallest roof.

Its trunk was expanding too. It burgeoned outwards, like a bloated stomach. Where the bark couldn't quite keep up, it cracked and spread, fissures breaking across the rough surface. I almost expected small woodland creatures to appear but if there were any about, they were keeping their distance.

When the pavement and then the road broke apart from the force of the trees' roots, I could understand why. So many trees were growing at such a rate that the ground started to shake.

There was a tremendous roaring sound. At first, I couldn't work out what it was but when tiles dropped from the roof of one of the terraced houses near Rubus's lair, I finally realised. Right in front of my eyes, an oak burst through the house towards the sky. From deep within the house, we could hear terrified screams.

I stopped gaping and started moving, pushing open the car door and sprinting for the house. At the rate that tree was going, whoever was inside was likely to become part of the root system.

Within moments, Morgan was next to me. We flung ourselves at the house, yanking open the door. What greeted us, however, wasn't a neat hallway. All we could see was the continually expanding tree trunk straining against the walls. I could make out plaster cracking and warping. We had only moments before the entire structure collapsed and all that remained was tree.

I jumped back and peered upwards. The tree was slanting to the right. To the left, there was a window on the first floor. Suddenly it swung open and the terrified face of a young woman appeared.

'Help!' she shrieked. 'Help me!' Her wide eyes frantically searched the street before alighting on us. She waved her hands desperately. 'I can't open the bedroom door! My children are in the other room! I can't... I can't...' She gulped in air, her anxiety taking over.

'We're on our way,' I yelled. 'Stay calm!'

Easy for me to say. Now we could hear screams from the streets nearby, though they were barely audible over the noise of the rupturing roads and pavements.

'Give me a boost,' I said to Morgan. 'I'll get inside and see what I can do.'

He nodded and formed a foothold with his palms. I hopped onto his hands, threw myself upwards and managed to grab the edge of the window frame.

Gasbudlikins. However much I wished it were different, I didn't have sufficient strength in my arms. My legs writhed in the air as I did everything I could to avoid losing my grip. It was only when I braced my toes against the wall of the house that I managed to haul myself upwards so I could squeeze through the window.

The woman, still in full-blown panic mode, had abandoned her post and returned to her bedroom door, yanking at it to try and open it. From deep within the house, I could hear children crying. I dusted myself off and gritted my teeth.

'How many children are there?'

The woman didn't answer. She was too focused on frantically trying to tug the door open.

I placed a firm hand on her arm. 'How many people are in the house?'

Morgan was clearly rubbing off on me because something about my stern, school-mistress tone finally got through to the woman. Although she kept her hands on the door handle, she stopped flailing and answered. 'Two. Two children. Bertie – he's only three. And Jess. She's...' The woman choked. 'She's just a baby.'

'Where are they?'

'Their bedroom. It's only a few metres away at the opposite end of the house. I can't get to them.' Her voice rose again. 'I can't get to them! I can't...!'

'Hush. They're crying so that means they're still alive. I've got this. It's only a tree. This will be a piece of cake.'

I'd barely finished speaking when there was a tremendous crunch. The wood panels on the door bulged and splintered. I pulled the woman back just in time before a branch shot out and pinned her to the far wall. She screamed again. Her shrieks were rather off-key – and off-putting.

I vaulted over the branch and grabbed her. If she hadn't been so surprised, she'd have put up more of a fight. As it was, I managed to get her to the window.

'Morgan!' I yelled. 'Incoming!'

I shoved the woman out. I heard an oomph and glanced down. Morgan had caught her – but he was now sprawled on his back with the woman on top of him. From the way she was moving, she was fine. From the glower on Morgan's face as he gazed up at me, so was he. I flashed him a grin and a tiny wave, then scooted for the door.

I tried the same as the panicking mother had done, tugging on the door handle with all my might. The door frame was already buckling but, even with the shattered wood through which the branch had sprung, there was no way in this godforsaken demesne I was going to manage to open it.

I cocked my head and listened. Fortunately the tree seemed to have stopped its growth – at least for now. The children were still crying. After listening to their mother, I could see where they got it from.

'Well, Madrona,' I muttered to myself, 'the doors are blocked. There's no way through. You're just going to have to find another way.'

Unwilling to let loose any magic without rooting it in anything real first, I stepped back and gazed upwards. From this angle, I could see the massive hole in the roof that the tree had created. If I couldn't go down and I couldn't go across, I'd darn well have to go up.

Without wasting any more time, I grabbed the dressing table and hauled it over before leaping onto it. If I jumped, maybe I could launch myself upwards to grab the side of the tree and get onto the roof.

The building was rattling now. Whether the tree had stopped growing or not, I suspected that the entire structure was not long for this world. I had to move – and move fast.

I used the dressing table as a launch pad and sprang upwards. All I succeeded in doing was plastering myself against the wall. My fingers barely scraped against the now-visible roof timbers. That wasn't any good. I got back to my feet, clambered on the dressing table again and readjusted my thinking. Snapping my fingers, I realised I had it.

I sprang up again, this time using the protruding branch as a sort of trampoline. The tree was healthy and young, so there was enough give on the branch when I landed on it to shoot me upwards an extra foot. It did the trick.

Letting out a loud, ululating, Tarzan bellow, I swung my legs up and hooked them onto one of the slanting cross beams in the roof. It was a tight squeeze but there was enough of a gap so I could push myself out onto the roof. After the claustrophobic, tree-filled house, it was a blessed relief to be outdoors again – though I couldn't take the time to savour it.

I edged forward, intending to circle round the tree to reach the other side of the house. As soon as I moved, however, my foot slipped on one of the moss-covered tiles and I went flying.

My hands scrabbled at the air and my life flashed in front of my eyes. Fortunately, at the last minute the tree itself saved me. While I swung out with nothing but air between me and the hard pavement below, one of the slimmer branches snagged on my baggy T-shirt and held me back. It stopped me falling. Gasbudlikins. That was close.

I swayed to my right, hoping to use the same branch to get back to relative safety. I could already hear the fabric of my T-shirt ripping; I didn't have long. With one deep breath – and just as the T-shirt gave way – I threw myself forward and wrapped my arms round the tree trunk to avoid falling again.

Done.

I shimmied around until I was on the section of the roof where I needed to be. There was another loud creak; I could swear the building was swaying. As this was a terraced house, I prayed that it wouldn't take down a dozen other houses with it when it fell. This was not the time for dominoes.

'Morgan!' I yelled.

His voice drifted back up to me. 'Are you alright?'

'I'm fine! You need to get the neighbours out. This building is about to collapse!'

I heard a moan from the mother but I didn't have time to worry about her. Morgan could do the evacuations and tea and sympathy; the Madhatter would do the action.

I pivoted slightly. Unfortunately, the gap in the roof here was considerably smaller. Without a decent diet, I doubted it would be as easy to squeeze down on this side as it had been to squeeze up on the other side. I pursed my lips. The next house along had a skylight; that would have to do. With any luck, the adjacent wall had been destroyed and, once I was back inside, I could get through.

Reaching for a branch to keep my balance, I shuffled over to the skylight. It was firmly closed. I'd have to smash it to get in. Cursing the human who invented double glazing, I angled my heel downwards and slammed it onto the glass. It cracked and a spider's web of tiny fissures appeared. I was going to need more than that.

Raising my knee, I kicked the glass again. This time, my entire leg went through, shards scraping through my jeans and piercing my flesh. I ignored the pain and the blood and set about clearing away as much of the glass as I could before lowering myself inside.

'Maddy!' I heard Morgan shout. 'You need to...' The rest of his words were swallowed up by the sound of approaching sirens. You had to feel for the fire brigade, I thought. They'd probably only just finished putting out the fires caused by the crazed rain from earlier; now they had trees with minds of their own to worry about. I bet all those burly firemen wished they had someone like me to help them out.

The neighbours' house was in an equally sorry state. Branches from next door had punched through the walls. I darted over to the most damaged part and started yanking at the crumbling plaster to create a large enough gap to squeeze through. When there was enough space I dived through headfirst, hitting a small cot and knocking it over as I landed.

Gasbudlikins. Heart thumping, I leapt to my feet. The room was covered in fallen debris and it was almost impossible to see a thing. It would be ridiculous if I'd fought my way in here to rescue babies and then hurt those very babies because of my own actions. I ducked under another low-lying branch that was poking through the wall and heaved away the cot. No baby.

'Bertie!' I shrieked, my voice now reaching the same pitch as their mother's. 'Jess!'

There was no longer any crying. The house felt as if it were alive, breathing and creaking and moaning in the final gasps of its life, but of the children there was no sound. Was I in the wrong room? Were they hiding? Was...?

'Maddy! Get the hell out of there! The whole place is about to collapse!'

I frowned and craned my neck round. There, outside the open window, was Morgan. 'The children...'

'They're safe. They're out.' He outstretched his hand towards me. 'Come on!'

I squinted. 'Are you hovering in mid-air? Can we actually fly after all?'

He rolled his eyes. 'Don't be ridiculous. I'm on a ladder in the garden. One of the neighbours gave it to me.'

I got up to my feet, turned slowly and put my hands on my hips. 'You got a ladder.'

'Yes.'

'From a neighbour.'

He glared at me impatiently. 'Yes! Come on. We have to get out of here.'

I sniffed. 'I've been clambering around the roof, risking my neck, possibly kicking a kid out of its bed, and you calmly got a ladder and put it in the back garden?'

'Can we talk about this later?'

I tossed my head. 'I'd like to talk about it

now.'

There was a loud rumble. I let out a small yelp and threw myself at Morgan. His arm wrapped round my waist and, flipping me over his shoulder fireman-style, he pulled me through the window and down the ladder.

We only just made it to the ground in time. A moment later, the house collapsed in on itself as if it were a punctured balloon.

Morgan ran, taking us both a safe distance away from the cloud of dust and debris. He carried me to other side of the street, which was now a mess of gnarled roots and fallen bricks. Blue lights from the fire engine flickered outside several houses as more residents were rescued. Then something hit Morgan and I was squashed between him and the wall.

'Thank you! Thank you! You saved my children!'

'You're very welcome,' I said, my voice muffled somewhere around Morgan's arse.

He dropped me gently to the ground. I brushed myself down and turned. By the time I'd done so, Bertie and Jess's mum was hugging Morgan tightly. She was no longer crying or shrieking or screaming, she was wrapping herself round him in abject gratitude.

'If it wasn't for you,' she gasped, 'they'd be dead.'

She pulled back and several other humans approached. 'Well done, mate,' said a burly man with a beard and what appeared to be dinosaur pyjamas. 'I don't know what shit is going down here but you're a hero. Well done.'

I folded my arms and glared. *I'd* entered the damned house. *I'd* clambered across the roof. *I'd* almost killed myself in the process. Morgan had borrowed a ladder, wandered up a few rungs and somehow become the arsebadgering superhero. Honestly. This was idiotic.

'Yeah,' I said with full-blown sarcasm. 'Go you.'

Several of the neighbours shook their heads. 'We've had enough. We're packing our things and getting out of here. The army has set up a boundary around the city. We're heading that way if anyone wants a lift.'

There were nods and murmurs and plans were made. After a few more handshakes with Morgan the wondrous saviour, people started to disperse.

Only when we were alone again did I speak. 'Maybe we should stop worrying about Rubus,' I said. 'It seems as if the apocalypse is already starting, regardless of the sphere.'

Morgan threw me a long, baleful look. 'It's only happening in Manchester,' he said grimly. 'Where the greatest concentration of faeries is. What happens if all this,' he waved a hand at the devastated street, 'starts happening in other places too?'

I considered. 'Well,' I said cheerfully, 'you'll

be busy. You are, after all, the hero of this piece.'

He smirked. 'Jealous?'

'No.'

'You look jealous.'

'I'm not...' Fortunately, I was prevented from having to defend myself. Further down, where Rubus's lair was situated, a small group was emerging. I spotted Rubus, Julie, Finn, Lunaria and various others.

My mouth flattened. 'Look who's decided to come out.'

Morgan turned, his expression shuttering. Without another word, he strode towards his errant brother. I caught up, keeping pace with him. At least Julie looked okay. That was something. It was a damned shame that Rubus hadn't had a tree slam him into a wall, though.

We drew up to Rubus and his crowd, maintaining a decent distance between us in case he decided to try anything. He looked relaxed, one eyebrow quirked as he gazed up and down the street. 'Have you been making a mess, Morganus?' he enquired.

Morgan growled. 'This is merely a taste of what will happen if you use the sphere, Rubus. People almost died on this very street. Goodness only knows what's happening across the rest of the city.'

Rubus clapped his hands to his cheeks in mock dismay. 'Goodness only knows indeed!'

'Our magic has done this,' I said, adding

weight to Morgan's words in a bid to prove to Rubus's minions that his lack of concern was criminal. 'This is *our* fault. We can't cast any more spells. Not if we want all this to stop happening.'

I spotted several pale faces but it was clear who was in charge. No one else spoke; there wasn't so much as a murmur from the assembly.

Rubus shook his head sadly. 'Madrona, Madrona, Madrona. Listen to yourself. You were so much more fun when you let your true self come to the fore. Heroism doesn't suit you.'

Maybe not, but altruism was something that Rubus would never understand. I exhaled and met his eyes. 'It's not about heroism, it's about self-preservation. You lot were lucky that a damned oak tree didn't suddenly sprout underneath your feet. You're lucky that the fire rain didn't set your hair alight.' I tilted my head. 'You weren't quite so lucky with those rats though, were you?'

Rubus was unable to repress a shudder. 'Nasty creatures. It's fortunate they didn't do more damage.' His mouth turned down. 'This is why we Fey need to exit this demesne *tout suite*. We need to save ourselves. Give me the sphere, Maddy,' he said. 'Put aside all this painful conscience stuff. It'll only ever make you miserable.'

'She doesn't have the sphere,' Morgan broke in. 'And the sphere is separate to this other business. We must agree to avoid using more magic so that what's in the atmosphere now can disperse safely.'

Rubus didn't answer for a moment. I couldn't read his expression. Frankly, it could have gone either way. Then he shrugged. 'I told the glamorous Julie here that I'd make sure none of my lot use magic unless it's an emergency. I can be magnanimous. If it comes to the sphere and me, however, all bets are off. And I'm only laying off spells because I don't want anyone to be hurt.'

'You mean *you* don't want to be hurt,' I snapped.

He tutted. 'Oh, Maddy. So much anger. This side of you really isn't fun at all.' He lunged forward without warning, one hand swiping at my face. Morgan leapt in front to block him. Rubus pulled back and laughed. 'Of course,' he added, 'I don't need magic to hurt you. I can do that without any spells.'

Julie took a step towards us. 'Darling,' she drawled, 'you need to relax.' She waved an airy hand. 'I recommend gin. It works wonders.' She blew a kiss towards Rubus and then, with Finn flanking her, joined us. It was a miracle that the large Redcap restrained himself; after all, Rubus had killed his brother in cold blood. I had to give him kudos for self-control.

Rubus clasped his heart and kept his eyes on Julie. 'Bye, darling.'

She smiled. 'Bye.'

I sneaked a quick peek at Lunaria. She looked even more wan and miserable than she was earlier. Poor thing. It seemed that all of us, in our own ways, were trying our best to succeed and none of us were managing it. Apart from Julie – but she had a good century and a half's experience on the rest of us.

'Julie!' Rubus called. 'Don't forget what I told you!'

Her expression dropped for the briefest second and I realised that I was wrong: she was holding on to a mask like the rest of us.

I bit back the temptation to ask Julie what he meant; I wouldn't give Rubus the satisfaction. I kept walking. We'd done all we could for now.

Chapter Twelve

It took us far longer to get to Manchester Cathedral from Rubus's street than it should have done. With virtually every road torn up by the sprouting trees, and people bundling their belongings into their cars to make their escape from the horrors of the city, the streets were almost impassable by motor vehicle. In the end we nabbed enough free city Mobikes to cycle there.

Towering trees dotted the landscape, with foliage and leaf cover making many of the streets even darker than they would usually be at this time of night. More and more helicopters filled the sky; when we spotted a tank turning down one of the main thoroughfares, it was clear that the army was no longer waiting till dawn to make their move into the city.

'Everyone stay calm,' bellowed a tinny loudspeaker attached to the tank. 'We are in control and there is nothing to worry about.'

I gave a loud, derisive snort. I understood what was going on and I knew that the British military was most definitely not in control. There was a great deal to worry about.

'All current events are occurring only within

the city of Manchester,' the loudspeaker burbled. 'Until the situation is resolved, all citizens must remain indoors unless it is not safe to do so. Due to flooding, the suburb of Burnage is being evacuated but other areas are deemed clear.'

I cycled round a massive sinkhole that had opened up smack-bang in the middle of the road. 'Clear?' I eyed the dark chasm, wrinkling my nose at the fetid stench rising from its depths.

'They don't know what to do,' Morgan said quietly. 'The humans like science, they like to be able to explain things and use logic to reason their way out of problems. There's nothing logical about magic.'

'There's nothing logical about your brother either,' Finn tossed over his shoulder.

'He promised me that he would lay off the hocus pocus, darling,' Julie said.

Finn's expression was sour. 'I wouldn't trust him an inch. No promise of Rubus's is worth a damn.'

Actually, I suspected that despite his blithe languor Rubus was as shaken by what was going on as the rest of us. Of course, he would use these events as further evidence that the power of the sphere needed to be unleashed so that all us Fey could travel back to Mag Mell as quickly as possible. But he must have finally started to realise what chaos that would incur.

'What did Rubus mean, Julie?' I called out. 'When he said not to forget what he told you, what was he talking about?'

'Oh, just some nonsensical acting tips,' she said, taking one hand off the handlebars for a moment to wave it around and indicate that his words were worthless. 'Honestly, I get that sort of ridiculousness all the time. Everyone thinks they have it in them to be the next Greta Garbo.'

Finn frowned. 'Who's Greta Garbo?'

'Sorry, darling,' she drawled. 'I'm showing my age. Do you know, I met her once?' She launched into a long tale which, unsurprisingly, involved copious amounts of gin.

I cast a quick glance in Morgan's direction. His jaw was set and although his shoulders were loose, his knuckles were white as he clenched the handlebars of the bike. It couldn't be easy facing your evil brother and begging him to be temperate whilst also trying to stop him destroying the world.

I swerved slightly, narrowly missing some snaking tree roots that appeared from nowhere, and lowered my voice.

'I don't want to ruin the mood,' I said chattily, 'but I feel obliged to point out that you look like a circus bear on a tricycle.' I wasn't lying; although the Mobike was adult sized, it appeared pathetically small with Morgan's large frame perched on top of it. He was all knees and elbows. That was nothing compared to Finn, of course, but Finn was distracting himself by focusing on Julie. Right now, Morgan had nothing but me to take his mind off things.

'Does that make you the clown?' he sent back.

I felt my insides relax slightly. 'Don't be daft. I'm obviously the ringmaster; Julie is the magician's glamorous assistant; Finn is the clown. Any second now, he's going to tip his front wheel into a pothole and do a massive somersault followed by a crash of cymbals.'

Morgan raised an eyebrow. 'Have you ever even been to a circus?'

I shrugged. 'How the hell do I know? I can't remember.' I tapped my temple. 'But there are vast, hidden depths to my wondrous knowledge that even I can't contemplate.'

Morgan didn't smile. 'You must be desperate to regain your memories.'

Strangely enough I wasn't. Artemesia had told me that she was close to finding a potion that would resolve my amnesiac issues but I already knew everything I wanted to. I didn't need to remember who I was before, not any longer. And I didn't want a serious conversation with Morgan right now. What he needed was some light-hearted Madrona goodness, not heavy discussions about our souls.

'I'm fabulous enough even without my memory,' I crowed. 'I mean, look at me! I'm cycling through a deserted city to sightsee in a cathedral whilst avoiding army tanks and arboreal mishaps, with a famous soap actress, a man who looks like he's gone ten rounds in the boxing ring with a bin lorry, and the sexiest faery alive. Does it get any better?'

Morgan's grip on the bike eased slightly. His eyes met mine and he said softly, 'The company is indeed extraordinary.'

I smiled. Maybe I should deliberately crash my bike then I'd be forced to hop up behind Morgan. I could rub myself against his body, reach round and feel his muscles rippling underneath my fingers, bury my nose in his luxuriant, dark curls…

'There's the cathedral!' Julie sang out.

Reluctantly, I ripped myself away from the image of Morgan and I riding stark naked on the same bicycle and peered ahead. I'd spotted the cathedral several times over the city rooftops but I couldn't remember being close to it before. It was certainly an imposing structure, especially in the dead of night. From here, it didn't appear as if any of the trees nearby had damaged it. Given the cathedral's size, that was hardly surprising. I doubted if there was a single crazy, magical tree anywhere in the world that could damage it.

The four of us cycled up to the front entrance, dropped the Mobikes on the grassy verge and gazed up.

'The clock has stopped,' Finn said quietly.

We followed his gaze. He was right: the hands on the large clock on the east tower weren't moving. Time was no longer cooperating with the city of Manchester. I thought guiltily of the times I'd manipulated time for my own gain, slowing down the seconds so I could get the upper hand over my opponents. Then I shrugged; what was done was done.

'Where are the archives kept?' I enquired.

Julie chewed on her bottom lip then pointed over to the left. 'I'm pretty certain they're near that small side chapel over there.'

Morgan nodded grimly. 'At least we'll be able to rummage around without being disturbed.'

I glanced at the others. 'Well, let's vamoose. We've got ourselves a dragon to find.'

We loped up the steps. It stood to reason that the heavy cathedral doors would be locked tight at this time of night to avoid the risk of drunken partygoers messing up the interior or, heavens forbid, the odd homeless person bedding down. Strangely, the door to the left was slightly ajar.

I paused, tilting my head and listening carefully. 'There are people inside,' I said. 'Lots of them.'

We exchanged looks before I gently pushed the door open so we could peer inside. My ears hadn't been deceiving me – and it wasn't just one or two people inside the cathedral either; there were hundreds of them.

No one was speaking much, which was why we hadn't heard them earlier. Most of them were sitting silently in the pews and contemplating their surroundings, hugging friends or praying quietly.

'The church offers succour in times of need,' Finn murmured. He reached for Julie's hand and squeezed it. 'And I suppose a lot of people imagine that what's been happening is some sort of blight from God.'

Morgan's mouth tightened. 'We'll enjoy a day or two of this. People will seek comfort and help but it won't be long before their fear changes to something far uglier. Aggression. Vigilantism. If Artemesia doesn't manage to disperse at least some of the residual magic soon, there's going to be chaos.'

I squared my shoulders. 'Then let's get a bloody move on before that happens.'

I slipped inside and looked around for a way to the smaller chapel where Julie reckoned the archives were. Spotting a likely looking door, I marched towards it. None of the stricken worshippers so much as glanced in my direction.

I opened the door and gazed into the darkness within. 'Is this right, Julie?' I asked.

When there was no immediate answer I turned and realised, somewhat belatedly, that I was alone. Honestly. One would expect one's sidekicks to at least try and keep up.

Spinning round, I headed back. Julie was doubled over, with Finn's arm wrapped around her. Morgan was looking on grimly.

'What's wrong?' I asked, alarmed.

'She doesn't feel well,' Finn said, standing over her slight frame protectively. He could spread his legs all he wanted; that wasn't going to stop any kind of tummy bug.

Morgan licked his lips. 'Can you get her back home? Now we know where the archives are, Maddy and I will find the others and help them to continue looking. Julie should rest.'

Finn looked even more concerned about her that he normally did. He nodded and carefully helped her back to where we'd left the bikes. Morgan and I watched them go.

'It's affecting her badly, isn't it?' I said. 'She's a vampire. She's never really had any real powers. These strange magic surges aren't just disturbing the rain and the trees and the animals, they're disturbing her too.'

Grimacing, Morgan turned to me. 'That would be my guess, too. It can't be a coincidence that she was struck down right on the steps of a holy building.'

'She told me she's never had a problem with things like this before. I don't think she was lying.'

'No,' he agreed. 'Not then. But she's changing now.'

'I tried to speak to Finn about it but he refused to listen.'

Morgan sighed. 'That's understandable. He's taken all the love he felt for his brothers and given it to Julie. I dread to think what will become of him if something happens to her.'

'You mean something other than turning all fangy and trying to drink our blood?'

He shot me a look. 'We're not there yet.'

'*Yet* being the operative word,' I muttered.

'Come on. We can't worry about her now.'

Morgan nodded. From the look in his green eyes, however, he was just as concerned about Julie as I was.

***

Fortunately we didn't have to waste much time searching for the archives. The sound of the other people bickering reached our ears long before we reached them.

'Just look in that box,' Timmons was saying.

'The dust is getting in my eyes,' Jodie complained. 'I'm not a Fey, remember? It's harder for me. I possess human frailties.'

'Well, put those human frailties to good use,' he said. 'Even Opulus is doing his best.'

There was a chink of light underneath one of the doors. Morgan headed for it with me barely a step behind. 'I take it,' he said drily, 'that you've not found anything yet.'

Their faces brightened immediately. It was no wonder they were glad of the distraction: there were fusty and musty papers scattered all over the room.

'What happened?' Jodie asked. 'Did you see Rubus?'

'We did. He said he'll lay off magic for now.'

Timmons exhaled. 'Do you think he actually will?'

'We'll have to hope so,' I said grimly. 'Did

you see what happened to the trees?'

'We were inside at the time. We heard enough though.'

Jodie pouted. 'I didn't. I don't have clever faery ears like you lot.' She gave Timmons a sour glance. 'Or eyes.'

He sighed in exasperation and I regarded the pair of them with mild amusement. Timmons loved it here; he probably wished he were wholly human as much as Jodie seemed to wish she were wholly Fey. Naturally both of them probably wished they were more like me. Poor them.

'Did Arty manage to conjure up that potion?' Morgan asked.

From the far corner, Opulus grunted. His eyes remained red-rimmed but, of the three of them, he appeared to be doing the best job of looking for evidence of nearby dragons. 'She did. We deemed it best not to use it unless we had to. She said that most of the magic is bound up in the ingredients, so there shouldn't be a problem using it and releasing more into the ether. But we wanted to wait, just in case.'

In case they were blamed for the end of the world. Surprisingly, that was a sentiment I could get behind. 'How long have you been here?' I asked.

'A couple of hours. We did find reference to a beast who could control fire in one old book—' Jodie began.

'I found that,' Timmons interrupted.

She rolled her eyes. 'Whatever. It was

pointless anyway. It turned out to be nothing more than a salamander transported here by some wandering Crusader in the Middle Ages.'

'We need help,' Opulus said flatly.

I stretched out my arms. 'Never fear! The Madhatter is here!'

This time all of them rolled their eyes. I beamed.

Spotting a small vial sitting on top of a dusty shelf, I edged round Morgan and the teetering piles of paper and grabbed it. 'Is this the potion?'

Jodie and Timmons nodded. I raised an eyebrow in Morgan's direction. 'It's a calculated risk,' I said. 'The army is already starting to evacuate people. I reckon there are only hours – if that – before looting starts. We need to tie up the sphere so that we can focus on other problems. Much longer and there won't be any city left to save.'

'I thought the army was only evacuating Burnage,' Timmons said.

I shrugged. 'That's what they said. But they'll be trying to keep things orderly and prevent a mass panic, so they'll be doing it in stages to stop the roads from getting clogged up. I bet that by this time tomorrow, Manchester will be a ghost town.'

Timmons looked pained. 'My hotel guests have already cleared out. I don't want to have to relocate.'

I smiled at him. 'That's why we're doing this – to stop all faeries from relocating unnecessarily.' I unstoppered the vial and took a deep sniff. 'It smells innocuous enough. Shall we?'

Jodie waved a hand around the messy room. 'Anything's better than what we're already doing.'

Morgan looked unhappy. 'If Arty thinks there's a chance that using the potion will disperse more magical residue, maybe we should do this hard way instead.'

'They've been doing this the hard way,' I pointed out. 'All it's got them is at each other's throats. We don't have the time to waste.'

'All the same...'

I ignored him and raised the vial to my lips, glugging it down in one long mouthful.

'You're not supposed to drink it, Maddy!'

I made a face. 'I can see why. It tastes horrible.'

'It's supposed to be scattered around the room!'

'And instead it's scattered around my body. It will help contain the magic and prevent more residue from leaking out.' Maybe. What the hell did I know? It had seemed like a good idea at the time.

Jodie tutted loudly. 'Great,' she said. 'Just great. Now we've lost the only chance of finding the information we need. We'll have to go back to Artemesia and get her to make some more. Except that she's desperately busy trying to stop more magic build-up from destroying the city. She doesn't have time to take a break to help us save the world.'

There was definitely something incongruous about Jodie's statements but I couldn't concentrate. I pursed my lips. My stomach was starting to feel very strange, churning in a most peculiar fashion. My vision was also going blurry at the edges. I was going to be sick; I was definitely going to be sick.

'Maddy!' Morgan said, obviously alarmed.

I turned towards him. 'Wh – what?' Even to my own ears, my voice sounded slurred and slow.

'Are you alright?'

'Fine,' I mumbled. 'I'm perfectly fine. I just need to...'

It all came gushing out before I could stop it, a stream of greenish vomit that sprayed from my mouth. Jodie screamed and scrambled to her feet, darting out of the way. Even Opulus seemed alarmed.

I wiped my mouth with the back of my hand and let out a loud burp. 'That's better.' I blinked a few times and my vision returned to normal.

Morgan rounded on me. 'You never ever drink or eat anything like that again,' he commanded. 'It could do untold damage.'

I pointed at the vomit spatters. 'Unfortunately,' I said, 'I rather think it already has.'

'So much for the Madhatter,' Jodie said. 'Now it's not just dust and mountains of paper to get through. It's the contents of her stupid stomach.'

I had to admit that they weren't pleasant. The room was already airless; now it was airless and filled with sour stench of my half-digested dinner. I peered round. I supposed I should make some effort at cleaning up.

The worst of the sick was on a pile of old books lying against a rickety metal shelving unit. I stumbled over and started wiping the green puke off with the hem of my T-shirt. It had already been soaked and slimed and burnt and ripped today; a little intestinal fluid was unlikely to do it any more harm.

I patted ineffectually at the front cover of the first book. '*The Parish Records for Diggle,*' I said, reading aloud as the words gradually became visible. 'It sounds like a children's TV show, not an actual place.' I flipped open the first pages. 'May 12th, 1467 Baptism Richard Stiff.' I looked up at the others. 'Who on earth thinks it's a good idea to name their child Dick Stiff? Dick Stiff from Diggle.' I shook my head. 'Poor arsebadger.'

I flicked another page. 'George Lung. Blimey. Do you think he was mates with Dick Stiff and Willie Throat and Billy Nose and Boris Arse?'

I really shouldn't have downed that potion. We were never going to find what we needed.

Opulus, who'd been keeping quiet, rose abruptly to his feet. 'Say that again,' he said.

'Dick Stiff, Willie Throat, Bi —'

'Not that you foolish girl. The other one. The other name.'

I frowned. 'You mean George Lung?'

He snapped his fingers. 'That's it.'

Morgan's expression cleared. 'Do you really

think that's it?'

Opulus raised a single shoulder. 'It's where the potion led us.'

'It's where my vomit led us,' I said. I paused. 'Led us where, though?'

Morgan turned to me. 'Lung. It's a variation of Liung.'

I waited for more. When he didn't continue, I gestured impatiently. 'I'm going to need a little more than that.'

'*Liung* is Chinese for dragon.'

'That's a little tenuous, isn't it?'

'Actually,' Morgan said with a sudden gleam in his eye, 'I don't think it is.' He held out his hand. 'Give me the book.'

I passed it over. There was still a considerable amount of vomit on it. Morgan made a moue of distaste. 'Vegetables, Maddy. You need to eat fewer kebabs and Pot Noodles and more vegetables.'

'Well,' I told him, 'at least you can't ever say that you don't know me inside out.'

Morgan smiled slightly before flipping through the pages, his eyes scanning each one as he searched. When his body tensed, I knew he'd found what we were looking for. 'We have an address,' he crowed. 'He was moved from Diggle not long after he was born. This could be it.'

'You have an address from the fifteenth century,' I pointed out, peering over his shoulder. 'How useful is that going to be? Anyway, how can you read that? It's barely legible.'

'It's Moss Side,' Morgan said. He jabbed at the entry. 'That particular suburb has been around for centuries and dragons don't like to move unless they absolutely have to. As unbelievable as it might seem, there's a very good chance that our Mr Lung is still there. If the building is still standing, anyway.'

Everyone, Opulus included, suddenly appeared considerably brighter. I put my hands on my hips and grinned. 'Then let's go and find out.'

Chapter Thirteen

It was less than four miles from the cathedral to Moss Side where hopefully we would find our very own dragon. With the semi-destroyed roads, piles of rubble and massive potholes, it took us almost forty minutes by bike. The journey didn't dint my renewed optimism, however.

'We're all going on a dragon hunt!' I chanted for a good part of the journey. I was hoping for at least a little bit of fire-breathing and wing-flapping – otherwise what was the point of being a dragon?

Unfortunately not everyone possessed my *joie de vivre*. Jodie, in particular, was growing more and more nervous the closer we got. 'Is he going to be, you know, scaly? With big teeth?'

'Very big teeth,' I said. 'All the better to eat us with.'

Morgan rolled his eyes. 'If he's anything like Chen,' he said, 'he'll look like an ordinary man. And at five centuries old, he won't be particularly fast on his feet. There's nothing to worry about it.'

'Unless,' I added, 'the magic in the air is affecting him in the same way that it's been affecting Julie and he's now got actual scales and actual sharp fangs.'

'Thank you, Maddy.' Morgan didn't sound particularly grateful. 'I doubt that very much though.'

'And claws that will rip through a human's flesh with barely a swipe,' I continued. 'And a penchant for chewing on the skulls of his victims.'

He hissed through his teeth. 'It will be fine.'

Jodie didn't appear comforted by his words. Clearly she trusted my judgment more than Morgan's. My smile brightened even further.

We halted outside the address the parish records had given us. The building certainly looked old enough. It was an imposing structure made of red brick, with four storeys stretching upwards into the night sky. I noted the satellite dish plonked on the side and wondered whether dragons enjoyed watching television. I found it hard to imagine.

'How are we going to do this?' Timmons asked nervously. 'Do we sneak in or simply ring the doorbell? It is after three in the morning. Maybe we should wait until daylight.'

I waved a hand dismissively. 'Daylight schmaylight. The Madhatter works in all conditions.'

'The Madhatter talks about herself in the third person and possesses all the charm of a faeces-covered gnat,' he muttered.

I raised an eyebrow. 'Pardon?'

Timmons winked at me and I smiled back. It was good to see that he was growing in confidence when he talked to me. It made a pleasant change from seeing him cower in fear.

'This is what we'll do,' I said. I spoke with an air of command. I intended to lead my troops into battle with the best possible strategy. I was going to lead from the front like all the best generals did. 'First of all, we'll search the perimeter, seeking out all the entrances and exits. Jodie and Timmons will take up the rear on the off chance that our Lung fellow decides to make a run for it. It's unlikely, but we want to cover every eventuality. Morgan will ring the doorbell while I sneak inside via a handy open window. That way I can circle round Lung while he goes to answer the door. We're not letting him flap his dragon scales away into the night if I have anything to do with it.'

'And what's Opulus going to do?' Jodie asked. 'Because it looks to me as if he has his own plan.'

I frowned at her before belatedly realising that the grieving Fey had crossed the street and was knocking loudly on the red front door. Gasbudlikins. What was the point of having a wonderfully strategic mind like mine if you were going to be completely ignored? I'd spent entire seconds coming up with that plan.

We exchanged looks and then darted over to join Opulus. I didn't have time to admonish him or send him to the brig before the door swung open to reveal a man.

If anyone had asked me what I thought the human form of a dragon would look like, I would have described the man in front of us. He was wearing a red velvet smoking jacket with a cravat tucked neatly around his throat and tweed slippers on his feet. His hair was pure white, smoothly brushed back at the sides, and he boasted a frankly astonishing handlebar moustache that curled over his cheeks. Naturally he was smoking a pipe.

He raised an eyebrow at us. 'Faeries,' he grunted. 'About fucking time. Get inside before the neighbours see you. That witch across the street called the police last time someone knocked on my door at this time of night. If I want five blonde escorts to visit me wearing fishnet tights and stilettos, that's my business. It's nothing to do with anyone else.'

My grin stretched from ear to ear. I loved him already. 'I love fishnet tights,' I purred.

He looked me up and down. 'You don't have the legs for them,' he said matter of factly.

Arsebadger.

Morgan stepped forward. 'Mr Lung?' he asked. 'George Lung?'

The man clicked his tongue. 'It's Liung,' he said. 'Honestly. Years ago one damned priest spells my name wrongly and for ever more I'm plagued with people like you who can't pronounce a simple word properly.' He glowered. 'Now, get the hell inside.' He turned on his heel and walked away. 'And close the damned door after you!' he shouted over his shoulder.

We looked at each other and shrugged. Then

we did as the man suggested and entered the dragon's lair. Literally.

I'd had a vague inkling of what Chen's place was like before the fire from all the debris that was scattered around afterwards. Looking around Liung's house, I suspected it was remarkably similar. There were objects everywhere; there wasn't a surface that wasn't cluttered with stuff. Some things looked incredibly rare and expensive, such as the glittering jewelled egg on a side table that could only have been created by Fabergé himself. Other things, such as the neon-pink plastic truck that had probably come with a McDonald's Happy Meal, were less aesthetically pleasing or costly.

I reached out, brushing my fingers against a mink stole that was draped haphazardly across a china jug. From somewhere up ahead Liung barked, 'Don't touch anything!'

I touched it anyway. When Morgan sent me a warning frown I shrugged, but to avoid further temptation I stuck my hands in my pockets.

We passed several rooms that were filled to the brim with old newspapers. No wonder Chen's place had gone up in flames if it was like this. One match and it would be kaboom. And no wonder Liung's neighbours spied on him – they were probably terrified that he was going set the whole street alight.

'Isn't it dangerous having all this around when you're a fire-breathing dragon?' I asked when we finally arrived in a small study. I arched an eyebrow. 'If you're a fire breathing dragon?'

Liung settled himself in a cracked leather armchair and regarded us imperiously. The rest of us grabbed seats from the motley collection in the room. I ended up on a child's rocking chair. My arse barely fit inside it but I wasn't about to pass up the chance to swing myself up and down if I could help it.

'I am a dragon but I don't breathe fire,' Liung snapped. Then a shadow crossed his face. 'Well, not until recently, anyway.'

I sat up straighter, hoping for a demonstration. Unfortunately, Morgan didn't waste any time getting down to business. 'We're here because we need —'

'You need Chen's magical sphere to be destroyed,' Liung interrupted. 'Yes, yes. You should have come here the moment the sphere passed into your possession. I warned Chen that creating the damned thing in the first place would cause problems but he wouldn't listen to me.' He shook his head disdainfully. 'He never did.'

'You knew him?'

'Of course.'

'And you know about the sphere?'

'Naturally.'

I threw my up hands in frustration. 'Then why didn't you come to us?'

'I was waiting for you to come to me.' Liung didn't seem in the slightest bit bothered about the trouble he'd caused by not getting in contact. He leaned forward conspiratorially. 'Chen was quite the hoarder, you know.'

I looked around Liung's shelves; they had so much stuff crammed onto them that they were bending and warping. In this room the floor was relatively clear but there were seven or eight tables and a similar number of bureaux and bookshelves. Each piece of furniture was covered in stuff.

I glanced at the old dragon, who seemed to be taking satisfaction in revealing this supposed nasty secret about his compatriot. Pot. Kettle.

'Can you destroy the sphere?' Timmons asked. His body was hunched even though his chair, some sort of straight-backed, elaborately carved Chippendale affair, afforded him much more space than I had.

Liung nodded his head. 'I can.'

Morgan moved forward in his seat, a hard glint in his eyes. 'More to the point, will you?'

Liung didn't answer immediately. He knitted his fingers under his chin and regarded us all with mild amusement. 'Will I save this demesne from an impending apocalypse? Or will I let crazed faeries use the sphere and subject us all to the ensuing chaos and the end of the world, you mean?'

'Yeah,' Jodie said, finding her voice. 'That's exactly what we mean.'

Liung turned his head and examined her. She held her ground, refusing to shrink back. 'You are pretty,' he said finally. 'If *you* want to come and visit me wearing fishnet tights, you are very welcome to do so.'

There was no accounting for taste.

'If you put on fishnet tights first,' Jodie shot back, 'I'll consider it.'

Liung smirked. 'That can be arranged.'

From somewhere in the distance there was a rumble of sound, like a giant clearing his throat. We all tensed, even Liung. When the noise drifted away, I breathed out again.

'This is all your doing,' the dragon snapped, looking genuinely irritated for the first time and pointing a bony finger at us. 'You faeries, waving your magic around without thinking of the consequences. You've always been the same. Why don't you stay in your demesne where you belong? Goodness only knows what will happen next. I'm not abandoning my home just because you've fucked up. But if you make my favourite pizza delivery company shut up shop, I will seek you out and make you pay.'

'We're working on a solution,' Morgan said smoothly.

'Well, work harder! I've been around for five hundred years and the only time matters have been this bad was during the Black Plague. If you don't sort out things soon, there will be nothing left of this city to save.'

Liung was obviously getting worked up and his voice rose with every word until he began to choke and splutter. A hacking cough started up deep in his chest. He groaned as a puff of smoke and a single flame shot out from his mouth, almost singeing Opulus's eyebrows.

Rather than apologising, Liung glared again. 'See what you made me do?'

'That is seriously cool,' I breathed.

Opulus waved his hand in front of his face as if to ward off any lingering dragon germs. 'Can we destroy the sphere ourselves?'

Liung shook his head. 'Only I am capable of that.' He gave a nasty smile. 'Unless you can find yourselves another dragon. With Chen gone, I think I'm the only one in this country, however, so good luck with that.' He sniffed. 'But bring me the sphere and I will dispose of it for good.'

'Pinky promise?' I asked.

Liung folded his arms across his chest. 'I give you my oath. I do not … pinky promise,' he sneered. 'Next time you need my help, don't wait so long to contact me. Untold damage could have occurred because of your delays.'

'Oi!' Jodie said. 'It's not like we knew you existed! You could have called us!'

'I was busy. And you must have known I was here. Everyone knows who I am.'

'No-one knows who you are, mate,' Timmons scoffed. 'This world isn't for the likes of you. This is a human demesne.'

Liung's face darkened. 'It is *my* demesne.'

'No-one knows you're here.'

'I am famous! I am George Liung of the

Liung dynasty!'

'This is almost like hearing my own personality echoing back at me,' I said in an aside to Morgan. Then I addressed Liung. 'I am Madrona Hatter of the Madhatter dynasty and I've never heard of you either!'

Liung stopped puffing out his chest and stared at me. A moment later he let out a loud cackling laugh. 'You? You're Madrona?' he laughed harder. 'You're the one who's responsible for all this in the first place. It was your actions that trapped your kind here.'

I shifted uncomfortably. 'I don't remember.'

He snorted. 'Sure you don't.'

'I've got amnesia,' I informed him sniffily. 'Anyway, what I did or did not do in the past is irrelevant. We are concentrating on the future.'

The dragon's lip curled. 'If you have one.'

'If I don't have one,' I shot back, 'then neither do you.'

'Mbongo spice and avocado seeds.'

'Huh?'

'You heard me. Mix three parts to one and then you'll have the cure you need to remember everything.' His eyes gleamed. 'Of course, remembering might not be particularly pleasant.'

It occurred to me that Liung was the only person I'd met who hadn't been sceptical about my amnesia when I first mentioned it. My eyes scanned his face. He seemed smug and self-satisfied but I'd lay money on the fact that he was telling the truth about the memory concoction; he wanted me to remember because he wanted me to suffer from those memories.

'I told you already,' he said softly, 'I've been around for five hundred years. I remember everything I ever did – every nasty word, every mistake, every terrible thing. Why do you think I'm still awake? You lot have only decades of problems to mull over in your beds when you can't sleep. Imagine what it's like for me.'

'My heart bleeds,' Timmons said. 'Maybe the solution is not making mistakes or doing terrible things.'

Liung smiled. 'I hadn't realised I was in the company of saints. That has not been my experience of your kind in the past.' He glanced at Jodie. 'Or of humans. Or vampires. Or werewolves.' He sighed and briefly stroked his moustache. 'Or dragons.'

'I'm not afraid of my past,' I said. 'I'll freely admit to my mistakes.'

'Good for you,' Liung returned. 'Just remember you said that. You got the chance to wipe the slate clean and you started again. Very few people have that opportunity. It's a blessing, not a curse.'

I licked my lips. I was fairly certain I already knew the worst of what I'd done but I didn't know the details. I didn't remember the pain of abandoning Morgan for Rubus. I didn't remember the guilt of realising I'd been the one to force the borders to Mag Mell closed. But I wasn't a coward; I didn't want to be afraid of who I'd been or who I'd become. Our memories made us what we were, warts and all. I'd stopped worrying about my amnesia days ago but now Liung made me want to resolve the issue once and for all.

Morgan got to his feet, apparently concerned about the turn the conversation had taken. 'We shall retrieve the sphere and bring it you. You will destroy it.'

Liung remained seated. 'And you will sort out the infernal magic that's causing all these problems.'

'We will try.'

He sniffed disdainfully. 'I don't like people who *try*. I like people who do.' He cast us another disparaging glance. 'Then again, I don't like faeries either.'

'We are annoying little arsebadgers, aren't we?' I agreed.

'Yes,' he said flatly. 'You are. Bring me the sphere and I will take care of it. Stop your magic from destroying my city then our business will be concluded.'

We'd only just met and he already wanted to forget us. We'd got exactly what we'd come for, however, and far more easily than any of us had expected. It was probably best not to push our luck. Shame though. I really did think Liung was a man after my own heart.

Chapter Fourteen

It was hard to bank down the temptation to run and find Charlotte Page and nab back the sphere again but after the day we'd had, we were all running on empty. And goodness only knew what unfortunate delights the dawn would bring. By unspoken agreement, we all got back onto the Mobikes and cycled to Julie's house for a few hours' kip before the next round of madness began.

Unfortunately, when we rounded the corner onto her street, it was clear what that madness would entail. The screaming was audible even to Jodie's human ears.

'I need more!'

Morgan glanced at me. 'Is that…?'

I nodded. 'It's Julie.'

'Give me blooooooooood!'

I winced. There was no doubt that the magic build-up was bringing her well-buried vampire traits to the fore. Maybe she could explain it away later by telling her neighbours she was preparing for a new acting role.

I wasted no time in getting to her front door and entering. I found her in the kitchen, standing against a white-faced Finn. The heavy, metallic taint of blood hung in the air. Judging by the puncture wounds at his throat, Julie had decided that her hospital-donated blood bags were no longer enough. The idea that the small woman could overpower someone as large and hulking as Finn was worrying, to say the least.

As soon as I stepped inside, Julie sprang at me. 'Give me yours,' she begged. 'Give me your blood!'

'I rather like it where it is, thank you very much,' I said primly, arching an eyebrow over her shoulder at Finn.

'It's my fault,' the Redcap muttered. 'I offered her my veins. I thought it might help. Instead, she's gone a bit loopy.'

A bit loopy? I gazed at her flailing hands and the desperate entreaty in her crazed eyes. This usually sane woman was tipping over the edge. Fortunately, I knew a little something about madness. Not much, but enough.

Reaching out, I took her hands in mine, snagging them before her manicured nails raked the skin on my cheeks. Then I stepped her backwards while murmuring her name, until her legs pressed against a kitchen chair. She sank onto it while I waved urgently at Morgan, who'd come in behind me. The others were sensibly keeping their distance.

'Gin,' I told him. 'And lots of it.'

'I'm not sure that alcohol is a good idea,' he began.

'It is for this lady.'

'I don't want it! I want blood!' Julie screeched.

'Shhhh.' I knelt down in front of her, wrapped my arms round her waist and hugged her. She could probably have overpowered me if she'd wanted to and my jugular was there for the taking.

I was taking a calculated risk. Finn and Morgan would yank her off me if she attempted to drain me dry, Morgan because he didn't want me to get hurt and Finn because he wanted to help Julie. Giving her the suggestion of access to my blood without my permission enabled me to judge just how far gone she was. None of this was her fault. The magic in the air was simply worming its way into her every time she breathed.

It took several moments but eventually I felt the tension in her subside and she started to relax. She didn't try and bite me either, so that was a bonus.

Her ragged breathing was starting to come under control when Morgan thrust a gin and tonic between us. I grabbed the glass and took a few chugs then offered it to Julie.

She shook her head weakly. 'Actually,' she whispered, 'I think your boyfriend is right. Gin isn't a good idea. Could I have a cup of tea?'

I gazed at her suspiciously. She'd tried this trick on me before. 'Are we talking PG Tips or Long Island?'

She smiled. It wasn't a face-splitting grin but it was more like the Julie I knew. 'PG Tips,' she said.

'With lots of sugar.'

'I'll put the kettle on,' Finn said. He turned away but Julie reached out and took his hand.

'I'm sorry,' she said. 'I don't know what came over me.'

'It's not your fault,' he replied. There was no censure in his eyes, although his tone was rather gruff. 'You can't help it.'

Julie looked morosely at the blood soaking into his shirt. 'Your poor clothes.'

I snorted. 'His poor neck, more like.'

Finn stiffened but Julie's smile widened. 'Yes,' she said. 'His poor neck.' She sighed. 'You've been nothing but good to me, Finn. Don't think that I don't appreciate you.'

I beamed at them. 'Group hug?'

Finn gave me a sideways glance; apparently I still wasn't his best friend in the world, even if he now tolerated me. 'Maybe not,' he said. He looked at Julie. 'Me and you though?'

She nodded. I moved back so she could stand up and the pair of them embraced. Although things now seemed a lot calmer, I angled myself so I could watch her face for signs of snarling or elongating fangs but she kept both her eyes and her mouth firmly shut.

When she was relaxed enough to let go, Finn busied himself with the tea. 'We're not the only people daft enough to go outside with all this magic shit going on.'

'Tell me about it,' I said. 'Pimply teenagers

have no regard for their own safety.'

He shook his head. 'No. That's not who I mean.' He glanced at Morgan and me, looking distinctly unhappy. 'There was a hunter.'

Morgan drew in a sharp breath. 'A vampire hunter?'

Finn nodded. 'He was waiting outside for us to get back. He tried to grab Julie.'

Gasbudlikins. That was all we needed on top of everything else. I thought we'd got rid of those arsebadgers, at least for now. 'You'd think they'd have the sense to stay away.'

Morgan frowned. 'I suppose they think they can take advantage of the chaos to go after Julie again.'

'One track bloody minds.' I rolled my eyes. 'Why can't they just fixate on breasts and arses like other men in the world?'

'Was it just one hunter?' Morgan asked.

'Yep.'

Morgan's jaw clenched. 'Is he still out there?'

Finn shook his head. 'No. I'm pretty sure I've scared him off for now. I wanted to do more – you know, break his legs or hurt him enough that he'd get the message that Julie is off limits. But he scarpered pretty damn quickly.'

Having seen what Julie was like when we entered the house – as well as hearing her from the other end of the street – I was hardly surprised. All the same, I was pissed off. Why couldn't we have just one problem at a time to deal with?

'Bad things come in threes,' Morgan murmured, as if reading my mind.

'Bad things can piss off. I'm bad enough for all of us,' I returned.

He smiled at me but his expression was tinged with worry. I grabbed the glass of gin again and downed it. If the apocalypse was nigh, I wouldn't have to worry about a hangover.

'We need to get some rest before the next round begins,' Morgan said. He gestured at Finn. 'Are you okay with Julie?'

'We'll be fine.'

Julie frowned. 'I am still here, darling. I might be crazed with bloodlust but there's no need to talk about me as if I'm not.'

'I'm sorry.' Morgan ran a hand through his hair. 'It's been a long night but we've found a dragon – and he's willing to help destroy the sphere. For the first time there might be...'

I held up my hands in horror. 'No! Don't say it!'

'...light at the end of the tunnel,' he finished.

My shoulders sagged. 'You said it,' I muttered. 'Now we're definitely doomed.'

Apparently unconcerned that Morgan had consigned us all to hell with his sexy loose lips, Julie pointed upwards. 'The guest rooms are ready. Feel free to kip down wherever you want.'

I glanced over. In theory, grabbing one of Julie's beds and snuggling up to Morgan was my idea of heaven. The actress was bound to have some furry handcuffs kicking around somewhere; I could tie him up and have my wicked way with him. Unfortunately, the only thing I really wanted at the moment was sleep.

By unspoken agreement, we all headed upstairs. Morgan took my hand and gently steered me into a room. 'We're only sleeping,' he warned. 'We need to rest. But all the same, I want to know you're close.'

I gave him a tired smile. 'Oh, I'll be close all right. Drooling on your shoulder and snoring in your ear, but close.'

He smiled back. 'Paradise.'

I closed the bedroom door and wriggled out of my jeans. The bed was even more inviting than Morgan's broad chest. I was going to dive down, close my eyes and fall fast asleep in an instant. Or I would have if the front door bell hadn't suddenly rung, echoing round the house and making me jump.

I looked at Morgan, wide eyed. 'I can't think of any good reason why someone would ring Julie's doorbell at this time of night.'

His expression was grim. 'Me neither.'

I didn't wait but flung the bedroom door open and pelted back down the stairs. Finn was already there, gripping a steel baseball bat in his hands.

'You got our backs?' I growled to Morgan who was right behind me.

'I'm here,' he answered.

We exchanged glances then I reached for the door and opened it.

I was fully prepared for anything: bazookas, rampaging Fey minions, Rubus. What I hadn't expected was the sexiest-looking man I'd ever seen in my life lounging against the door frame and glinting at me with his baby blues.

As his eyes travelled down my bare legs, his grin widened and exposed a dimple in his cheek. He straightened up, a dark red curl falling across his forehead. 'Well, well, well,' he drawled with a faint Scottish brogue. 'If I'd known the faeries were this gorgeous I'd have come to Manchester sooner.'

Morgan pushed past me, temporarily blocking my view. 'Who the fuck are you?' he snapped.

The handsome Scot bowed. 'You rang and I answered. I am Monroe.' He said this with a flourish, as if we should instantly know who he was.

Finn dropped the bat. It landed on Julie's perfect parquet flooring with a clank and he bounded forward, gripping Monroe's forearm with his hand. 'Monroe! It's a pleasure to meet you!'

Monroe inclined his head. 'Indeed. And you are…?'

Finn beamed. 'I'm Finn. I'm a Redcap. I'm the one who called you!'

Monroe seemed to relax slightly. 'Well then, it's a pleasure to meet you.' He looked Finn's massive shape up and down. 'I can't imagine,' he murmured, 'that anyone ever says otherwise.'

Morgan cleared his throat, still unimpressed by our visitor. 'Finn, who is this?'

'Monroe!'

'I got that part,' he said drily. 'Who is Monroe?'

'The lead werewolf. The one from Scotland that I left a message for.'

'I prefer Alpha,' Monroe said. He looked up and down the silent street. 'I see that you wee people have been having some trouble so it's just as well you called us. It wasn't easy getting into the city unnoticed with the army around and I suspect that things are only going to get worse. We could feel the magic rippling twenty miles before we saw the city.' He shook his head, his shaggy red hair ruffling as he did so. 'What have you lot been up to?'

I popped my head round Morgan's shoulder. 'We?' I asked hopefully. 'There are more of you?' Hopefully they'd all be as good-looking as Monroe. Morgan was more than enough for me but that didn't mean I couldn't appreciate a bit of eye candy and do some window shopping, while still clinging onto my man.

Monroe gave me a long, slow, easy smile. Then he gave a low whistle. Seemingly from nowhere others appeared, detaching themselves from shadows and from behind cars and low-lying rooftops. I counted a dozen in total. They trooped in behind Monroe and waited for instructions. I was liking the werewolf more and more; I needed minions who behaved like this, too.

'May we come in? We've had a long journey.'

Finn nodded like an eager puppy and stepped aside. Morgan moved as if to enter and then frowned. The hairs on the back of his bare arms seemed to straighten and quiver, and his eyes narrowed to thin blue strips. 'What is this?'

'Julie,' I interjected hastily. 'She has a barrier in place. She needs to invite you in for you to come inside.'

Monroe frowned in suspicion. 'The only being capable of such a feat is a vamp—'

His word was lost as Julie herself appeared. She shuffled past me and peered at Monroe, obviously liking what she saw as much as I did. 'Well, hello, there.'

The werewolf king doffed an invisible hat. 'I know you,' he said.

She smiled. 'You might have seen me on television.'

I waited for the inevitable expression of delight but Monroe just pursed his lips. 'No. We've met before. I was just a bairn so you probably won't remember me but you came to my uncle's estate once.'

All at once, Julie's demeanour changed. She was longer smiling; in fact, her body language and her expression were icy cold. 'Oh yes,' she said. 'You're one of *those* werewolves.'

I glanced at her askance. When she didn't

immediately fess up, I nudged her. 'Go on.'

She sniffed. 'I went to the werewolves to petition them for help in dealing with the vampire hunters. They declined – and not very politely, either.'

Monroe shrugged, his muscles rippling as he did so. Mmm. 'We don't get involved unless our own livelihoods are threatened.'

Morgan crossed his arms. 'So why are you here?'

'Because our own livelihoods are threatened,' the werewolf answered smoothly. He shot an amused look at me and looked back to Morgan. 'Don't worry, mate. I can tell you've marked her. She's all yours.'

Marked me? That had better be a metaphorical mark. Morgan relaxed slightly. I felt rather smug that he was laying claim to me, despite his caveman-like leanings. 'Actually,' I said, 'I've marked him.' I put my arm around Morgan. 'So hands off.'

Monroe grinned. 'I don't swing that way – though I can see the attraction.'

I smirked. 'He is rather sexy, isn't he?'

Morgan growled something under his breath. I reckoned he'd been appeased enough. He really didn't have anything to worry about; the werewolf might be dripping with sex appeal but he was far too cocky for me. I'd strangle him before too long. I had enough cockiness to last a lifetime; I didn't need others to add to it.

Julie tilted her head. 'I'm not sure about this,' she said.

'We need their help,' Finn told her.

'I needed their help before. They declined.'

From the group behind Monroe, there was a growl followed by a deep snarl. I blinked and stared. One of the younger werewolves was sprouting dark fur all over his body. His face was changing shape too, his chin, mouth and nose elongating into what could only be described as a muzzle.

'The magic,' Monroe murmured. 'I strongly suggest you make a decision either way before Phil here becomes fully furry and tries to eat your neighbours.'

We all turned to Julie. Well, everyone else did – I couldn't tear my eyes away from the Phil the Furry.

'Fine,' Julie snapped. 'You may come in.'

Monroe smiled as if he'd expected nothing less. He stepped across Julie's threshold and then he was inside.

Chapter Fifteen

If I'd thought Julie's house was getting crowded with our small group, it was nothing compared to now. Rather than attempt to fit into her kitchen, we headed for the vast living room. I took a couple of minutes to put my jeans back on, not because I was embarrassed by my naked legs but because I knew it would make Morgan feel better. I was getting pretty good at this thoughtfulness lark.

By the time I got downstairs again, Monroe had made himself comfortable in a large armchair. He pointed to a man who looked more like a bear than a wolf with his massive broad shoulders and over-indulgence of facial hair. 'That's Malcolm.' The bear man inclined his head.

Monroe moved on. 'This is Dwight.' A smaller, bespectacled man smiled. Monroe shifted his finger, pointing at different werewolves in turn. 'Enright, Goddard, Matthew, Peterson, William...'

I held up my hand. 'I'm not going to remember. You might as well stop now.'

Monroe raised an eyebrow. 'You don't want to know the names of the people who are here to save you?'

'You're not here to save us,' I pointed out.

'You're here to help us save the world. If you snowflakes can't managed that without formal introductions, you know where the door is.'

Despite my words, my tone was pleasant enough. I knew I was being rude but I really wasn't going to remember all their names and I was bloody tired. I'd make it up to them once this was over.

Monroe gazed at me for a long moment and then shrugged. 'Fair enough. So,' he asked, 'how did all this happen? How did we get to the stage where the world needs saving?'

Morgan leaned forward and outlined what had happened, leaving out the teeny-weeny little fact that a great deal of our woes could be laid at my doorstep. Once he was finished, he fixed Monroe with a hard stare. 'We can't afford to worry about the welfare of a new group of people. We have enough on our plates as it is.'

Monroe snorted. 'You don't need to worry about us, little faery. We are werewolves. We are perfectly capable of looking after ourselves. We'll help you retrieve this sphere and ensure the dragon destroys it. Our strength and might will guarantee your success.' He sounded utterly confident.

I could feel Morgan bristling at both Monroe's self-assurance and being described as 'little'. It was time to put all this to bed – and to go to bed.

'It's settled then,' I said, standing up. 'We get a few hours sleep and then we head to Charlotte Page's house to get the sphere.'

'Assuming this little human still has it. Passing it to a cleaner was not a wise move.'

Now it was my turn to bristle. 'I used what means I had at my disposal to keep it safe.'

Monroe raised an eyebrow. 'If you'd contacted us earlier, we could simply have taken this Fey Ruby maniac out of the equation. That still might be the best move. We could move on him now while the rest of you have sweet dreams.'

'Except,' Finn pointed out, 'he's stronger than you think and he has numerous others faeries at his disposal who are more than willing to sacrifice themselves on his behalf.'

'And if he feels like he's in danger,' I added, 'he'll just let loose more magic and cause more havoc across the city. We have to tread carefully.'

'He won't be expecting us,' Monroe said. 'With the element of surprise on our side—'

Morgan interrupted him. 'He will already know you are here and will be preparing. He's not a moron. We do this our way, without alerting my brother to what we're up to, or we won't succeed.'

The werewolf shrugged. 'Suit yourself.' He looked around. 'I suppose a few hours' sleep won't be a bad thing.'

'Before you go,' Julie asked, 'how badly are you being affected by the magic within the city?' There was a strained expression on her face. Given how reluctant she'd been to allow the werewolves access to her house, and how quiet she'd been, I knew that the question was important to her. She really was suffering from her vampire side. We were all in unknown territory; for once it wasn't just me who didn't have a clue what was happening.

Monroe gazed at her, assessingly. Part of me expected a flippant reply but when he spoke, his response was gentle. 'I have extraordinary control over my wolf form,' he said, 'and even I'm finding it hard to keep the animal at bay. The magic in the air is seeping into my soul.'

Julie leaned forward. 'But how does it make you *feel*?'

He held her eyes. 'Like I could conquer the world.' There was a murmur of agreement from the assembled werewolves.

Julie nodded, apparently satisfied. 'I'll show you to the bedrooms. Some of you will have to share. My house is large but it's not that large.'

'Ma'am,' Monroe drawled, 'we appreciate your hospitality.' He paused. 'Perhaps you could show us which room has a lock on it and we'll sleep there.'

He didn't need to add that he wanted the lock to keep us safe from him and his wolves. I shivered. This magic crap was potentially going to be the end of us.

***

Four hours later, we assembled outside the address I'd scraped up for Charlotte Page, employee of Pixie Dust Cleaning Services. Morgan, me, and the pack of werewolves. If this wasn't enough back-up then we were screwed.

For a cleaning lady who probably worked for the minimum wage, she certainly lived in a genteel part of town. Her house didn't quite match up to the grandiose standards of Julie's but it wasn't far off. The façade was red brick, with a trail of ivy climbing up one side and curling round several of the shuttered windows. I counted three storeys. Maybe Ms Page owned Pixie Dust Cleaning Services as well as working for them.

Monroe arched a long glance upwards. 'I thought you said this chick was a cleaner? How many cleaners can afford digs like this?'

Morgan sniffed disdainfully. 'Perhaps you shouldn't be so quick to judge. Cleaning is an essential business. You shouldn't look down your nose at it.'

Monroe gazed back at him. His arms were loose at his sides but I suspected he was already growing mightily tired of my green-eyed Fey. 'I'm not denigrating her profession,' he said. 'I'm simply analysing the situation. We need to know what we're walking into.'

Morgan opened his mouth to respond and I stepped in hastily. 'I think perhaps it's best if I handle this,' I said. 'You lot stay out here.' Nice as it was to have my back covered by my lover and a pack of werewolves, sometimes it was easier to work alone.

This time both of them wanted to argue.

'Listen, arsebadgers,' I hissed. 'Charlotte Page is just a human woman who I've pulled into this mess. She's not the enemy. This will go much better if I deal with her. If she sees an army of angry men on her doorstep, she's liable to run.'

I didn't wait for either of them to answer but simply pulled back my shoulders, strode up to her doorstep and rang the doorbell. When I glanced back, Monroe, Morgan, Opulus, Vandrake and the rest had melted into the shadows. Good. It was about time someone paid attention to my superior strategic planning skills.

Charlotte answered the door far faster than I expected. The bright smile on her face disappeared almost immediately when she saw me. 'You're not the police,' she said.

My spine stiffened. Police? I bit back the million questions on my tongue and quickly dissembled. I was the Madhatter, after all. 'I'm the Community Liaison Officer responsible for this locality,' I said, making up a job title that I hoped sounded official enough to pass muster. 'The police, as I'm sure you can understand, are rather busy at the moment with the army in town and all the ... strange goings-on over the last twenty-four hours. I'm here in their place until they can visit.' I offered a perfunctory, business-like smile.

Charlotte frowned. 'Show me your identification.'

Gasbudlikins. Why did I have to get the smart, wary human? 'I don't have it on me,' I said, palms stretched outwards. 'It was eaten by...' I glanced around as if afraid that someone would hear me, 'a pink elephant.'

Charlotte's eyes went wide. 'You saw a pink elephant?' she breathed.

I wished. 'Yeah,' I nodded. 'It snatched my ID and lanyard with its trunk and ran away.' I leaned in. 'I didn't know elephants could run but that thing moved pretty darned fast.'

'They might not look graceful,' Charlotte told me, 'but they can shift when they want to.' She peered at me. 'Hang on,' she said. 'I recognise you from the police station.' She relaxed further. 'I *do* know you. We met in the toilets.'

I smiled. 'Yeah. You told me that weight lifters can lift more in blue-painted gyms.'

She shrugged. 'I'm full of odd facts like that. It's amazing what a little knowledge can do when you're betting.'

'Betting? You're a gambler?'

The corner of her mouth lifted. 'Only occasionally. And always legally, of course.'

'Of course.' I licked my lips. Learning more about her was all very well but it wasn't getting me any closer to my goal. 'So the reason you called the police...'

Her smile vanished. 'I'll show you,' she said. 'She's this way.' She stepped back into her house. With a surreptitious wave at Morgan and the others, who had no doubt been watching this entire exchange with bated breath, I hopped in after her.

The house was even grander on the inside. Morning sun streamed in through old stained-glass windows, creating pretty patterns on the bare floorboards. Unlike Liung, Charlotte had a discerning eye and there were only a few things dotted around. The minimalist style wasn't exactly suited to this mansion but I kind of liked it all the same.

'Nice place,' I murmured.

'I won it,' she called from down the corridor. 'Poker.'

Huh. Maybe I should have become a gambler instead of a fake superhero; it certainly paid better. Even villainy didn't pay dividends like this.

'It's more trouble than it's worth,' Charlotte said, pausing in front of a closed door. 'I can barely afford the council tax and something is always breaking down. The plumbing is a nightmare. And now there's this.' She put her hand on the doorknob and twisted it, revealing what was inside.

My mouth dropped open. What had once been a beautifully appointed room was now a scene of utter devastation, with torn curtains, slashed walls and overturned chairs. It wasn't the mess that shocked me, though; it was the creature standing in the centre of the room and snarling that surprised me.

It was more than two metres long and one metre wide, and covered in dark fur. Two large horns sprouted from its head, curving to the sides in opposite directions. Its muzzle was elongated, like a duck's bill. I'd have said it was some kind of deformed animal were it not for the empty plate in its large paws and the human expression in its eyes. It swung its head towards us and gazed at us with a tragically sad expression.

'I'd have called the RSPCA,' Charlotte said, 'but they've got their hands full with other matters. I have a few friends in the police force who said they'd send someone to help.' She bit her lip. 'Besides, I don't think this is an animal. I think it's my housemate.' She cast me a sidelong glance. 'Unless it's eaten her. That's always possible.'

I blinked. This was entirely outside my experience. 'Your housemate?'

'Lizzy. She's from Brisbane, Australia. She's been studying in Manchester for a year or so and I let her kip here. I've got plenty of room and the rent, when she pays it, is welcome.' She hesitated. 'Watch her lips.'

I focused on the creature's mouth. I couldn't hear any sound but it appeared that it was trying to say the same thing over and over again. I scratched my head. 'Uh…'

'I'm an expert in lip reading,' Charlotte confided. 'It helps with scoping out the lay of the land when I'm preparing for a big bet. I can read trainers' words from a hundred metres away. I've managed to avoid several dodgy gambles as a result. There was this one horse that —'

I held up my hand. 'Perhaps another time.' I pointed at the bizarre, furry duck-dog creature-thing. 'What's it saying?'

'She. Not it. I think.' Charlotte grimaced and whispered in my ear. 'Vegemite. We've run out.'

'What's Vegemite?' I asked with a frown.

Lizzy, if that's what the thing in front of us was, opened her mouth in a sudden scream and lunged forward. Charlotte yanked me back into the corridor and slammed the door shut. 'Don't say it aloud in front of her!'

'What? Vegemite?'

Lizzy threw herself at the other side of the door, splintering the wood. I jumped back, alarmed. Charlotte glared at me. 'You're supposed to be helping.'

'Sorry,' I muttered. 'This is my first time with an Australian monster.'

'Lizzy's not a monster. She's just having a bad day.'

It wasn't my job to deal with this. Even if I *were* some sort of police liaison officer – or the arsebadgering police commissioner – it wouldn't be my job to deal with this. I was here to retrieve the sphere and get the hell out again. However, given that Lizzy's transformation was no doubt caused by the build up of Fey magic in the Manchester atmosphere, it was arguable that it was my fault. And if it *was* my fault, I was honour-bound to help.

I tried to summon up my evil-bitch persona but Morgan had rubbed off on me too much. Either that or I was simply too wonderful to abandon both Charlotte and Lizzy to their fates – even though I had no idea how to help either of them.

My indecision must have been evident because Charlotte gazed at me, a frown marring her smooth, freckled forehead. 'You're not with the police. I'm usually good at reading people and your air of self-importance suggested you were a copper – but you're not.' She sighed. 'Great. Who are you and what do you really want?'

She seemed more exasperated than anything. I raised my shoulders. 'Okay, Charlotte,' I agreed. 'I'm not with the police but I reckon I can probably help. Or I know someone who can.'

'Charley,' she said.

'Pardon.'

'Call me Charley.' She folded her arms. 'How long will it take to get hold of this someone?'

I smiled. 'Just give me a minute.'

Chapter Sixteen

Morgan wasn't impressed at being left out in the cold when I beckoned in Monroe. I gave my love bunny a quick, reassuring smile and blew him a kiss. The fact that his jealousy was still affecting him was rather nice. Yes, I'd get tired of it fairly quickly but right now it showed that he cared for me.

I'd never thought of myself as someone who needed to be told repeatedly that I was loved. I was still learning about myself, I supposed. I still had amnesia, after all.

Monroe the werewolf swaggered inside the house as if he owned the place. As soon as he stepped across the threshold, he lifted his nose, sniffed and recoiled. 'What is that?'

Charley appeared. Monroe looked her up and down, apparently unimpressed by her blue hair. 'What are you?' he hissed.

'The woman whose house you're in,' she said. She looked at me. 'Is this the best you can do? This guy with the ego the size of a blimp?'

I winced. 'Give him a minute. He has, uh, a sensitive nose. It's probably affecting him adversely.'

I'd barely finished speaking when Monroe

stalked towards her. He paused in front of her, his nostrils flaring. 'Sunshine,' he muttered. 'You smell of sunshine.' He flashed her a disarming smile. 'Despite your hair, you're rather pretty,' he purred. 'I like the freckles.'

His abrupt volte-face did little to impress Charley. 'Be still my beating heart,' she said. 'What a wondrous compliment.'

Monroe drew back and inspected her again. 'Sarcasm doesn't impress me.'

She raised her eyebrows. 'Oh no. I'm devastated.'

I watched the pair of them. I knew next to nothing about either of them but I'd seen a gentler side to Monroe already. The fact that he was ramping up the machismo factor suggested to me that Charley's 'sunshine' affected him more than he wanted to admit. I couldn't tell what she was thinking. No wonder she was a gambler; she really did possess a poker face.

Apparently realising that he was laying it on too thick, Morgan stepped back and gave her room to breathe. 'I apologise,' he said. 'The magic in the air is causing my ... animalistic side to gain dominance.' He grinned at her. 'Next time I'm rude, feel free to slap me around.' He bowed. 'Thank you for inviting me in. I'm only here to help.'

Charley looked slightly confused. 'Magic? Is that what you're calling all this spooky shit?'

Monroe waved a hand around. 'It's *just* what I call it.'

Charley's eyes narrowed. Yep, she was far too smart for our good – and Monroe was far too careless.

Taking a breath, I pointed at the closed door. 'The problem is in there,' I told him.

The werewolf squared his shoulders. 'Excellent,' he said. 'This won't take long.' He strode past Charley and opened the door, his face dropping in shock when he spotted Lizzy.

'Maybe I should wait for the real police,' Charley said to me.

'They won't be able to help your housemate.' I glanced around. 'Do you mind if I use your toilet while Monroe sorts this out?'

Charley flicked a look over her shoulder. 'Your Monroe doesn't look like he's sorting anything out at all.'

She had a point. He hadn't moved a muscle; he was still staring into the room, with a blank look on his face.

'Anyway,' Charley continued, 'help yourself. Top of the stairs, turn right. If you want to snoop around, my bedroom is the next floor up.' I blinked at her and she laughed. 'You're here for a reason and it's not to help Lizzy. Even if I weren't a gambling girl, I'd bet my eyeteeth that you want something from me. Just be warned,' she said, 'I don't have much to take. It's not been a very productive month.'

'I'm not here to steal anything.' I was taking back what was already mine. Sort of. 'Neither am I

221

here to hurt you. Or do anything bad. Or mess up your life. Or…'

'I get it,' she said drily. 'If that caveman friend of yours helps Lizzy, I don't really care why you're here. Do what you want.'

I stared at her. 'Really?' This was a nice house; it would be kind of fun to mess around for a bit and let off some steam. The thought of sliding down the banister of the grand staircase was particularly tempting.

Charley shrugged. 'After the last twenty-four hours, and with half of the British Army currently patrolling the streets, I'm not sure I have any worry left. What will be will be.'

I could learn a thing or two from this woman. I stuck out my hand. 'I'm Madrona,' I said.

She took my hand and shook it. 'Hi.'

I gave her an awkward smile. 'In the interests of honesty,' I said, 'I've not actually seen a pink elephant. Just on television. But if you know where one is, tell me. I'd love to get up close.'

'Yeah,' Charley admitted. 'Me too.' She grinned at me and I grinned back.

I was tempted to ask her for a cup of tea then we could sit down and properly chin wag, but I reminded myself that I had an apocalypse to avert. I could make new friends later.

I headed for the stairs. I'd been under the impression that Monroe, for all his swagger, had been stunned into a shock by Lizzy. He hadn't moved or even twitched since he'd opened the door and seen her. As I passed by, however, I could see that Lizzy was lying on her back, her belly presented towards him in submission.

'Bunyip,' he muttered.

I raised an eyebrow. 'Pardon you.'

He tutted. 'No. *She's* a bunyip. An Australian creature. I've not heard of one existing for centuries. It must be in her ancestry – the magic has drawn the beast out of her.' He shook his head. 'Amazing.'

I thought she looked like an overgrown mastiff who'd been mated with a giant duck. I patted Monroe on the shoulder. 'Great. Continue with the fabulous work.' It was important to keep the staff happy. I tripped up the stairs and left him to it.

I could have asked Charley to find the sphere for me but it seemed prudent not to give away too much of the game unless I really had to. With her relaxed nature and her invitation to look around, she'd proved amenable – but the lady was a gambler at heart. If she knew she had an object in her possession that had unquenchable power, she might be tempted to do something stupid with it. I was no longer taking any chances – not when I had the future of the whole world in my dainty hands.

I scoped out various rooms on the first floor. Most were empty, apart from the aforementioned bathroom and a large bedroom emblazoned with a gigantic Australian flag. Call me Sherlock Holmes. This had to be Lizzy's room.

When I'd satisfied myself that there was

nothing to be seen on this floor, I loped up the next flight of stairs. Again, there was only one room that appeared to be occupied. There was a vast four-poster bed with elaborately carved posts, unmade sheets and very little else. No wonder Charley wasn't bothered by the fact that I was poking around – there was nothing to poke around in. There was, however, a laundry basket in one corner that was brimming full with dirty clothes. I darted over.

I drew out the clothes one by one. There was no sign of the work clothes I'd seen Charley in at the police station although I admired the other clothes she had. There were a lot of sparkly, revealing tops and short skirts. I didn't have to speak to her to know her game; no doubt she wore alluring clothing to put off her fellow gamblers. If they were too focused on peering down her cleavage, they'd be less inclined to pay attention to what she was up to her with her cards. Score one for the blue-haired betting lady. My admiration for her dress sense and strategic skills didn't help me right now, however. The trouble was, there was nothing else in this room. If she'd left her work clothes at work, this was a completely wasted visit.

My eyes fell on the unmade bed. Hang on a minute. I lifted up the corner of the duvet and my heart skipped a beat when I saw the crumpled tunic and trousers underneath. From the looks of them, Charley had collapsed into bed while fully clothed and wriggled out of them before getting dressed this morning.

I extricated the clothes from the sheets then fumbled in the front pocket of the tunic. My heart sank into the pit of my chest when I realised the sphere definitely wasn't there though. Gasbudlikins.

Trying to remain calm, I searched around. At least with the lack of furniture, it didn't take long. I got down on all fours and checked under the bed, then in each of the four corners of the room and underneath the laundry basket. There was no sign of the sphere. I pursed my lips and looked around. Maybe it was in Charley's bed.

Whipping off the duvet, I checked the sheets. Nada. I was on the verge of giving up hope altogether when I saw the sphere nestled against one of the pillows. It must have rolled there when I took off the duvet.

I sprang towards it and snatched it up. Praise be. Charley had obviously slept with it all night, like in some bizarre princess and the pea situation. Or gambler and the object-to-end-the-world situation anyway. It didn't matter; I had the arsebadgering thing back in my possession. All I needed now was Liung to come through and the world would be safe. I breathed out. Madrona the Madhatter wins the day. Natch.

I tripped out of Charley's bedroom and headed downstairs. The closer I got, the louder the bickering became.

'She might transform again at any point. It's

vital she comes with me and my team so that we can keep her safe.'

'She's my housemate. Unless she says that she wants to go with you, she's staying here where she belongs.'

'She'll be safer with us than with you.'

'Hello? Have you got your head buried under your own ego? Have you seen what's going on outside? The army has issued a declaration. No one is supposed to leave their homes unless otherwise directed or in an absolute emergency.'

'You don't think that transforming into a bunyip is an absolute emergency? What does an emergency constitute in your book then? Is it when you run out of hair dye?'

I paused. The sensible choice would have been to head for the nearest window and jump out of it so I didn't get involved with these two. Unfortunately, I suspected that we would need Monroe and his werewolves in the hours to come. And I couldn't just leave Charley alone with her hairy housemate.

I sighed and stuffed the sphere into my bra. It meant I had an unsightly bulge, as if I'd suddenly grown a massive boil on my breast overnight but I knew it was safe there. Only Morgan had access to my breasts, thank you very much.

I walked down the remaining stairs. Monroe and Charley were glaring at each other. 'Hey!' I chirped cheerfully. 'I found the toilet!'

Neither of them looked at me. Well, that

wasn't very nice.

'I had a lovely long pee,' I informed them. 'Now I feel much better. How is Lizzy doing?'

Reluctantly Charley turned away from Monroe towards me. 'See for yourself,' she said.

I jumped down the last couple of steps and peered into the room. Where there had been a snarling furry creature, there was now a tall blonde woman hugging her knees and looking distraught. Given the expression on Lizzy's face, I thought things had been better when she was a bunyip.

'Are you okay?' I called. I wasn't venturing inside until I knew there was no chance she'd transform again and try to munch on me. I would be a particularly tasty morsel.

'Mmm.'

'Lizzy,' Monroe said, 'why don't you get some clothes and come with me? I'll keep you safe.'

'I hate to put a spanner in the works,' I murmured, 'but we do have an apocalypse to avert.'

Charley frowned. 'So this really is the end of the world? From what I heard it was just local to Manchester.'

'It's not the end of the world,' Monroe snapped.

'But it could be if we don't get a move on,' I told him. 'Lizzy needs to make a decision. If she's okay here, I think she should stay here.'

He opened his mouth to speak just as the doorbell rang. We all jumped; Lizzy added a whimper for extra effect and drew further into herself.

With a grim look on her face, Charley marched to the door and flung it open. I was right behind her. I could see Morgan hovering behind a parked car. I gave him a tight smile and a nod so that he knew I had the sphere in my sweaty little palms. He relaxed slightly and beckoned me but I couldn't leave yet, not now that Manchester's finest were here too.

DC Jones blinked at me. 'Well, well, well. Ms Hatter. Trouble just seems to follow you around, doesn't it?'

'Actually,' I told her calmly, 'I follow trouble, not the other way around. Charley here was in a spot of bother so my friend and I came to help her out. Because you guys were off having a doughnut or whatever.'

Next to her, DI Mulroney rumbled in irritation. 'What are you doing here?'

I stared at him. 'I just explained. Weren't you listening?'

'Thank you for coming,' Charley said to the pair of them, ignoring the renewed tension in the air. 'I think things are under control now.'

I smiled and pointed. 'See? I did that.'

Monroe appeared behind us. 'Actually, it was all me.'

Mulroney tsked. 'I don't care who brought things under control,' he said. 'I just want to know what happened and whether it's likely to happen again. We're fighting fires across the city and we came here as a favour to you, Charley. If you don't need us, there are other places we can be.'

Jones didn't seem to hear her partner's words. Her eyes were fixed on Monroe and two high spots of colour were rising in her cheeks.

'Yeah,' Charley said, 'he's good looking but don't waste your time. He's an absolute bastard.'

Monroe's eyebrows snapped together. 'After what I just did for you, you should be more grateful.'

'You mean fall at your feet in worship?' she enquired.

He shrugged. 'It's a start.'

I rolled my eyes and stepped out to join the police. I closed the door behind me but I could still hear Monroe and Charley arguing. 'Sexual tension,' I said. 'They'll work it out if we give them time. And maybe a matching pair of ball gags.'

Jones looked faintly alarmed but Mulroney appeared interested. Then he seemed to realise that his thoughts were visible on his face and his expression closed off. 'This area is the next one to be evacuated. The army will be moving residents out within the hour. I suggest you join the evacuation. You seem to be creating more problems. If I see you again, I'll have to arrest you.'

I folded my arms. 'I understand that I am indeed an arresting vision but I think that's taking things a bit far.'

Mulroney rolled his eyes. 'We don't have time for this,' he said under his breath.

I glanced at Jones. She still appeared to be shaking off the vision of Monroe and his dimple. 'Thank you,' I said. 'For going to the bogles' estate and helping them.'

She shook herself. 'Bogles?'

Uh-oh. That was the second time I'd mentioned them to her. I really ought to be more careful. 'The people near Boggart Hole. I'm sure your intervention was well received.'

Mulroney glowered. 'I thought that was an anonymous tip off. Was that you as well? There was virtually a Mexican standoff in the street.'

'Are they all okay?'

'What's it to you?'

DC Jones interrupted. 'Everyone's fine. But,' she added, with a warning frown, 'we are now working alongside the army and taking our orders from them. We can't get involved as easily as we could before.'

She said that as if she thought I was planning to arrange for more life-or-death showdowns. This was becoming irritating. Why wasn't it easier to save the world? Why did people always have to question what I was doing?

'Look,' I said, trying not to sound impatient and failing miserably, 'I'm on your side here. I'm...' I broke off as my eye caught something at the end of the street. Gasbudlikins. 'When did you say the army would be here?'

'In the next hour. Sooner probably.' Jones narrowed her gaze. 'Why?'

I opened the front door again, ignoring both Charley and Monroe who were standing so close together I was surprised they still had room to breathe. 'There's an Australian woman in there who really needs your help.'

I grabbed Monroe's arm and hauled him out then unceremoniously shoved Mulroney and Jones in. 'It's been lovely knowing you both!' I called. 'Help Charley and Lizzy, and stay inside till the army gets here and all will be fine.' Before any of them could protest, I slammed the door shut again. If they knew what was good for them, they'd do as I said.

Monroe glared. 'What are you doing? I was talking to that blue-haired bug of a woman.' He pushed past me as if to enter again.

'You idiot werewolf,' I hissed. 'Stop thinking with your cock and start paying attention.'

'I am pay...' Monroe's voice trailed off as he caught sight of the masses of faeries gathering at both ends of the street, blocking off our exits. Morgan and the others were already on their feet and heading into the middle of the road. 'Is this Rubus?' he asked.

'Yes,' I answered shortly. I hopped down the pavement and ran to Morgan's side. 'How did he find us?'

'Might have been magic,' he grimaced. 'Might have been old-fashioned look-outs. You have the sphere?'

I nodded grimly. 'I do.'

'Then you need to get out of here any way you can, Maddy. Keep yourself and that thing safe. We'll keep Rubus busy.'

I shook my head. 'I'm not getting out of here any more than you are.'

Charley's front door opened and Mulroney peered out. 'What on earth is going on?'

Monroe snarled at him, whiskers and fur springing out all over his face. For what was possibly the first time in his life, Mulroney did the sensible thing and stepped back inside.

'Stay there!' I screeched at him. We didn't need more collateral damage.

I met Monroe's eyes and he nodded at me, understanding. He was already more wolf than man but he still managed to snap his fingers at several of his werewolves and send them to guard Charley's door. Then he bounded back over to us. 'Have you grown a third boob?' he enquired, gazing at the lump protruding from my chest.

Morgan growled. I grinned. 'While you were flirting with Charley, I got the sphere,' I told him. 'Now all we need to do is to get it – and us – out of here.'

Monroe smiled. 'Well, it's fortunate you brought me along to be your faery godmother then. Your wish might just come true.' He exploded into full wolf form. Suddenly he was a gigantic beast with ice-blue eyes and snow-tipped fur. All around him, the other wolves did the same.

'If only wishing made it so,' I muttered.

I leaned up and kissed Morgan on the cheek. Then we all readied ourselves for the onslaught.

Chapter Seventeen

I'll say this for Rubus: he didn't hang back and let his henchmen deal with all the trouble. He enjoyed the limelight far too much to let others do the dirty work. I could appreciate that, much as it galled me.

He strode forward from the left, his thumbs hooked into his belt. He had clearly come dressed for action; he was wearing khakis and an army jacket. I doubted anyone would mistake his loose-hipped swagger for that of an uptight soldier's, however.

'Hello, brother.' He grinned as he got close. He blew me a kiss. 'And Madrona too.' He swung his gaze round us, including the assembled werewolves. 'I see you've been making new friends. That's sweet.'

Morgan's expression remained stoic and calm but I sensed him seething underneath. 'You keep turning up at the most inopportune moments, Rubus. This isn't a good time.'

Rubus smirked. 'Oh, I think it's the perfect time. It took me a while to work out how Madrona had spirited away my sphere from the police station without Carduus noticing but I worked it out.' He paused. 'With a bit of magical intervention.'

My mouth twisted. 'You said you wouldn't perform any spells. We told you what would happen if more magic was released.'

He dismissed my complaint with an airy hand. 'Yes, yes. I know what I said. I thought about it a bit more, though, and decided I didn't care. This demesne is doomed whatever happens. All that matters is getting us back home before it implodes. I really don't understand why you're all so keen to stop that from happening.' He blinked at us earnestly. 'Don't you want us to survive?'

Morgan growled under his breath. 'This is about everyone's survival. Not just ours.'

'The humans have been doomed for generations. If our magic doesn't kill them, they'll kill themselves before too long. We're doing them a favour by not prolonging their misery.'

Monroe snarled, baring his teeth.

Rubus raised an eyebrow. 'Hello, doggy,' he cooed. 'I assume that what you'd like to say – but can't – is that your kind aren't human.' He shrugged. 'I tell you what. I'll arrange for your lot to come back with us to Mag Mell. You can't say fairer than that. You'll enjoy all the benefits that our demesne has to offer. You won't have to hide your existence or your true nature any longer.' He leaned forward slightly. 'And I bet you've noticed just how beneficial the magic in the air has been to you and your kind.' He tapped his mouth. 'Let me guess. You're stronger. You find it easier to shapeshift. You don't need to wait for that pesky moon to go all furry.'

Around us, the other werewolves began growling and snapping. I could swear that several of them were drooling.

Rubus's grin grew wider. 'You are werewolves, right? I've not come across you before but you don't look much like lap dogs to me.' He glanced at Morgan. 'Even if that's what you're acting like.'

Morgan put his hands in pockets, evincing utter casualness. 'Insult away,' he said. 'We're leaving and you can't stop us.'

'Leave if you want to,' Rubus returned. His expression hardened. 'Just give me my sphere first.'

'We don't have it.'

'You always were a terrible liar, brother. Hand over my sphere or suffer the consequences.'

The more times we confronted Rubus, the more it seemed that he spent his time watching bad Hollywood movies so he could learn the lines that the villains uttered. He was like a caricature rather than a really bad guy. That thought would have been comforting if it weren't for the fact that he was standing in front of us. He never seemed to quit. And I didn't know how to make him.

'We don't have the sphere,' I said.

Rubus gazed at me fondly. 'You're better than Morganus but I'm still a more accomplished liar than you, Maddy. I can see right through you.'

By my side, Morgan gritted his teeth. 'Don't call her Maddy.'

Rubus snorted. 'Because you've laid claim to that name? Because you own her and her name? I offered her freedom. You're just another ball and chain.'

I placed a hand on Morgan's arm. 'You never wanted me, Rubus. You just wanted to piss off Morgan.'

Rubus appeared to consider this for a moment. Then he shrugged. 'Yeah. Too true.'

The longer we debated, the more chance there was that the army would show up and give us the chance to get away unscathed. However, it appeared that Monroe had a different idea. His snow-tipped fur was standing on end and his muscles were bunched up, as if he were getting ready to pounce.

'Down, boy,' I said.

I was too late. Either Monroe's wolf form wasn't as sentient as he liked to pretend or he didn't hear me. Either way, he launched himself at Rubus, his large jaws clamping down on his arm.

Monroe's action gave the other wolves the excuse they needed. Half of them peeled off towards the Fey at one end of the street and half peeled off towards those at the other end. The scene exploded – fur, blood, snarls, calls … and more arsebadgering magic.

Rubus raised his free hand and muttered something under his breath at Monroe. A bolt of green magic flew towards him and smacked him on the muzzle. The werewolf instantly let go. I tried not to feel too satisfied at the blood staining Monroe's muzzle and the trickle of blood dripping from Rubus's arm and splattering onto the tarmac below.

The Fey was in more pain than he was letting on. 'You'll pay for that,' he snarled.

From both ends of the street there were howls and screams. It was impossible to tell who was winning, Rubus's Fey or Monroe's wolves. There was nothing I could do to help them, not with the sphere stuffed into my bra and everything to play for.

Out of the corner of my eye, I saw the wolves guarding Charley's door straining at the bit to join the fray. And it wasn't just Charley's house we had to worry about; up and down the street, nervous faces peeked out of windows. I suppose it wasn't every day that gang warfare suddenly erupted, not when the going price for these houses had to be upwards of half a million pounds. I sucked on my bottom lip. We had to find a way to calm things down.

'You're never going to stop, are you, Rubus?' I said eventually. 'We're never going to win.'

'Finally, you're getting it.' He nodded. Blood continued to drip onto the road but it looked as if the wound were already healing. Arsebadgering faery skills.

I looked at Morgan. 'I'm tired,' I said. 'Let's just hand over the sphere and get on with it. We might as well yield to the inevitable.'

Rubus let out a crow of laughter. 'She's got you there, brother. I'm never going to quit. I'm going to take our people home no matter what happens.'

I couldn't tell whether Morgan believed me or not. His eyes scanned my face as he tried to work out what I was thinking. 'We can't give up, Maddy. Not with the wolves on our side. At least now we have a fighting chance.'

Fighting chance was right. This street was already soaked in blood and the fight had barely begun. I wasn't convinced there would be any wolves left after this bout. Or any faeries.

'We've run out of options, Morgan,' I told him. 'This is already a bloodbath.' I drew in a breath and met Rubus's eyes. 'We've taken the sphere to a bank and dropped it in a safety deposit box.'

Rubus sighed deeply. 'Oh, Madrona, just when I thought you were starting to see the light. The banks – and the shops – have been shut for the last two days. You must think I'm a complete idiot. Tell me where my sphere really is and I might be tempted to let you go.'

'The pink elephant took it. Snapped it right up with its pretty pink trunk and inhaled it.'

Rubus tutted.

'No? We dropped it in the ocean. It sank to the deepest, darkest part. It's swimming with the fishes now.'

He crossed his arms.

'We gave it to an astronaut.' I pointed up to

the sky. 'It's closer to the moon than it is to us right now.'

'I'm getting really fucking tired of this,' Rubus snapped. 'Just hand it over.' He paused, a light dawning in his eyes. 'You're stalling for time. Why?'

'Maybe,' Morgan said, stepping in, 'you should wait and find out.'

Rubus lunged towards him but yet again Monroe leapt forward and knocked him backwards. Rubus fought back, blasting more magic towards the werewolf, but Monroe avoided the worst of it. I winced, though, when he caught a bolt on his hindquarters.

Rubus raised his arm. From the left hand side of the street, a single Fey peeled off. He wove in and out of the fighting and strolled towards us. I squinted, then my heart sank. Carduus. That was all we needed.

'Find it!' Rubus roared. 'Find my sphere!'

Carduus reached into his pocket and drew out a small glass bottle. He uncorked it and sniffed the contents, a smug expression on his face. As he did so, Charley's door opened and DI Mulroney appeared.

'You will stop this at once!' he bellowed from behind the wall of wolves that was guarding him. 'I am the police and I order you to stop!'

DC Jones and Charley appeared behind him. Rubus, unperturbed by the interruption, flicked out a hand and sent yet a bolt of destructive magic towards them. Charley only just yanked Mulroney back in time.

Rubus wheeled round, pointing his finger in an arc around us. Within moments a barrier of fire surrounded him, Morgan and me. Flames were licking at us. Rubus had trapped us inside the circle of flames with him. And Carduus was almost here too.

Monroe had rolled away and escaped the ring of fire. I flung my hands out in the direction of the Fey scientist and screeched at Monroe. 'Get him!'

The werewolf didn't need any further telling. He ran towards Carduus and knocked him off his feet, sending the bottle smashing to the ground. Glass and green liquid went everywhere. I dreaded to think what the concoction was but at least Monroe was keeping Carduus busy for now.

Morgan, Rubus and I were alone in the centre of the flaming circle. Unfortunately, the sphere was also with us. I suspected it wouldn't take long for Rubus to work that out.

Rubus drew his gaze up and down Morgan's body then his eyes flicked to me. When he spotted the bulge at my chest, his mouth curved into a nasty smile. 'Well, well, well. Either you have an unsightly growth, Madrona, or I've just found my sphere.'

He wasted no more time and leapt towards me with outstretched hands. I tried to move away but the force of the flames at my back prevented me from going far.

Morgan pushed me to one side, acting as a barrier between Rubus and myself. 'Leave her alone.'

Rubus smiled even more broadly. 'I will if she gives me my sphere.' He moved forward again. When Morgan continued to block his way, Rubus shrugged. 'This is very tiresome.' He drew back his fist and, with all the force he could muster, slammed it into Morgan's face. 'See how you like that, pretty boy,' he snarled.

Morgan staggered. Blood dripped from him nose but he raised his head and met Rubus's eyes. 'It doesn't matter what you do to me but you can't hurt Maddy and you can't get the sphere. We won't let you.'

Rubus tsked. 'You aren't very bright, are you, dear brother? I'm the one with all the power. Not you.' He regarded Morgan slyly. 'If you're going to keep getting in my way, you're leaving me with no choice.'

He grabbed Morgan by the throat and spun him round, tightening his hold. Morgan was no more able to fight back than a kitten could fly. His fingers scrabbled at Rubus's arm but the truce meant that he couldn't retaliate. And neither could I.

Rubus grinned at me. 'Whatcha going to do now, Maddy?'

'Would you kill your own brother?' I asked. 'Is that really who you are, Rubus?'

His smile disappeared. 'If he worked with me instead of against me, I wouldn't have to hurt him.' He loosened his grip on Morgan's neck and for a second I relaxed. I should have known better. Rubus moved his hand to Morgan's arm and, in one swift movement, bent it backwards. Morgan's mouth opened in a silent howl of agony as the bone snapped.

I leapt forward, prepared to do everything I could to save Morgan but the truce held me in mid-leap. Pain flashed through my body. There was nothing I could do. Short of talking Rubus into being a good guy, I was powerless to stop him. At this point, we all were.

'Give me the sphere and I'll stop this,' Rubus purred. 'Or don't give me it and I'll kill him in front of your eyes. Then I'll kill you.'

There was no way out. The fire beat against us from all sides. Morgan was barely clinging to consciousness. All the power was in Rubus's hands.

I hated not being on the winning side.

I licked my lips. It occurred to me that things went better for me when I stopped trying to be good and gave in to my wicked side. When I was an evil bitch life smiled down on me. I'd been right before: kittens couldn't fly – but I could still pick one up, fling it into the air and give it a damned good try at flight.

I tilted back my head and moved my hands, as if reaching into my bra to pull out the sphere. I pretended not to notice the gleeful expression on

Rubus's face.

'No,' Morgan croaked.

I wished he'd stop worrying. At the last moment, I reversed my course and stretched my hands upwards instead of inwards. I grabbed all the magic inside me that I could muster and sent it flying up into the atmosphere. Bolt after bolt of flaming colours stretched upwards in a kaleidoscopic rainbow.

Rubus frowned. 'What are you doing?'

'You started it,' I said, as I continued to pelt magic into the sky. 'You've got your Fey using spells, even though we know the consequences of that. I'm just helping out.' I concentrated harder. Hopefully, this would be enough.

Rubus dropped Morgan and jumped towards me. I sidestepped, singeing my hair as it swung towards the fiery barrier that was holding us in, but I didn't stop releasing magic. Sooner or later, something would happen. It had to.

'I don't know what you think you're playing at,' Rubus growled. 'But—'

A strange sound came through the air. I didn't know what it was but I knew as soon as I heard it that my plan had worked. By adding to the magic in the atmosphere, I'd made another magical event occur. Yes, more people might die as a result, and yes, that made me an evil bitch. But faced with total annihilation or another magically-induced plague, what was the choice.

Unfortunately, plague was the right word. A

gigantic black cloud appeared over the horizon, blotting out the remaining sunlight as it stretched from one end of the city to the other. Even Rubus stopped his snarls to stare. 'What the fuck is that?' he breathed.

The noise got louder. It was almost electric in tone, like a buzzing. It wasn't until it was almost upon us that I realised what it was.

'Locusts,' I whispered, half to myself, half to Morgan, who was staggering up to his feet and cradling his broken arm. 'A plague of arsebadgering locusts.'

I'd barely finished my sentence when they were upon us. I shrieked and threw my arms over my head to protect myself. I ducked down, taking Morgan with me.

I felt the locusts crawling over my scalp and my back, getting into my clothes and biting my skin. I was sure that the others were screaming too but I couldn't hear them over the swarm's cacophony. Hundreds of them sizzled as they flew into Rubus's magic fire.

I don't know whether the shock made Rubus release his hold on the circle of fire, or the locusts smothered it by the sheer force of their numbers, but it wasn't long before Morgan grabbed my upper arm and hauled me away. He dragged me out from the middle of the street towards the relative safety of the houses opposite.

'What do we do?' I yelled at him, waving my hands in front of my face to see what was happening. The cloud of locusts was so dense that it was impossible to see more than a few inches.

'We run,' Morgan shouted. 'We have to.'

With his good arm, he took my hand and held it tightly, as if he were afraid to let go. A moment later, we were running down the street. Whether it was away from Rubus or into more danger, I didn't know; the only thing I was certain of was that we had to get away.

When we reached the end of street, I stumbled over a fallen body. A Fey. One of Rubus's, then. I reached down to yank him upwards but whoever he was didn't move – and if I dallied too long I was liable to join him on the ground. I couldn't afford that; the world couldn't afford that.

I yielded to Morgan's insistent tugging and we kept going. We curved round the side of one of the houses just as the trundle of a heavy vehicle hit my ears. There was a bellow from a loudspeaker, barely audible over the sound of the locusts. 'We are preparing for evacuations! We are…'

Whatever else was said was lost. Morgan and I kept running, our heads down as we faced the battery of flying locusts. At some point I realised that we weren't alone and that some wolves were by our side. I hoped they'd all made it out.

At that point, all I could do was hope. Any action beyond fleeing was lost to me.

Chapter Eighteen

It felt like an eternity, although it was probably only minutes, before the locusts disappeared back to whichever magical hellhole they'd sprung from. All the same, our little group continued to run until we found ourselves in a sheltered back alley. We paused for breath and to take stock.

Monroe almost immediately transformed, abandoning his wolf form with its protective fur for his naked skin. He was covered in welts and burns, and there were two long brands down his body where Rubus had seared him with his magic. I couldn't take the time to appreciate the werewolf's tanned, naked splendour because I was too busy shaking out locusts from the folds of my clothes but I rather thought that I preferred Morgan's lean goodness to Monroe's tattooed muscles.

'Everyone is here,' Monroe said grimly. 'Everyone made it out.' He jerked his head towards a few of the stragglers. 'Set up a perimeter to watch for anyone approaching while we take stock.' They bobbed their heads and immediately peeled off.

Monroe stalked over to another wolf – Dwight? William? I couldn't remember and it didn't really matter – and clicked his fingers. The wolf transformed back into human shape and the pair began to murmur. I was tempted to eavesdrop but frankly I had greater concerns.

I grabbed Morgan's face in my hands and stared into his eyes. 'Are you alright?' I demanded.

He smiled. 'I am.'

'Your arm…'

'It'll heal.' He dipped his head towards mine for a brief kiss. I thought it was rather restrained of me not to grab him for a proper snog; he certainly deserved it. 'We made it out and we have the sphere. We're halfway there already.'

'That was all me,' I told him. 'By throwing magic into the sky, I brought those locusts upon us.'

'You did what was necessary.' He brushed a curl away from my face.

I met his eyes. 'You don't have to keep making excuses for me, you know. If there are other people out there who were caught up in that storm…'

'I'm not making excuses. You thought on your feet and did what you had to.' He grimaced. 'To be honest, I wish I'd thought of it. Anyway, the locusts have gone now. Maybe they'll have done some good in stripping all those crazy trees of their foliage and halting further growth.'

'You're being very optimistic.'

His eyes held mine. 'Thanks to you. We can only deal with each problem as it comes and in the best manner that is presented to us at the time. We're all fumbling here, Maddy. All of us.'

Monroe sniffed. '*I'm* not fumbling. And next time you feel like unleashing a plague of locusts on us, darling, perhaps a heads-up would be a good idea.' He grimaced. 'I'm still itchy.'

There was a shout from behind us. 'Incoming!'

I stiffened. Monroe cocked his head. A moment later, a message was relayed by a runner. 'Faery. Female. Heading straight this way.' The wolf messenger frowned. 'She's taller than a freaking maypole.'

I looked at Morgan. 'Lunaria.'

Monroe whipped round. 'Is she a friend?'

I wrinkled my nose. 'Difficult to say at this point. Tell me where she is. I'll go and speak to her alone.'

Monroe opened his mouth to protest but I shook my head. 'It's best this way.' All the same, I plucked out the sphere and passed it to Morgan with a meaningful glance. He nodded and slipped it into his pocket.

Squaring my shoulders, and adding an extra sway to my hips to suggest that everything was going exactly as I'd planned, I headed out. When I saw Lunaria standing in the middle of the next street looking somewhat lost, I took a deep breath and strolled up to her.

'Hi, Mads,' she said, as if we'd just bumped into each other while out for a jaunt. Her head swung from side to side. 'I can hear them. Can you hear them?'

I peered at her. Despite her nonchalant tone, she didn't look well. Her face was pinched and drawn and her eyes were almost ghoulishly large. 'Uh,' I said, hesitating, 'do you mean the wolves?'

'They're everywhere,' she whispered. 'All around us.'

I cocked my head and listened. Admittedly, it did sound rather intimidating. Heavy breathing and rapid heartbeats sounded from all corners. It sounded as if we'd stumbled into some sort of bizarre alfresco porn scene. Instead, it was a bunch of werewolves who dripped machismo and attitude but were utterly terrified about what was going to happen next now that they'd met Rubus in person. I had no doubt that they were fully prepared to take out Lunaria if she so much as twitched. They probably felt the same way about me too; after all, I'd brought the locusts down on their furry heads. Literally.

'Don't worry about them,' I said briskly. 'Let's focus on you. Were you back there with Rubus? Did you get hurt?'

Lunaria seemed confused for a moment. Her forehead creased then she shook her head. 'No. I stayed back. I was watching, though.' She clutched my arm. 'Rubus is okay. He didn't get hurt. I'm so worried though, Mads,' she said. She started scratching her arms, her long nails raking her skin and leaving behind painful red weals. 'Things aren't right here. He's still not right.'

That was the understatement of the year. I

took her hands in mine to stop her from doing herself real damage. 'What's happened to you?' I asked. 'You were struggling before but now it seems like you're barely clinging on.'

'It took me a long time to realise but we're not supposed to be here,' she said, gazing into the distance. 'We're screwing up this demesne and it's screwing us up.' She blinked and looked at me again. 'I mean, look at what it's done to you.'

Compared to her, I was pretty darned awesome but I suspected this wasn't the time to point it out. 'Mmmm,' I said non-commitally. 'But you do realise what will happen if we use the sphere to go back to Mag Mell? We've spoken about it many times. This entire city – this entire *world* – will be destroyed.'

Lunaria touched her chest with her fingertips. 'It hurts. It hurts so bad.'

I knew what she was talking about. The homesickness we felt for Mag Mell was as much about physical as emotional pain. Thanks to my amnesia I didn't feel it as acutely as the other Fey but I still understood it.

I felt a twist of guilt. A couple of days ago, I'd manipulated Lunaria into taking some pixie dust. There was a good chance that she was pining so badly for home because of that. Another thing to blame myself for.

I sighed. 'Making ourselves feel better isn't right if it will kill everyone else.'

'I don't want anyone to die.' Lunaria's voice

was slow and languorous, as if it were an effort to get the words out. She pulled her hands away from me and turned her head. Then her mood changed without warning. 'Rubus is in trouble. We have to help him. He's going to hurt himself. He's going to do something he'll regret. You've got to help me help him! You have to do it, Mads!'

Er... 'I'm trying to help him,' I said reasonably, trying to think of a logical way out of this. The trouble was that any semblance of logic appeared to have long since left Lunaria's frazzled brain.

'He's very fragile, Mads,' Lunaria said, earnestly. 'If everyone in this demesne dies as a result of his actions, I'm not sure he'll be able to live with himself.'

I just managed to stop myself from rolling my eyes. The solution was simple: all he had to do was *not* kill everyone and all would be well. 'How do we stop him, Looney?' I asked softly, praying she might have an insight into Rubus's psyche that the rest of us had missed. Not that I agreed with her assessment of him as fragile; an arsebadgering matriarchal buffalo was more fragile than Rubus.

She wrung her hands. 'I don't know. I tried to talk to him but he just yelled at me. I used to think he shouted because he didn't like me but now I know that he acts like that because he's too afraid of the truth. He's too afraid to let all of us down. He doesn't want to hurt any one of us and he's suffering so badly for it.'

Poor baby. I opened my mouth to tell her exactly what I thought of Rubus. That's when I spotted the bruise snaking out from under her collar. I stared at it. No locust caused that. 'Lunaria,' I said quietly. 'Has Rubus hurt you?'

Her hand went to the purple mark. 'He's wrestling with demons. I have to help him with that.'

Gasbudlikins. I gritted my teeth. 'You have to get away from him. As you've said, he's not in a good frame of mind. He's already killed other Fey. If he hit you—'

'He didn't hit me.' She didn't sound in the slightest bit convincing.

'Lunaria…'

She rounded me, her eyes suddenly blazing. 'You're so focused on Morgan that you can't see what really counts! Rubus needs us! He's in pain and I don't know how to help him!'

I swallowed. 'Is that why you came looking for me? Because I have to say, I'm not sure that I can—'

'No.' She turned her face away and her shoulders slumped, as if she'd finally realised that I wasn't going to be Rubus's saviour. Neither was she. The arsebadger was completely irredeemable. All we could do was save ourselves from him.

Lunaria continued. 'I came here to tell you that he sent people to sort out your friend. He likes her and he doesn't want to hurt her, so if something happens and she ends up dying, he'll feel even worse. I have to help him. I can't let him hurt himself any more.'

The blood in my veins ran ice cold. 'He's sent people to sort out my friend?' There was something so chilling about that phrase that I found myself barely able to speak. 'You mean Julie?'

'I don't like her,' Lunaria said, her lip curling. 'I don't care what happens to her. But if she does end up getting hurt then Rubus —'

I didn't wait for her to finish speaking. I wheeled round and started running in the opposite. Gasbudlikins. Was all this crap ever going to stop?

***

All this apocalypse-avoidance stuff was doing one good thing: it had made me considerably fitter than I was even a week or so ago. I sprinted most of the way back to Julie's house even though it was at least ten miles. Okay, five miles. Three or four, certainly. If you rounded it up.

Morgan and Monroe and his wolves fell in behind me, shouting after me. I didn't have the breath to run and explain what was happening the same time. If Lunaria was telling the truth, they'd work out the problem sooner or later.

I smelled the problem long before I saw it. Julie's vampire nature meant that no one could cross her threshold without her permission. If they smoked her out, however, she'd have no choice but to leave and face whoever was out there. Given the thick banks of smoke blowing down her street and the strong smell of burning, someone was already laying waste to her home.

I covered my mouth and nose with my arm and ran forward. There was no sign of any people; I assumed they'd already been evacuated by the army and were out of Manchester altogether. That was something – but it didn't help Julie or Finn or any of the others who were holed up with her.

Part of me expected a Fey army to be in front of her house, complete with burning torches and pitchforks and perhaps a crucifix or two. When I saw it was only one man – and realised who it was – my mouth dropped open.

'Come out, vampire!' Dave the human yelled. 'Come and meet your maker! I am a vampire hunter and I am going to stake you through the heart and make sure you never sink your deadly fangs into anyone ever again!'

Despite the broken windows on the ground floor and the fire inside, I slowed to a walk and continued to stare. I hadn't seen Dave since Morgan and I came across him in an old warehouse that Rubus had reportedly once used as a hideout. Dave and Rubus had some sort depraved quid pro quo agreement: Dave sold pixie dust to hapless Fey not already on Rubus's side, not to mention attempting to spike Morgan with the stuff at the same time; Rubus, in return, gave Dave a selection of human drugs to enjoy personally and to sell on the streets.

I'd rather liked Dave the first time I met him.

Now I knew what a pathetic excuse for a human being he really was.

I dragged my eyes away from him and glanced upwards. I spotted Finn hovering on the second floor, a window open to allow him to breathe. His expression was worried but, when he caught sight of me, he gave me a brief thumbs up. When the wolves and Morgan pitched up behind me, Finn began to wave enthusiastically. He was still alive and, judging by his reaction, so were the others.

'Hey Dave,' I called, 'whatcha doing?'

At first he didn't hear me. He was so intent on burning Julie out of her home that I could probably have screeched in his ear with a loudspeaker and he wouldn't have noticed. 'I'm hunting you down! You're not getting away this time, bloodsucker! Vampires don't scare me! You're an abomination in the eyes of God!' He sang out each sentence with abandoned glee. It was quite disturbing how much he was enjoying himself.

'Davey boy!' I yelled.

He jerked, the fact that he was no longer alone finally registering in his dim brain. He turned slowly towards me, blinking through the smoke. 'You,' he said. He frowned. 'What are you doing here? Did Rubus send you?'

I'd almost forgotten that I'd lied to Dave and pretended that I worked for Rubus just like he did. 'Yeah,' I said. 'Yeah. He told me to tell you that you've done enough and he wants to meet you back at headquarters.'

'No way! I've still got three Molotov cocktails. Vampires are evil! That woman deserves to be put down.' He shrugged. 'Besides, I never liked that stupid soap opera.'

'Vampires aren't evil, Dave,' I told him, slowly moving closer. I hoped he would focus on me and not on the werewolves who were getting closer to the house to get everyone out. 'I'm sure Rubus told you they were but they're really not.'

'Dracula,' Dave said smugly. 'He was evil.'

'He wasn't real.'

'Kiefer Sutherland in *The Lost Boys*.'

'Again,' I said, 'not real.'

'Kiefer Sutherland isn't real?'

Heaven help me. 'No,' I said, trying to stay patient. 'He's real. But he was acting a part. Besides, Count Duckula was a good guy.'

'Stop trying to fool me. He's not a guy,' Dave said. 'He's a duck.'

I tried to smile. 'Yeah, you got me there.'

Dave had been a lot smarter the first time I'd met him. Clearly all those drugs were addling his poor boy's brain. I straightened my shoulders and eyed him sternly. 'You need to cease and desist, soldier. No more of this.'

'Madrona's right,' Morgan said, coming up behind me. 'You shouldn't be doing this, Dave. You should get out of the city. Bad things are afoot.'

'Bad things like vampires!' Dave yelled. He reached down for another petrol-filled bottle.

Gasbudlikins.

I sneaked a quick glance at Morgan. 'Let me handle this,' I murmured.

'Because having a conversation about animated vampire ducks was helping matters?' he enquired.

I sighed. 'You're right. Let's stop this tomfoolery and just take the idiot down. Can you manage with your arm?'

Morgan grinned. 'Believe me, it'll be a pleasure.'

'What are you whispering about?' Dave said. 'I don't like it when people talk behind my back.'

'You take the left side,' I said to Morgan, 'I'll take the right.'

He nodded. 'Three, two—'

There was a shout from inside the house. 'Opulus!' I heard Timmons shout. 'No!'

There was a loud crash and then the front door was flung open. Standing there, his entire body alight, was the unmistakable figure of the grieving Fey. Even his hair seemed to be on fire. He ran towards Dave and leapt on top of him.

Dave shouted and tried to wriggle free but flames were already licking at his clothes. He squealed and choked as Opulus stopped moving and collapsed. Morgan and I sprinted forward and rolled the burning body of the Fey from Dave.

Dave staggered to his feet. I jumped at him again, trying to put out the flames. He pushed me away but it was a wasted effort. He fell to his knees, his skin blackened and the sickening stench of burning flesh ripe in the air. Then he fell forward. It appeared that Rubus had just created another victim.

Morgan checked Opulus and shook his head grimly. Make that two victims. Lunaria thought Rubus was fragile; I knew that he was a monster. My shoulders sagged with the pointlessness of it all. Why on earth had Rubus taken it upon himself to attack Julie of all people? It didn't make any sense. He liked her; I'd have gone so far as to describe him as an ardent fan. What the hell was going on?

The werewolves had creating a sort of human ladder. They barely glanced in Dave or Opulus's direction as they helped Finn, Julie and Timmons clamber down from the high window.

Julie's face was pure white. 'They came at me in my house,' she whispered. 'I'm supposed to be safe there.'

Monroe's mouth flattened. 'I'm starting to think nowhere in this city is safe,' he muttered.

I looked around. 'Where's Artemesia?' My chest felt tight. Was she still inside, in that burning building?

'She went off to her lab,' Finn said. 'We couldn't stop her. She said she had to get some books and she didn't care if anyone of us tried to get in her way.'

That was something then; at least she was alright. For the moment. I gestured helplessly at Morgan. 'What now?'

He swallowed, his expression tight. 'Nothing has really changed. We have the sphere and we still have to see it destroyed.' He drew it out gingerly before passing it to me. 'Keep it safe, Mads. We'll contact Liung and set up the meet.'

I took the sphere with some reluctance, shoving it into my pocket for now. 'And in the meantime? Before we get hold of him?'

Morgan ran a tired hand through his hair. 'We find Arty and pray that she's found a way to let off some magical steam. It's probably just as well she ran back to her lab, even though I expressly told her not to. If she hasn't found a way out of all this, the city might be lost for good no matter what we do.'

Julie and Timmons gave tiny whimpers; Finn just looked grim. As if by unspoken agreement, some of the werewolves went to their sides. 'Don't worry,' one said, patting Julie on the arm. 'If all else fails, you can come and live with us in Scotland. We'll accept your petition this time.'

I glanced at Monroe, half expecting him to argue, but he just looked tired. He nodded tersely. 'Lead the way to this Arty fellow. I, for one, can't wait to get out of this shithole.'

Chapter Nineteen

Because Morgan was Fey, his broken arm would heal quickly; I only hoped it would be quickly enough. We were marching quickly towards the denouement of our chaotic plans and if he wasn't fully fit it would be that much harder to succeed.

Even though we were in the relative safety of Artemesia's little apothecary lab, the mood was downbeat. Every time we turned around, it seemed as if there were another disaster and another death to deal with. Although we were within touching distance of putting down Rubus's plans for good, the future still appeared bleak. The continued mess of magic was barely being kept in check; rioting and looting in the city seemed to be increasing, despite the continuing evacuations and ever-growing army presence.

'You know what I think I should get?' I said to no one in particular. 'A hat. In the stories, the Madhatter always wears a fabulous hat. I reckon I could get an impressive one. I wouldn't even have to pay for it, I could just smash a few windows of select boutiques and take my pick.' I patted the top of my head thoughtfully. 'Something tall and large. I could hide all manner of helpful objects inside it.'

Morgan offered a faint smile but I could tell

his heart wasn't in it.

'We could all get hats,' I continued. 'It'd be like Ascot but for the apocalypse instead. Dressing for death,' I proclaimed. 'It'll be an internet sensation.'

'Except,' Jodie said, 'there will no longer be any internet.'

Monroe sniffed. 'I do not dress for death. You know why?'

'Why?' I had a feeling I knew what he was going to say.

'Because I don't die. I don't lose. And I don't let a bunch of trumped-up faeries who are feeling a bit homesick get the better of me.' He drew back his shoulders. 'I am Monroe.'

He certainly seemed to be feeling a bit better. I looked around for a set of drums or at least a handy pair of cymbals to crash. The best I could do was a teaspoon and saucer. I tapped the spoon onto the china, immediately sending a spider web of fine cracks across its surface. Oops. Clearly, I didn't know my own strength.

'Well,' I said, pretending not to notice my minor act of destruction, 'I'd hate to end your winning streak. We're going to have to do something about Rubus to avoid any further problems.'

'Agreed.' Monroe got to his feet. 'I'll get my wolves together and we'll head to his lair straight away.'

I noticed that the few wolves behind him

went pale. The magic and destruction they'd already faced appeared to have put the fear of Fey in them.

'Let's not do anything rash,' Morgan said. 'We're not going to beat him with brute force. He has the numbers. And the magic. We have to be smarter.'

'Rubus is on the edge,' I said. 'He's teetering on the brink of all-out insanity. Much more of this and he'll be completely loopy.'

'Sounds like someone I know,' Jodie muttered.

I didn't take offence but I did turn to her with raised eyebrows. 'While he maintains an element of sanity,' I said, 'his actions are predictable. If he goes psycho, even he won't know what he's going to do next. We can't afford to sit around and twiddle our thumbs. We have to move quickly.'

'We've hardly been twiddling our thumbs,' Artemesia said.

'I know,' I replied. 'I'm just pointing out that…'

Morgan put a hand on my arm. 'Let's focus on the important points, shall we?' He flicked a look at Artemesia. 'Have you found a way to release the magic pressure in the atmosphere?'

She grimaced. 'Sort of. It's risky but I'm not sure there's much choice at this stage. I didn't want to go ahead until I'd spoken to you about it first, though.'

I nodded wisely. 'That makes sense. My

superior intellect will see through any gaps in your plan.'

Artemesia raised her eyes heavenward. 'Give me strength.'

I flexed my muscles. 'I don't have much,' I admitted, 'but what I have is yours.'

She tutted. 'Anyway, before the Arndale Centre was built, there was a restaurant-cum-nightclub called the Wishing Well. As you might surmise, it was built on the site of a wishing well. A real wishing well, with all the power and magic that you might imagine it would have. I suspect that, several generations ago, a bunch of faeries from Mag Mell created it.'

Jodie frowned. 'Aren't wishing wells super-dangerous?'

Timmons nodded. 'Yep. We try to keep their locations hidden. There's no telling what could happen if the humans visited them regularly and made wishes.' He grimaced. 'You think things are chaotic now? Imagine what it'd be like when you could wish for whatever you wanted and it would be granted.'

'Kebabs,' I said dreamily.

Timmons smiled. From our earlier conversations, I had a feeling that he shared my appreciation of a good spicy kebab dripping with tasty grease.

'They are indeed dangerous, as Begonius says,' Artemesia interjected.

'Timmons,' he told her. 'Not Begonius.'

She waved a hand. 'Whatever. My records indicate that one of our more sensible ancestors persuaded the humans that the well was indeed dangerous. They filled it in and demolished the building above it. However the well went very deep and had various caverns inside it, which still have pockets of air and space within them. There might even be a secret passageway or two leading underneath Manchester. If those passageways exist, their locations are no longer known.' She patted the pile of books next to her. 'Even these babies can't help.'

'What you're proposing,' Morgan said, 'is to use the old magic of the wishing well to contain the new magic that's built up over the city.'

Artemesia nodded. 'You've got it in one. In theory, the well will contain any power I filter down into it.'

Monroe didn't look impressed. 'In theory?'

She tugged at her earlobe. 'Until I try, I won't know for sure.'

'What's the worst-case scenario?' I asked. 'If it doesn't work and the magic seeps out?'

'The whole city will collapse into a giant sinkhole.' She said this so matter-of-factly that it seemed a very real possibility. Ah. 'The well is the best I could come up with on my own and with such short notice. I'm sure you've noticed that our magic-related problems, even without the sphere, are growing worse by the hour.'

I looked away and began to whistle. Not my

fault. No sirree.

'You should do it,' Morgan said. 'I'm not sure there's any other choice.'

'Will it take a long time to arrange?' Finn asked, while Julie stared, unmoving at Artemesia.

Artemesia shook her head. 'I'll need to get into the Arndale Centre and locate the right spot but once I'm there it'll be easy.' She pointed to a small radio. 'Getting inside shouldn't be a problem. There's been a lot of looting and most of the windows and doors into the Centre are already broken.'

Morgan folded his arms. 'Looters don't have any care for either their own safety or for others. It's not safe for you to go alone. We'll all go. That way we can be sure you're protected.'

'No.' Artemesia set her jaw. 'You have to meet Liung and deal with the sphere. Sorting out the magic in the atmosphere is pointless if we don't get that damn thing destroyed.'

Timmons got to his feet. 'I'll go with her. I'll make sure she's alright.'

I blinked at him. That was impressive; two weeks earlier he'd been a terrified weasel of a faery and now he was volunteering to face down an angry mob of humans.

When he continued speaking, I was even more shocked. 'Once we've sorted out the magic and sent it to the well,' he said, 'Artemesia and I will go to Rubus and do whatever we can to keep him in place. He keeps turning up at the worst moments. You can't afford for him to interrupt the meeting with Liung as well.'

I gazed at him. From dodgy hotel manager to potential hero of the hour. That was my influence. I'd rubbed off on him and now he was almost as wonderful as I was. Either that or he was just good in an emergency.

Monroe frowned. 'I have no problem with facing down Rubus again. We were taken by surprise last time but that won't happen again.'

'He's got magic and he's not afraid to use it,' I reminded him.

'Big deal. We are wolves. We're not scared of him.'

Much as I appreciated some overblown bravado, I hoped those words wouldn't come back to bite him on the arse. 'Just so long as you don't leap in and claim all the glory for yourselves,' I said. 'We are the ones who've done all the hard work.'

Monroe winked at me. 'I wouldn't dream of it, darling.'

'We'll all escort you to the Arndale Centre,' Morgan said, ignoring us both. 'Then we'll meet Liung and rid ourselves of the sphere once and for all.'

I rubbed my palms together. 'Sounds like a plan.' Then, because I wanted to prove that I was in this with Morgan and that the sexy Scottish werewolf was merely an aside, I leaned over and kissed my man heartily. Mmmm. Amnesia or not, one thing I'd certainly not forgotten was how to snog.

Before I spontaneously orgasmed in front of everyone, I pulled back and glanced at Artemesia. 'One other thing,' I said. 'Liung said that the cure to my, uh, memory issues, involved something called hmmbongo and avocado.'

She started. 'Mbongo?'

I shrugged. 'If you say so.'

Artemesia's eyes gleamed. 'That could actually work.' She jumped to her feet, darted to some nearby shelves and began rummaging. 'Here!' She pulled out a jar of something that looked like shrivelled penises. Ick. Then she grimaced. 'I don't have any avocado seeds.'

'You've got hmmbongo but you don't have avocado?'

She tapped her mouth. 'Maybe I can pick some up when we're at the Arndale Centre.' She looked at me. 'I think the wily old dragon might be onto something.'

I swallowed, hoping I didn't look as nervous as I felt. Once my memory returned – *if* my memory returned – I'd be forced to face all the facets of my personality and my past, regardless of what warts both might contain. I could do it, though; if I could beat Rubus, I could beat myself. I nodded awkwardly at her and stood up.

As soon as I did so, there was an odd trumpeting sound. I spread out my arms. 'Look! Even the angels are singing a chorus for me!' I beamed.

'Darling,' Julie said, her voice barely a whisper, 'I think that came from outside.'

We exchanged glances. Morgan got to the door first, hauling it open and peering out. 'Wow,' he whispered.

I nudged him aside and gazed out. When I saw what had made the noise, my mouth fell open and I clapped my hands in delight.

Jodie blinked. 'Is that a pink elephant?'

I beamed. 'It is! Not just slightly pink either. Or that sickly baby pink. That creature,' I said, as the elephant trundled past, its trunk and tail swinging, 'is proper pink.' It was also bloody massive.

Tempting as it was to rush out and greet it properly, I decided that getting trampled wasn't on today's agenda. All the same... 'It's a sign,' I declared. 'We will emerge from this day fully victorious.'

Morgan took my hand in his. 'Let's hope so,' he murmured. 'Let's certainly hope so.'

Chapter Twenty

I twitched more than once. In fact, my left eyelid was ticking and twitching so rapidly and so often that I was beginning to think I had a parasite in my eyeball. Morgan pocketed the shell and gave me a brief smile. 'That was Artemesia. The old wishing well worked a treat.'

I wished that made me relax. If anything, my eyelid flickered even more furiously. I tried to smile but it was more like a grimace.

Registering my nerves, Morgan took my hand and squeezed it reassuringly. 'One problem at a time. Julie is fine, despite the best efforts of Rubus to burn her alive. Artemesia has solved the issue of the magical build-up. I can't feel the prickle across my skin any more, so she must have been successful with the ancient wishing well. There's no sign of Rubus. The magical sphere is by far the largest problem but in thirty minutes we won't have to worry about it any more.'

'Assuming Liung really is trustworthy, does what he said and destroys it,' I said.

'For all his gruffness, he seems trustworthy enough.'

I had to agree but I couldn't deny the sense of

foreboding that was burgeoning deep inside me. I curled my fingers tighter round Morgan's. 'I feel sick,' I admitted.

He nodded. 'Me too.'

'And my chest hurts.'

'We're at Castlefield. This is the main border crossing back to Mag Mell. The closer we are, the more the pangs of homesickness kick in.'

I growled. 'Liung chose the spot for the meeting to taunt us. By handing him the sphere we might be saving the world but we could also be consigning ourselves to an eternity here.' I sighed. 'I might not remember Mag Mell but I do understand the ache. I feel it. It's growing. Suffocating me. And it's all my fault.'

'You weren't to know that the borders would remain closed. You had good intentions when you used your magic to shut them. You wanted us faeries to recognise that our visits were potentially harmful and that we didn't belong in this demesne,' he reminded me gently. 'You didn't mean all this to happen.'

I sniffed. 'We don't know that for sure. Maybe this is exactly what I was aiming for.'

He smiled. 'No. I know you.'

'I'm an evil bitch.'

'You pretend to be. But you're not.' He leaned in. 'And soon you'll be the person who saved this entire world from destruction.'

Well, me and Morgan and Liung and Finn and Artemesia and Julie and Jodie and... Okay.

Mostly me, though. 'I suppose,' I said, 'I did achieve what I set out to do. I did prove that faeries shouldn't be here. Go me.'

'Go you indeed.' His shoulders tensed and he lifted his chin. 'The others are back.'

I followed his gaze and spotted the small group wending their way towards us. I waved.

'The werewolves are in place,' Finn reported.

Jodie still appeared rather star struck. 'Monroe has the pack organised. He'll make sure there are no interruptions.'

'Great. And I have to say I'm thrilled that you made it to join us for this,' I chirped. 'You're all going to be witness to my brilliance at saving the world!'

Jodie looked irritated. 'Does she have to be here?' she asked Morgan.

I answered for him. 'I'm the heroine in this storyline.'

'You are the one who started all these problems.'

I shrugged. 'So I'm the villain too.' I grinned. 'I guess it's all about me.' Despite my flippancy, I felt a small part of my uneasiness slide away. I was indeed both – and it was indeed possible to be both. I met her eyes, for once with perfect sincerity. 'We all have a touch of villainy inside us. We're all selfish beings who make mistakes. But if we can right those mistakes and work towards making more of ourselves and being better people, we've already succeeded.'

Jodie stared at me then at Morgan. 'I can't believe I'm listening to a lecture on morality from Madrona the Madhatter,' she muttered.

Finn cleared his throat. 'Can we get to the point? Is he here yet?'

We all knew who he was referring to. Morgan and I shook our heads. 'No sign of Liung yet,' Morgan said.

'What do we do if he doesn't show?'

I shrugged. I'd happily show Morgan that I was feeling nervous but I wouldn't show anyone else. 'I'll take the sphere to the deepest, darkest ocean and drop it in.'

'We should have done that in the beginning, darlings,' Julie said. She fluttered her hands. It was good to see that she was almost back on form. There was even some healthy colour in her cheeks.

'Too many variables,' Morgan grunted. 'Like getting to the ocean without Rubus stopping us.'

'Speaking of your darling brother, have we had any word?'

Morgan's expression was grim and I noted him touch his sling briefly as if to remind himself of what his brother was capable of. 'Nothing. I spoke to Begonius ten minutes ago. It appears that Rubus is tucked up for the night. Monroe and his wolves will probably have a quiet time.'

'Timmons,' I said softly. 'Not Begonius. He prefers to be known by his human name.'

Morgan squeezed my hand reassuringly. 'Timmons,' he agreed, with a gentle glint in his eye.

'You're more kind-hearted than you realise for remembering that.'

It was only a name; it wasn't rocket science.

'You'd be surprised,' Morgan continued, 'how many people don't listen or pay attention to small details like that.'

'Many people aren't me.'

He chuckled. 'That is very true.'

I was no longer convinced I was being complimented. Perhaps it wasn't wise to pursue this line of conversation for too long.

I checked my watch. It was almost time. 'He should be here by now.' I craned my neck, scanning the Roman fort and the grassy banks. 'Can anyone see Liung?'

Finn and Jodie scanned the area while Morgan pursed his lips. Julie reached into her coat pocket and drew out a delicate silver hip flask. She took a sip and smacked her lips. 'Fortification, darling,' she murmured. I could tell from the scent rising into the air that it wasn't gin and, when she tucked the flask away, her lips were faintly stained with red.

'I can't see him anywhere,' Finn admitted, still pretending to search around so that he didn't have to notice what Julie had been doing.

Morgan continued to frown. 'Can you hear that?' he asked.

'I can't hear anything,' I started to say. Except then I did.

There was an odd thrumming sound in the

air, as if the distant clouds were beating. It got louder and louder. I spun in the direction it was coming from. From over the horizon, behind a copse of old oak trees, a speck appeared in the sky.

Jodie's mouth fell open. 'That's...'

The speck grew closer. And bigger. 'A dragon,' I breathed.

We watched as the shape, growing more massive by the second, flapped towards us. He was the size of house and dark red in colour. Oddly, his features were still similar to Liung's human face.

'You know,' I said, as he circled over our heads, 'none of the storybooks or films ever said much about a dragon's genitalia. It does rather ... hang down unpleasantly, doesn't it? Not to mention that, proportionally speaking, I ain't all that impressed.'

Julie tilted her head backwards to get a better look. She'd regret it. 'I see what you mean.'

Liung opened his mouth and roared, rather pointlessly in my opinion. He somersaulted before landing directly in front of us, his massive claws slamming into the earth and raking up great clods of mud. Now he was just showing off.

He stretched out his neck. He widened his jaws in our direction, and snapped for effect. Then, before our eyes, his body transformed. With a crunch of bones and heaving scales, he shrank into the wrinkly and flabby form of an old pensioner who'd seen better days.

Unperturbed by his nudity, he stretched his

arms wide. 'I am dragon!' he bellowed. 'Hear me roar!'

I rolled my eyes. 'Yeah, yeah.'

Morgan nudged me. 'Jealous?' he asked with a mischievous glint that didn't often light his eyes.

'Are you kidding me? I would totally rock being a dragon. I'd be far better at it than that old codger.'

Liung paused long enough to glare at me. 'There's only room in this city for one dragon and that it is me!'

I tsked. 'Whatever. I'm the only person around here with a proper nickname. That makes me the best, whether you can flap your dry, scaly wings and breathe fire or not.'

Liung's smile grew. 'I've been thinking about that. What do you think of Liung the Lawless?'

My lip curled. He shrugged. 'Liung the Lucky? The Lovable Lurker? The Lively Lark?'

I snapped my fingers. 'I've got the perfect one. The Lugubrious Lugworm.'

Liung frowned. 'Too long.'

I opened my mouth to make another helpful suggestion but Morgan beat me to it. 'I take it that the fact you flew here as a dragon means that the magic hasn't left your system, even if it has left the atmosphere?'

'You take it right indeed, sir!' Liung sang. As much as it galled me, I had to admit that he suited his newfound skills. He seemed far happier and more light-hearted. 'If anything,' he continued, 'I'm feeling more powerful, not less.' He cracked his knuckles and started stretching his legs as if he were limbering up for some sort of bizarre naked marathon. 'There's virtually nothing I can't do.'

'Except put on clothes,' I muttered.

Liung shook his groin in a most unappealing manner. 'Modesty is for fools. If you've got it, flaunt it.'

I shrugged. 'If you insist.' I started to pull my T-shirt over my head. It was only Morgan's arm reaching across me that stopped me.

'Let's stick to the point, shall we?' He cleared his throat. 'You're here, Liung. We have the sphere. Will you stand by your promise to destroy it?'

The old man gave him a long look. 'Why else would I be here? Pass the thing over.'

Morgan resisted. 'We need you to do it now. We have to know that it's gone for good.'

'Yes, yes,' Liung said impatiently. 'That's fine. I'll get rid of Chen's dratted thing in a jiffy. Just get it out.'

Morgan nodded. Without saying a word, Finn and Jodie flanked Liung. Julie stayed where she was, an oddly lascivious look on her face as she watched the old dragon. Her eyes kept drifting towards his jugular. To be fair, I couldn't help wondering myself whether dragon blood would taste the same as Fey or human blood – and I barely had any tastebuds to speak of.

Liung stiffened. 'Do you think I'm about to run away with it?' he enquired.

I thought of how Rubus had fooled us by creating a glamoured version of an old dragon. 'We can't afford to take any chances,' I said. I dusted off my palms and made a show of rolling up my non-existent sleeves, as if to prove that I was here for more than just tit-for-tat with the creepy old arsebadger.

'I gave my word,' Liung growled. 'What more do you want?'

'We just want the sphere destroyed,' Morgan replied.

Finn and Jodie edged closer to Liung, Jodie's hand straying to her hip where her knife hung. Her fingers twitched and I could feel her anxiety. My left eyelid was flickering even more intensely. Another few minutes, I told myself. Another few minutes and all this would be over.

Morgan kept his gaze on Liung while I put my fingers in my pocket and drew out the sphere. It was cool to the touch, despite my body heat warming it for some time. I rolled it around my fingers; all this trouble for such a small thing.

I lifted my eyes up to Liung's, noting his covetous gleam. For a moment, I almost changed my mind and took a step back – but we had to do this. Part of Liung wanted to own the thing for himself and bind it to him like his other daft objects and dragon paraphernalia, but that didn't mean he wouldn't get rid of it for us. In fact, the way that he wasn't masking his feelings about the sphere gave me more hope that this would end the way we needed it to. At least he was being honest about his desire to own it; if he'd been blasé, I'd have suspected his intentions far more.

I took a deep breath and held it out. Liung lunged towards it and I snatched it back in the nick of time. 'Tell me,' I said. 'Exactly how will you destroy it?'

He ground his teeth in frustration. 'Under ordinary circumstances,' he said, 'I would have to take it away and spend several days crushing it. The magic imbued in that little thing is powerful. Once I extinguished the invisible power, I could melt it with ordinary fire.'

He smiled, displaying his yellow teeth. 'However, all your little faery spells have caused such havoc in our fair city that I can actually get rid of the sphere far more quickly. Now that I can transform into a real dragon, and have more power at my own disposal, all I have to do is breathe fire onto it for a few seconds and I suspect both the sphere and the magic linked to it will be obliterated for good.'

I raised my eyebrows. 'Wow. I know you have appalling halitosis but that's some feat.'

Liung's eyes narrowed. 'Don't push it, girly, or I might change my mind.'

The more time I spent looking at him, the more I knew that Liung was prepared to do everything necessary to vanquish the arsebadgering sphere, regardless of what he said. He really did love Manchester. He certainly spoke about it enough. He didn't want to risk his beloved city, let alone the rest of the world. His bluster was the same as mine; it concealed his worry about what disastrous potential the little metal ball held within its smooth exterior.

I held it out again. This time, when Liung reached for it I let him take it. Perhaps there was something to be said for Liung's nudity, after all. His body language was certainly easy to read. Although the light in his expression suggested there was still a part of him that wanted to keep the sphere, the tension in his body suggested that he also wanted to be rid of it as quickly as possible. It was a painful dichotomy – to want something so badly but to know that it was bad. I felt the same about greasy kebabs.

Liung inhaled deeply, raising the sphere to his nostrils before examining it carefully. 'It truly is a work of art,' he said softly. 'It's supposed to be impossible to create a perfect sphere that is symmetrical down to the last nanometre but Chen did it.' The dragon shook his head in amazement. 'He excelled himself. Such a shame that an object of beauty can be so destructive.'

I flicked a quick look at Morgan, who was very still and staring at Liung as if he were ready to snatch the sphere back at a moment's notice. 'Is he talking about the sphere now?' I asked. 'Or about me?'

Jodie sighed in exasperation but my words did the trick. As if by common consent, everyone relaxed slightly. Julie giggled and even Finn, towering over Liung with his hulking frame, dropped his shoulders and his deeply etched frown smoothed over. Liung appeared vaguely amused; he abandoned his perusal of the sphere and dropped his hand to his side.

'Do you need to transform back into a dragon to breathe enough fire to destroy it?' Morgan asked.

'I don't know,' Liung answered honestly. 'I'll try as I am now and then transform if I need to.' He dropped his eyes and a melancholy sadness crossed his face as he gazed at the sphere for one last time. Then he drew in a breath.

A loud crack ripped through the air. At first I thought it was part of Liung's act but when I saw the confused expression on his face, I realised I was mistaken. A dribble of blood left his lips and trailed down his chin. The sphere dropped from his hands and rolled on the ground as he fell forward into Morgan's arms. As he collapsed, I saw the massive wound on his naked back. As if they were tied together, Julie and Jodie spun round to see where it had come from.

'Grab the sphere and get out of here!' I yelled to them. 'I'll get this!' I shoved them away and strode forward.

Finn sent Julie a terrified glance as she scooped up the sphere. 'Run! Both of you!' Then he squared his shoulders and joined me. All for one and one for all. Or something. Julie and Jodie had better run damned fast though.

Rubus appeared from out of the darkness on the other side of the Roman fort. I could see a gun held lightly in one of his hands; he was dragging a bloodstained and barely conscious Monroe with the other.

'Well, hello there,' he drawled. 'Fancy seeing you lot here. We must stop meeting like this.'

Chapter Twenty-One

Rubus laughed, a long and slow sound filled with grating, smug self-satisfaction. 'What?' he called. 'You didn't really think those faeries you sent to watch me were going to get in my way, did you?' He shook Monroe. 'Or this fool of a werewolf and his pack?'

Morgan let Liung's naked body fall to the ground. His face was white with both the pain from his broken arm and shock at Rubus's untimely appearance. 'If you have killed either Artemesia or Begonius, I'll —'

'You'll what?' his brother sneered. 'Run away like you did when I ended Viburna?' He snorted derisively. 'You can't do a thing. Artemesia is fine. She has skills that I need and I don't want her to get hurt. Her Uncle Carduus doesn't have her extensive knowledge and, despite his loyalty, I want more. As for Begonius, or Timmons as he stupidly insists on being known, he's out for the count. All it took was a little force-feeding of pixie dust.'

Rubus grinned manically. 'I'm not a complete despot. I won't kill people if I can use them – and sooner or later I'll be able to use Begonius as I wish. When I get him and the rest of us back to Mag Mell, he'll swear blind that I did well by him. He'll be too high on dust for anything else. He'll see the truth, just like everyone else. He'll recognise that I'm trying to help us, that I'm trying to get us back home. You're the one who wants us to suffer.'

'What about the werewolves?' I asked.

Rubus shrugged. 'The dogs are dead.' He sniffed at Monroe, releasing him so that he crumpled into a heap. 'Apart from this one. I thought I might keep him as a pet. To be honest,' he said, as if confiding a secret, 'I was expecting more from their kind. I thought they'd put more of a fight. They're almost easier to slaughter than Redcaps.' He winked at Finn. 'Blades slide into Redcap flesh remarkably easily.'

There was a sudden howl of anguish as Finn flung himself from behind us and launched himself towards Rubus. I leapt forward to try and help him – or at least to save him from getting shot point-blank in the head.

I wasn't fast enough. I saw Rubus's lip curl before he raised his arm and a single jet of magic smacked Finn in the chest and he crumpled like a deck of cards.

Morgan snarled, rushing forward until he was barely a metre past me. His fists clenched and I could see the veins on his neck bulging as he strained to attack his brother. It wasn't going to do any good; the truce still held for Morgan just like it held for me. Rubus could slaughter every single one of us and we wouldn't be able to so much as scratch him back.

'So full of rage,' Rubus murmured. 'I keep telling you, Morganus, it doesn't have to be like this. All I'm trying to do is get us back home.' He shook his head in mock sadness. 'I just want us all to be safe in Mag Mell and you seem determined to continue torturing us and forcing to stay here.' He sighed. 'Look at how much you're hurting right now. I don't have to hit you for you to feel pain. You're already hurting yourself.'

He took a step towards Morgan. My heart hammering against my ribcage, I bellowed and jumped in front of him so that I would take the blow.

'Why are you with him?' Rubus asked me. 'I can give you so much more, Madrona.' He dropped his eyes, sliding them with nausea-inducing lust across my body. It was all for show; he only acted like he wanted me in order to piss off Morgan.

Morgan didn't know that, though. He growled and stepped out from behind me. 'Leave her alone, Rubus. This is between you and I.'

'Morganus,' Rubus tutted. 'Oh Morganus. You're my brother. I'm sorry I hurt you before. I promise I won't lift another hand against you. But if you insist on getting in my way at every turn then I will destroy everything that you care about.' He smiled at me. 'And that means her.'

Morgan's nostrils flared. I didn't think I'd ever seen such fury reflected in the depths of his emerald eyes. If only looks could kill.

'Where is the sphere, Morganus?' Rubus said. He raised one hand and pointed it at my chest. 'Tell me where it is or the Madhatter gets it.'

We'd been in this situation before but on that occasion the roles were reversed and I'd refused to hand over the sphere to help Morgan. I could only pray that he would refuse now. I resisted the urge to glance back, trusting that Jodie and Julie had the sphere safe and were already skedaddling back into the bowels of the city with it.

I breathed deeply, forcing myself to stay calm and think things through. Brute force was not going to win the day; we had to be smarter than Rubus. I played for time until the answer struck me.

'Your heart is crammed with skid-marked underpants, Rubus,' I said, shaking my head with deep sadness. 'Your soul is stained with faeces. Not the healthy kind, either. I'm talking about the sort of half-runny, half-solid crud that includes random bits of sweetcorn and the smear of rectal blood.'

Rubus gazed at me. 'You're actually a masochist,' he said. 'Forget the Madhatter part. There's nothing more to you than the desire to inflict pain upon yourself. I should have realised that sooner. No wonder you spent so much time with me when all you ever wanted was to be with *him*.' His voice dripped with disdain. 'Morganus the saintly do-gooder. You could have been my queen. Instead you'll be nothing more than a footnote in history.'

I raised my hand towards Morgan and

pressed my fingers against his forearm with just enough pressure to warn him to back off. I had this. I was the Madhatter, no matter what Rubus snorted to the contrary.

Monroe let out a tiny moan. It was barely audible, even to my Fey ears, but it gave me the ammunition I needed.

'You're alone,' I said.

Rubus glared at me. 'So?'

'This is supposed to be your moment of glory, Rubus. This is when you snatch the sphere and use it to free every faery from a lifetime of greasy kebabs, daytime television and Uber taxis. But no one is here to witness your triumph Given your past performances, that's not the way you work.' I scanned the horizon behind him. 'Monroe and his wolves got you, didn't they? You might have been victorious in the end but I bet my freckles that all your lieutenants are either bleeding out or already dead. You don't have anyone left to take back to Mag Mell, do you?'

Something flashed across Rubus's face. It was brief but I was too smart to miss it. 'I'm their keeper,' he shot back. 'I'm keeping them safe. They're back at the hide-out, snug as bugs and safe as houses.'

I raised an amused eyebrow. 'Are they? I reckon you're telling porkies. Big ones. I wonder what the faeries in Mag Mell will say when you're the only one to return. Will you be feted as a hero then?'

Beneath my fingers, I felt Morgan's muscles relax slightly. 'Maddy's right,' he chimed in. 'One of the elders will perform a Truth Draw, which you won't be able to resist. When it's discovered that you've killed our own, as well as countless others from other species, you'll be thrown in the darkest dungeon. You'll be vilified. The footnote in history will be you. And you won't be a martyr like Viburna, you'll be the monster that's used to scare children.' He smirked. 'You're no saviour, Rubus. You never were.'

I stared hard at Rubus. He was growing angrier by the second and the glint of madness in his eyes was becoming more visible. 'There are plenty of people here!' he yelled. 'I'm holding them back until my glory is assured! I'm going to save them all! I'm going to return us to Mag Mell. You … you…'

His voice faltered as he lost all semblance of rationality. His cheeks were flushed scarlet and his fists were tightly clenched. His chest rose and fell rapidly with his erratic breathing.

I barely managed to hold my ground. We were no longer facing Rubus; the creature in front of us was more like an enraged animal on the verge of extinction. And yet he still retained the upper hand. He could still hurt us.

Rubus waved his arms around. 'Come out!' he shouted. 'I command you all to come out and face the bastards who don't want you to return home!'

We all glanced over but when I saw who emerged from the ruins of the old Roman fort, and realised my guess about Rubus's troops had been correct, I felt only sadness. There was no triumph to be gained from watching the limping, blood-soaked, raggle-taggle group that hobbled towards us.

I didn't know how many Fey had been working with Rubus but there were very few of them left. No wonder they'd not appeared until now. Most were limping. All of them were covered in blood.

I cast a quick glance at Monroe. He might have suffered a catastrophic defeat but he and his werewolves hadn't gone down without a fight. I mentally applauded what he'd achieved, although with very little enthusiasm.

Rubus didn't appear to notice the sorry state of his clan. He waved an exultant hand. 'See? I have more Fey on my side than you have on yours.'

I scanned the group. 'Where's Carduus?' Then I realised I already knew the answer. It was the real reason why Artemesia hadn't been killed; Rubus needed her because Carduus hadn't made it. Maybe it was Monroe in front of Charley's house, or maybe it was the locusts. It didn't really matter. Carduus was one Fey whose passing I wouldn't mourn.

'Carduus is fine,' Rubus snapped. He held out his palm. 'Now. Give me the sphere.'

'It's not happening,' Morgan answered.

Rubus bared his teeth. 'I was hoping you'd

say that.' Without warning, he pointed and threw out magic in my direction. I spun, using my shoulder to block the worst of the blow, but it still knocked me off my feet.

Morgan let out a strangled cry. I opened my mouth to tell him I was okay and realised, rather belatedly, that I couldn't speak. I couldn't move either. I was face down in the dirt and totally paralysed. Strangely, I couldn't feel any pain – but somehow I didn't think that was a good thing.

'I'm going to kill you,' I dimly heard Morgan say to Rubus over my head. He was very angry. That was nice.

'You know you can't,' Rubus responded serenely. 'She's not dead, though. She still has a chance. Whether she gets it or not is up to you.'

'I—'

Whatever Morgan was about to say was interrupted. There was a calm shout from behind us. If I could have, I would have frowned. What was Julie doing? She should have been long gone by now.

'Let Mads be,' she called out. 'I have what you want.'

She was bluffing and she was doing a damned good job. I felt a twinge of smug delight. It was a good thing the actress was on our side and not on Rubus's.

'I knew you'd come through and do the right thing.' There was a smile in Rubus's voice.

That wasn't right. I struggled to move, every

atom of my body straining. I managed to wiggle my little toe. That was hardly going to cut it.

'Stop her!' Jodie's voice screamed. 'She's got it. She's going to...' Her words faltered mid-sentence and there was a dull thud. I clenched my jaw and tried to move. What was happening? What was going on?

'Julie,' Morgan cried, anguished. 'What are you doing?'

'What I should have done all along.' Her voice sounded very close, as if she were hovering over me. My last flicker of confidence in my soap-star friend started to ebb. Surely not? Surely she wouldn't betray us? She'd be killing herself and destroying her own demesne.

I strained to move again. Were my muscles returning to life or did I just need to pee? It was hard to tell.

Rubus spoke again. 'Thank you, Julie.'

There was the sound of a scuffle, followed by a loud oomph of pain. 'Don't!'

It was the horror in Morgan's voice that gave me the impetus I needed to turn my head so I could see what was going on. I still didn't have enough control over my limbs to save the day but I was able to focus for long enough to spot Julie passing the arsebadgering sphere into Rubus's waiting palms.

No.

Dread filled me. What was she doing? This was crazy. I was supposed to be the mad one but it was starting to seem as if I were the only person who was sane.

Morgan stared at Julie in horror. 'Why?' he whispered.

She didn't look even slightly guilty. 'You have no idea what it's like,' she said. Her bottom lip trembled but her voice was firm. 'To be afraid all the time. Not to know who's going to come round the corner and attack you for who you are. I have no control over my vampirism. The only reward I have is that I get to live forever – assuming I'm not killed by a bunch of vampire hunters.'

I wet my lips. I was regaining control of my facial muscles if nothing else. When I spoke, however, it was little more than a hoarse whisper. 'But we took care of the hunters. You're safe.'

Julie shook her head. 'One came at me only a few hours ago. It was only by luck that I survived. My house has been burnt down. My *sanctuary*, Mads!'

'That was Dave.' I tried clearing my throat but it didn't make my words any louder. 'He worked for Rubus, for gasbudlikins' sake.'

A brief tremor of doubt shivered across her and I felt hope flare. Then she squared her shoulders and her resolve appeared to stiffen. 'He was proving a point. As long as this demesne remains as it is, I'm in danger. The magic build-up, which was created by *your* loss of control and *your* spells, showed me what my potential is. It showed me that I don't have to be weak, I don't have to live every minute of every day in fear, downing gin and tonic by the bucket just to get through. With magic flooding this world, I can finally win.'

'At the expense of billions of lives,' Morgan pointed out.

'It's not my job to worry about the world,' Julie said. 'It's my job to worry about me. I can't take this life any longer.'

'You might not survive the transition.'

She smiled. 'Oh, I think I'll manage.'

Rubus was dancing from foot to foot, almost beside himself with glee. 'Protest all you want, brother dear. The sphere is mine.' He reached for it, ready to grab it from Julie's outstretched hand.

Morgan threw himself forward, lunging to get to the sphere first. Julie snapped her jaws and I realised for the first time just how sharp her teeth had become. She tore at the flesh on Morgan's hand with her incisors and blood spurted everywhere.

I strained again, doing everything I could to move, but my limbs were leaden. No matter how hard I tried, I wasn't going anywhere.

It was over very quickly. Rubus rounded on Morgan and slammed his fist into his nose. There was a sickening crunch of bone, then Rubus pulled back and held the sphere triumphantly aloft. 'I have it!' he crowed. 'I finally have it!'

There was a murmur from Rubus's few remaining followers then one of them elbowed her way through. Lunaria looked even paler than usual, apart from two high spots of colour on her cheeks. When I saw the expression in her eyes, I swallowed.

The madness reflected there was even more obvious than the craziness in Rubus's emerald depths.

I licked my lips. 'Morgan,' I croaked. I swung my gaze round, searching desperately for him. He was curled up into a foetal position, with Rubus's foot resting on his hip as if he'd just bagged himself some prey. I could hear Morgan's ragged and uneven breathing. He wasn't dead but he wasn't going to be any help.

My fingers twitched as life stirred in my body. I gulped in air and continued to strain while Lunaria strode forward. Just as the numbness in my legs began to dissipate, she drew out a long, curved dagger. It was already stained with blood.

Rubus, finally sensing her approach, turned. 'Ah, you're there,' he said. 'That's good. You can be by my side when I use the sphere. When we finally get back home to where we belong.' He smiled, savouring his triumph.

Lunaria raised the dagger aloft, holding it high over her head.

'Darling,' Rubus drawled, 'I told you. I don't want my brother dead. Anyway, you can't kill him because the truce still holds.'

The crazed light in Lunaria's eyes intensified. 'I have to help you,' she muttered. 'You need help.'

'I'm perfectly capable of managing without you.' Rubus grinned at the sphere, its smooth metal surface gleaming in the dull moonlight. 'I have everything I need right here.'

I pushed myself up to a sitting position.

Lunaria didn't glance in my direction.

The only other person who seemed to appreciate what the lovesick Fey was planning was Julie. 'Wait,' she began. 'I think…'

Her words were drowned by the inarticulate sob that ripped from Lunaria's mouth. She sprang forward, bringing the dagger down with heavy force onto Rubus's exposed chest. His glee was replaced with an expression of surprise.

'What?' he asked. 'What just happened?'

A moment later, he keeled over on top of Morgan, his fingers curling round the sphere as he fell. Even in his death throes, he couldn't let go of it. Lunaria's dagger was buried in the centre of his chest, right up to its hilt.

The air around us froze. Lunaria seemed astonished by what she'd done. She fell to her knees beside Rubus and stroked his hair. 'It was for you,' she murmured. 'It was all for you.'

Julie, whose face had been a blank mask of shock, started to shriek. 'You stupid bitch!' she yelled. 'What have you done?' She lunged forward, scrabbling around Rubus's fallen body to get to the sphere.

I staggered to my feet, swaying and unsteady. I took a step forward and stumbled, while Julie prised Rubus's fingers away from the sphere, peeling them off one by one until the object was returned to her own grasp.

'What do I do?' she shouted. 'How do I make it work?'

Rubus didn't answer. It didn't take a genius of my proportions to realise that he would never answer anyone again, even though Lunaria pulled his head into her lap and continued to coo at him.

Julie swivelled and kicked his leg. 'Rubus!' she screamed. 'How do I get it to work?'

I moved slowly towards her. I couldn't hurt Rubus but I could hurt Julie. Whether she was my friend or not, and whether she was having a temporary bout of insanity or not, I'd kill her if it prevented her from using the sphere and flooding this demesne with magic. I threw my arms out and grabbed her wrists in a bid to yank her towards me.

She pulled away. 'Fuck off, Madrona! I have to do this!'

I shook my head. 'No, you don't. You know what will happen to this world – your world – if you do.'

'I don't care!' But she was shaking her head as she spoke.

'You do care. Using that arsebadgering sphere will kill every human on this planet and probably kill you too. Magic doesn't belong here. You know that.'

Julie's eyes held mine. 'But I can feel it inside me. I can feel it surging through my blood. The power, Mads. It's like nothing I've ever felt before.'

'That doesn't make it right.' I held out my palm. 'Give me the sphere, Julie.'

A single tear rolled down her cheek. 'I'm just so tired of being afraid all the time. I don't just act on set, I act every single minute of every day. Why the hell do you think I drink so much? It's the only way I can cope. With this little sphere, I can make those feelings go away.'

I kept my own gaze steady. 'You'll make every feeling go away, Julie. You'll make everyone go away. For good. I understand you feel like shit but this isn't the answer.'

Her voice dropped to a whisper. 'Rubus said it would be fine.'

'Rubus was a psychotic maniac who didn't care about anyone or anything other than his own glory. Give me the sphere. It doesn't have to be like this.'

From the ground, Morgan let out a soft moan and my heart wrenched. He moved slightly. With one eye on Julie, I stepped over and helped him up.

'Maddy's right,' he whispered. 'This isn't the way. You're not going to solve any problems by using the sphere. We'll find another way to help you and make you strong so you don't have to be afraid. Destroying your own world won't help anyone.'

Julie choked. For the first time, it seemed as if the layers were peeling away and the real Julie was being exposed. She wasn't a glamorous actress or an all-powerful vampire, she was just scared. Gasbudlikins. She wasn't the only one.

I didn't waste a second. Taking full advantage of her wavering, I leapt forward. I'd over-estimated my own recovery from Rubus's magic bolt, however, and ended up colliding with her. Both of us crashed to the ground, narrowly avoiding landing on Rubus and Lunaria.

Sprawled underneath me, Julie yelped loudly.

'Sorry!' I rolled off her. 'I wasn't trying to hurt you! I just wanted to get the sphere...' My voice trailed off as Julie kicked the sphere away.

It was glowing. Blue light bounced off of it, casting a tremendous haze into the air.

'I didn't do anything,' she stammered. 'I didn't set it off. I didn't mean to! Stop it, Mads. You have to do something!'

I shielded my eyes and sprang towards it. Morgan did the same but I pushed him back. Feeling the sphere burn through the skin on my fingers, I grabbed it and covered it. 'Stop!' I yelled at it. 'Stop that!'

Unfortunately, the magic paid me no attention. Despite my attempts to cover it, the light increased. Even Lunaria paused in ministering to Rubus's corpse to stare, while his bedraggled group of blood-soaked minions gaped.

'We're going home,' one of them whispered.

Not if I had anything to do with it. 'Tell me what to do!' I shouted, rounding on Morgan.

He shook his head, growing horror in his eyes. 'I don't know! I don't know how to stop it!'

'Destroy it,' whispered Monroe, from where he lay on the ground. 'Stamp on it. Use your own magic. Just do something.'

He was right. I flung the sphere to the ground before bringing my foot crashing down on top of it. Nothing happened. If anything, the freaky blue light only intensified. I raised my hands and sent a jet of magic towards it in a bid to cancel it out but again my efforts only seemed to make things worse. It was as if the entire city of Manchester was now bathed in the blue magical glow.

'Look,' Julie whispered.

I turned and followed her gaze. There, just beyond the Roman fort, a ghostly horde of people suddenly became visible. Fey: lots of them. They were just beyond the border with Mag Mell and they were watching us. Some appeared to be shouting, although their words were inaudible, and most of them were gesticulating frantically.

'What are they saying?' I screeched at Morgan.

'Destroy it. They want us to destroy the sphere.'

I rolled my eyes. 'I'm fucking trying.' I turned back and gazed in frustration at the tiny ball of chaos. Then, without thinking, I snatched it up again and swallowed it.

Morgan stared at me. 'What the hell have you done?'

I retched. That was harder than I thought it would be.

A strange heat spread through my chest and down into my stomach, like the world's worst case of indigestion. I'd already thought this would be a bad idea when I'd considered it back in the police station several days ago. Now I knew it was. I opened my mouth but no words came out. It felt as if I were burning from the inside out.

Julie's mouth dropped open. 'Your eyes are blue,' she said. 'And your fingers...'

I looked down. Blue light shone from each digit. The magic was growing; it was inside me but it was still growing and there was nothing I could to stop it. The heat was getting more and more extreme. I was going to explode.

I reached out and grabbed Morgan's hand, squeezing it tightly. 'I'm sorry,' I whispered. 'I'm so sorry.' Never had an apology been so weak or so insignificant. The world was ending and all I could do was mumble that I was sorry. Gasbudlikins.

I squeezed my eyes shut. I really was very, very sorry. The Madhatter had really fucked things up this time.

Chapter Twenty-Two

There was a lot of screaming. Of course, that was probably fitting for the end of the world but it was hurting my ears. I hoped that it would be over quickly and the people here wouldn't suffer too much.

Then Morgan leaned over and I felt his lips brush against mine. I opened my eyes and blinked. 'We're home,' he said, cupping my face in his hands. 'We're in Mag Mell.'

The screaming continued. All around us, Fey were hugging Fey. What I was hearing were not screams of fear or pain or horror, I realised rather belatedly. Quite the opposite: everyone seemed utterly delighted.

I stared at Morgan in horror. 'It's happened,' I whispered. 'The human demesne ... the world...'

An elderly Fey man pulled me from Morgan and hugged me tight. 'You did it, Madrona! I knew you would!' He squeezed me. 'You have no idea how much I've missed you. To not know how you were or what was happening...' He sniffed. 'It's been so hard.'

'I caused the apocalypse,' I mumbled into his shoulder. I didn't know who this guy was but right now I desperately needed the hug. All those people, all dead.

'No, you darling girl! You stopped it!'

Hope flared in my chest. I stepped away from him and he pointed. 'Look.'

I blinked and followed his finger. Seemingly only metres away, albeit as if I were looking at flickering shadows, I could see Castlefield. It looked exactly as we'd left it. A vast vista was displayed in front of us, the border rippling between us, but my friends visible. There was a slight blue hue, which I supposed was because we were watching from a different demesne. But nobody was dying. My eyes skimmed over each figure.

I shook my head. 'I don't understand,' I whispered. 'Did it really work then? Are they really going to be alright?'

'As you see,' Morgan said. He glanced at me with a small, relaxed smile then swept an arm across. 'Unless we're both hallucinating, the human demesne has survived – and it's all still standing.'

'The people too,' I breathed. All of them. I squinted, focusing on the shadowy shapes. 'That's Julie!' I yelled. My erstwhile friend was on the ground on all fours, a look of anguish on her face. Not far from her, Monroe was picking himself up. He staggered over to the crumpled form of Jodie and poked her. Her head turned slightly and I relaxed further. Even Finn was stirring. Morgan was right. They were suffering but they were still alive. A slow smile spread across my face. 'I saved the world.'

The elderly man smiled, his eyes crinkling at the edges. He was remarkably good looking for someone of his age. 'Indeed. The humans are still there and they're all fine. We could feel what was happening though. For the last few days we've been able to watch as well.' His smile was replaced with a flash of rage. 'So we all saw what Rubus was just doing. The shifts in power and magic over the past few days have been felt by everyone in Mag Mell. It's why we're all here. We knew something was happening with the border. I prayed it was going to re-open but I couldn't allow myself to really believe...' His voice cracked slightly and he gave himself a small shake. 'That magical thing you swallowed was about to blow. When the dust has settled, you're going to have to tell me what it was and where it came from.' He patted me on the arm. 'Don't worry though, sweetheart. You saved all those humans. You saved that entire demesne, Madrona.'

I sensed rather than saw a brief ripple of tension from Morgan. 'The blue ...' he muttered, half to himself.

The old man grimaced. 'Magic.'

I gulped. 'Magic? But that means...'

He brushed my cheek with the back of his hand. 'Some leaked out from that thing. You couldn't possibly contain it all. It doesn't appear that there's enough to seep out beyond Manchester though.'

I yanked myself away. That was *my* city. My home. 'It doesn't belong there.' My voice was rising. 'It will cause so many problems. It—'

'Normally,' the old man said, with a strangely fond expression, 'I'd have agreed with you. The human demesne shouldn't be able to cope with that level of magic. Maybe we've underestimated it all along.'

Maybe. There was a lot they wouldn't have seen from here though.

Morgan ran a hand through his hair. 'Perhaps the build-up of magic created by all those spells prepared Manchester for what was to come. The city made itself strong enough to withstand the onslaught that the sphere created. You stopped the sphere before anything worse happened.' He glanced at me, obviously trying to be reassuring.

'Definitely,' the old man said briskly. 'There's nothing to worry about. Watch them. From what I can tell, the humans are going to cope just fine.'

I didn't know who this guy was and I had no reason to trust him. I stared at Morgan, aware that panic was causing my nostrils to flare it what was probably a less than attractive expression.

Morgan understood me instantly. He reached out and took my hand. 'I think it's true,' he said. 'Manchester will never be the same again – you can see that from the very visible magic in the atmosphere. But it's been contained. *You* contained it. By swallowing the sphere, you prevented the magic from leaking out further. The humans in

Manchester – and the vampires, werewolves and the rest – will be okay. Their lives will be changed but they will survive and they can leave if they wish. The rest of the world is going to be fine. If the apocalypse had been going to happen it would have already.'

The old man sent me an anxious look. 'Believe me, since the day you left, I've been here almost every morning trying to find a way through to help you get home. I had to get you back. I've missed you so much. An hour ago...' He choked slightly. 'An hour ago when I felt the borders start to weaken further, I knew it was going to be fine. I knew you'd find a way. You always do.' He leaned forward and kissed my forehead. 'You're amazing.' Inexplicably, he then wiped away a tear.

I stared at him. He obviously did know me rather well. After all, I really *was* amazing. 'Who are you?' I inquired.

He laughed and hugged me again, even tighter than before. Over his shoulder I gazed at Morgan in confusion.

'Father,' he mouthed.

I pulled back. Huh. No wonder he was so stately and good looking. And pleased to see me. A million questions sprang to my mind but instead I shook myself. Family reunions were all well and good but I had to get back; I had to be in Manchester. The people there needed me.

'How do we get back there?' I asked. 'I have to help them. If there's magic all across the city then…'

The man who was apparently Daddy Dearest shook his head. 'You can't. The borders are closed for good now. The magic surge caused by the sphere opened them just long enough for all the trapped Fey to return. But they won't open again. You're all back here for good.'

I swallowed, my stomach dropping. 'But…' I briefly squeezed my eyes shut. No. No matter how much I wanted to be there, I didn't belong in that demesne. No faeries did. The problems our presence had caused would have repercussions for generations. I dragged my gaze across the forlorn band of people across the border, feeling sick. In effect they were struggling because of me. They might be alive but they'd still almost died because of me.

Morgan growled under his breath. 'Stop it.'

I jumped. 'Stop what?'

He turned to me, his green eyes holding mine. 'All of us were there. What happened in Manchester is on all of us, not just on you. We're all to blame. We all have to shoulder the burden. You might not remember it but you used to argue until you were blue in the face that we didn't belong in that demesne and that we shouldn't visit it at all. You were right all along.'

Yeah, I had been right all along. I didn't exactly feel vindicated at the moment though – not when it had so obviously been my efforts which had hastened, if not caused, almost outright disaster.

My father – whose existence still seemed difficult to get my head around - stroked my hair. 'You've been so brave,' he murmured. 'And so good.'

'I've been a bitch.' It was the truth.

He smiled at me. 'You always were headstrong.' He dipped his head. 'I like to think of it as assertive intelligence and bracing wit.' He winked. 'Your mother would be proud.'

I was going to have to spend more time with him. He was good for my already enhanced ego. And with any luck, he'd be rich too. I smiled in vague reassurance that I wasn't about to spend the rest of my days parading around in a sack-cloth and ashes and looked around. I could see Artemesia embracing an older couple. She looked tired but otherwise alright. Paeonia was on her knees and sobbing. Other Fey I recognised were kissing the ground. Vandrake was clutching his chest in relief, the perpetual ache of faery-induced homesickness gone for good.

I realised I also felt good. There was a warmth pulsating through my veins caused not by swallowing the sphere but the by the happiness of being back home on my own soil in my own land. I blinked at Morgan who was still watching me. Perhaps for the first time I understood what it meant to be Fey. I understood just why Rubus had been so desperate to get back here.

'You promise?' I said, addressing both my father and Morgan. 'You promise they're all okay back in Manchester?'

'They will be.'

Morgan nodded. 'They might have to adapt to a new world but they'll be fine.'

Despite their assurances, I felt a sense of foreboding. I pointed across the border towards the ravaged figures of my friends. 'We still caused that. Faeries invaded their demesne, fucked it up and then left the humans to deal with the fall-out.'

Morgan's jaw tightened and I could see pain reflected in his face. 'We can't go back. The borders are sealed again. Whatever is happening back there, the humans will find a way to deal with it. They usually do.' He looked around us. 'And maybe they won't be completely alone. Not everyone is here,' he murmured. 'I don't see Bego— Timmons, I mean.'

I stiffened, my own head swinging around and searching for him. Morgan was right. There was no sign of the human-loving Fey hotel manager. I crossed my fingers tightly that he was alright. And that if he remained back with the humans, his presence wouldn't cause any more problems. I scanned the rest of the Fey crowd. I couldn't tell if anyone else was missing. What I could see, however, sitting quietly in a corner and with Rubus's head still cradled in her lap, was Lunaria.

'She killed him,' I whispered. 'She killed Rubus. How? How could she break the truce?'

Morgan smiled sadly. 'She didn't break the truce. She couldn't have.'

I watched her for a moment. 'Of course,' I

breathed. 'She was worried about Rubus and what would happen to him if his plan succeeded. She killed him in order to save him. It's a twisted logic, but to Lunaria it made perfect sense. She wasn't trying to hurt him, not deep down. That's why she was able to kill him.' I paused. 'She's going to need our help.'

Morgan lifted up his chin. 'We'll be right by her side.'

I nodded fervently. 'We owe her everything.'

'No,' he said. 'We owe you everything.'

I sniffed. Yeah, okay then. 'That goes without saying.'

With Morgan at one side of me and my father at the other, I pulled my eyes away from the strange diorama of the human world and looked around Mag Mell. Everything seemed brighter. The greens were greener; the sky was bluer. In the distance, a golden city glittered in the sunlight.

'It's beautiful here,' I said, the understatement of the century.

'We've tried so hard to bring you back and to re-open the borders,' my father said. 'Nothing worked. It was clearly a terrible malfunction.'

My eyes flew to Morgan's. Er... 'It was my fault.' I looked down awkwardly. 'Or so Rubus said. I can't actually remember.'

'Maddy's got amnesia,' Morgan interjected.

My father blinked. 'Seriously? How did that happen?'

'Long story.' I still couldn't quite look him in

the eye.

'You must remember Mag Mell,' he said.

'No.'

'You must remember me.'

'No.'

He spread his arms wide. 'Come on, Maddy. I'm your dad. Not to mention that I'm utterly unforgettable.' He spun round in a circle for effect.

Morgan leaned in to my ear. 'The apple didn't fall far from the tree.'

I tried to smile but couldn't. I had to tell the truth – the whole truth – and right now before I lost my bottle. 'I'm the one who made the borders close,' I said. 'Apparently I was trying to prove a point.' My expression soured. 'And look at what I achieved. Ten years of exile and goodness knows how many catastrophes.'

My father blinked. Then he laughed. 'Oh, Madrona, darling, you are funny!'

My eyes narrowed. 'Funny ha ha or funny strange?'

He continued to chuckle. 'Both. You wouldn't have had the power to keep the borders closed for more than a day at most. You don't have the magic to force them shut for a decade. What a thought!' He shook his head.

I put my hands on my hips. 'I've got plenty of magic!' I argued.

'Not that much,' he said, still amused. He patted my arm. 'You still have so much to learn. We don't know what made the borders close but it certainly wasn't you. All we know is that now they are closed for good.' He beamed at Morgan and me. 'It's probably not a bad thing. I'm going to check on the others. I'll be right back.' He ambled off in the direction of the nearest group hug.

'It was me,' I said stubbornly. 'I do have enough magic.'

'I know,' Morgan murmured. 'I don't think he realises quite how powerful you really are.'

'Or how foolhardy,' I added with a dark scowl.

He smiled slightly. 'It's not a point I'd continue to argue about, Maddy. Maybe it's for the best that no-one will actually think it was your fault.'

I glared at him. 'But it was. I'm going to re-vamp my Madhatter costume. When I've got my cape and mask on, people here will see that I'm not to be trifled with.'

'I can't imagine that anyone would ever think that.' He smiled and leaned in, endowing my lips with another kiss. 'Does it really matter?'

I sighed and thought about it. 'I guess not,' I muttered. 'It just ... it just doesn't seem right that things have ended this easily. That all those people are still going on with their lives back in Manchester and we're here. What's Julie going to do now? Or Jodie? How hard did Julie hit her? Is Monroe going to make it?'

Morgan took my arm and gently turned me, then pointed at the border and the flickering view of the human demesne beyond. 'We can still see them. If they come to Castlefield, they might be able to communicate.'

I watched as Jodie struggled up to her feet and began yelling and gesticulating angrily towards Julie's crumpled figure. At least I presumed she was yelling. I couldn't actually hear her. I balled my fists up in frustration. 'We can't talk to them.'

'There's always sign language,' Morgan said. 'We've got a lifetime to learn a way to communicate with them.' There was an intense expression on his face, as if there were something he desperately wanted to ask.

I focused on the silent image of Julie, breathing out as she finally stood up and gazed blindly towards us. Her expression, a grimace of pain and anguish, didn't change. 'They can't see us, Morgan. We can see them but they can't see us.'

He sighed. 'No. It doesn't look like they can.'

I wrinkled my nose. 'So even sign language is a waste of time. Whatever happens there, we can't do anything about it. We can't affect it in any way. We'll never be able to communicate with them again. And the borders have to remain closed. We can't afford to re-open them and negatively impact on their demesne again.'

His expression dropped. 'No.' He hesitated. 'I'm sorry.'

A smile spread across my face. It hurt but I gave it my best effort. 'It'll be like the world's greatest television show. We need popcorn. Now.'

Morgan drew me close. 'You don't have pretend in front of me, remember?' he murmured in my ear.

I realised I was shaking. 'Julie was scared,' I whispered. 'It wasn't her fault.' I paused. 'It was her fault but she was only acting on instinct. She's not evil. She's really not. She ...'

'Hush,' he said. 'I get it. She realised what she'd done right at the end. She knew it was wrong.'

I clenched my fists. 'Manchester is still in trouble. Whatever daddy dearest over there says, there shouldn't be magic there. Look at all that blue. They're going to be in trouble. They're going to need us.'

'They're stronger than you think. They'll manage. Manchester will manage. Besides, all of them have skills. They can do this without us.'

I certainly bloody hoped so. 'There's no choice is there?'

He shook his head. 'It appears not. But if the city is still standing now, after all that's just happened, then it's going to survive.'

I scanned across the flickering images of our friends. I wasn't the only hero. Morgan was right; Manchester would survive and so would they. Even without me and my fabulousness.

I put my arm round Morgan's waist and inhaled his scent. 'For what it's worth,' I told him, 'and to answer your unasked question, yes, I'll be here by your side making you miserable for a lifetime.'

He didn't smile back but his eyes lit up with both triumph and delight. I pushed myself onto my tiptoes and went in for a long, deep, slow kiss.

'I'm sorry about Rubus,' I said, when we finally broke apart. 'He was your brother after all.'

Morgan ran a hand through his hair. 'Is there any other way it could have ended?'

I sighed. 'I don't know. I really don't know.' I glanced round at Rubus's old, and now rather forlorn-looking, allies. Their moment of triumph wasn't quite as sweet as they'd hoped it would be. They weren't the heroes they'd believed themselves to be. 'There's a lot of mending to be done.'

Artemesia appeared beside us. 'I heard that.' She drew out a small vial with a colourless liquid inside. 'It's lucky I managed to sort this before Rubus pulled all of his crap. There should be enough to do the trick.'

I stared at it. 'Is that…?'

She nodded. 'It will restore your memory. I've checked and double-checked. Liung spoke the truth. This will do what is needed. Just down it in one and *adios* amnesia.'

A large part of me didn't want to. I still had doubts as to who I was and what I was, or what I'd been. I couldn't be afraid, however. I was the Madhatter.

I took the vial. 'Before I drink this,' I said, 'I have a question for you both. A serious question.'

Morgan stilled. 'Go on.'

I turned to him with sombre eyes. 'I swallowed the sphere. It's inside me right now.' I pointed to my stomach and dropped my voice. 'What happens when it comes out the other end?'

Artemesia shrugged. 'By swallowing it, you halted the magic. When it, uh, ejects itself, it'll be like it was before. Just hand it over to one of the elders for safekeeping. I imagine it's already been rendered useless by the journey across the border but it doesn't hurt to be sure.'

'Yeah but...'

'What, Maddy?' Morgan asked.

'We're in Mag Mell. Is there such a thing as double-quilted toilet roll here? I mean, I've experienced a ring of fire after a few spicy kebabs but having a magical sphere pop out of my arse brings arsebadgering to a new level. I mean...'

Artemesia made a face and walked off.

Morgan cut me off with another kiss.

'Maddy,' he said, 'shut the gasbudlikins up.'

About the author

After teaching English literature in the UK, Japan and Malaysia, Helen Harper left behind the world of education following the worldwide success of her Blood Destiny series of books. She is a professional member of the Alliance of Independent Authors and writes full time, thanking her lucky stars every day that's she lucky enough to do so!

Helen has always been a book lover, devouring science fiction and fantasy tales when she was a child growing up in Scotland.

She currently lives in Devon in the UK with far too many cats – not to mention the dragons, fairies, demons, wizards and vampires that seem to keep appearing from nowhere.

You can find out more by visiting Helen's website:
http://helenharper.co.uk

Other titles

The complete *Blood Destiny* series

Bloodfire

Bloodmagic

Bloodrage

Blood Politics

Bloodlust

Blood Destiny Box Set (The complete series: Books 1 – 5)

Also
- Corrigan Fire
- Corrigan Magic
- Corrigan Rage
- Corrigan Politics
- Corrigan Lust

The complete *Bo Blackman* series

Dire Straits

New Order

High Stakes

Red Angel

Vigilante Vampire

Dark Tomorrow

The complete *Highland Magic* series

Gifted Thief

Honour Bound

Veiled Threat

Last Wish

The complete *Dreamweaver* series

Night Shade

Night Terrors

Night Lights

Olympiana stand - alone

Eros

The complete *Lazy Girl's Guide To Magic* series

> Slouch Witch
>
> Star Witch
>
> Spirit Witch
>
> Sparkle Witch

Wraith stand-alone

The *Fractured Faery* series

> Box of Frogs
>
> Quiver of Cobras
>
> Skulk of Foxes

63695364R00197